FLOCKS OF PRAISE FOR THE MEG LANGSLOW NOVELS OF DONNA ANDREWS

STORK RAVING MAD

"Meg grows more endearing with each book, and her fans will enjoy seeing her take to motherhood."

—*Richmond Times-Dispatch*

SWAN FOR THE MONEY

"As usual in this hilarious series . . . a good time is guaranteed for everyone except Meg." —*Kirkus Reviews*

"Andrews always leavens the mayhem with laughs."

—*Richmond Times-Dispatch*

"The Meg Langslow series just keeps getting better. Lots of cozy writers use punny titles, but Andrews backs them up with consistently hilarious story lines." —*Booklist*

SIX GEESE A-SLAYING

"Fans will enjoy [this] entry in Andrews' fine-feathered series." —*Publishers Weekly*

"Fans of comic cozies who have never read Andrews' Meg Langslow mysteries have a real treat in store. . . . Lots of silly but infectious humor and just enough mystery."

—*Booklist*

COCKATIELS AT SEVEN

"Suspense, laughter and a whole passel of good clean fun."

—*Publishers Weekly*

"Andrews has mastered the art of writing farce with style and wit."
                                                    —*Mystery Scene*

NO NEST FOR THE WICKET

"Fun, lively, charming."   —*Publishers Weekly*

"Andrews strikes just the right balance between comedy and suspense to keep the reader laughing and on the edge of one's seat . . . Fans of this series will no doubt enjoy this installment, while new readers . . . will be headed to the bookstore for the earlier books."
                                    —*Romantic Times BOOKreviews* (4 stars)

"Any day when I start reading about Meg is cause for delight. Ending the book makes me yearn for more than one per year. Hint."   —*Deadly Pleasures*

"As usual, Andrews is a reliable source for those who like their murder with plenty of mayhem."   —*Kirkus Reviews*

"Andrews' talent for the lovably loony makes this series a winner; to miss it would be a cardinal sin."
                                          —*Richmond Times-Dispatch*

OWLS WELL THAT ENDS WELL

"A loony, utterly delightful affair."   —*Booklist*

"It's a hoot . . . a supporting cast of endearingly eccentric characters, perfectly pitched dialogue and a fine sense of humor make this a treat."   —*Publishers Weekly*

"Death by yard sale epitomizes the 'everyday people' humor that Andrews does so well . . . for readers who prefer their mysteries light . . . Andrews may be the next best thing to Janet Evanovich." —*Rocky Mountain News*

"Andrews delivers another wonderfully comic story. . . . This is a fun read, as are all the books in the series. Andrews playfully creates laughable, wacky scenes that are the backdrop for her criminally devious plot. Settle back, dear reader, and enjoy another visit to Meg's anything-but-ordinary world." —*Romantic Times* (starred review)

WE'LL ALWAYS HAVE PARROTS

"Laughter, more laughter, we need laughter, so Donna Andrews is giving us *We'll Always Have Parrots* . . . to help us survive February." —*Washington Times*

"Perfectly showcases Donna Andrews' gift for deadpan comedy." —*Denver Post* on *We'll Always Have Parrots*

"Always heavy on the humor, Andrews' most recent Meg Langslow outing is her most over-the-top adventure to date." —*Booklist*

"I can't say enough good things about this series, and this entry in it." —*Deadly Pleasures*

"Hilarious . . . another winner . . . keeps you turning pages." —*Mystery Lovers News*

CROUCHING BUZZARD, LEAPING LOON

"If you long for more 'fun' mysteries, à la Janet Evanovich, you'll love Donna Andrews' Meg Langslow series."

—*Charlotte Observer*

"There's a smile on every page and at least one chuckle per chapter."

—*Publishers Weekly*

"This may be the funniest installment of Andrews' wonderfully wacky series yet. It takes a deft hand to make slapstick or physical comedy appealing, yet Andrews masterfully manages it (the climax will have you in stitches.)"

—*Romantic Times*

REVENGE OF THE WROUGHT-IRON FLAMINGOS

"At the top of the list . . . a fearless protagonist, remarkable supporting characters, lively action, and a keen wit."

—*Library Journal*

"What a lighthearted gem of a juggling act . . . with her trademark witty dialogue and fine sense of the ridiculous, Andrews keeps all her balls in the air with skill and verve."

—*Publishers Weekly*

"Genuinely fascinating. A better-than-average entry in a consistently entertaining . . . series."

—*Booklist*

MURDER WITH PUFFINS

"Muddy trails, old secrets, and plenty of homespun humor."

—*St. Petersburg Times*

OTHER MEG LANGSLOW MYSTERIES BY DONNA ANDREWS

The Real Macaw

Donna Andrews

St. Martin's Paperbacks

This is a work of fiction. All of the characters, organizations, and events portrayed in this novel are either products of the author's imagination or are used fictitiously.

THE REAL MACAW

Copyright © 2011 by Donna Andrews.
Excerpt from *Some Like It Hawk* copyright © 2012 by Donna Andrews.

For information address St. Martin's Press, 175 Fifth Avenue, New York, NY 10010.

ISBN: 978-1-250-00864-0

Printed in the United States of America

Minotaur hardcover edition / July 2011
St. Martin's Paperbacks edition / June 2012

St. Martin's Paperbacks are published by St. Martin's Press, 175 Fifth Avenue, New York, NY 10010.

10 9 8 7 6 5 4 3 2 1

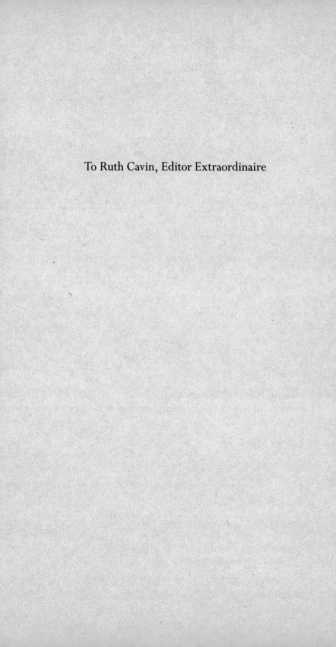

To Ruth Cavin, Editor Extraordinaire

Acknowledgments

Thanks to all the usual suspects:

The folks at Minotaur, including (but not limited to) Andy Martin, Pete Wolverton, Hector DeJean, Matt Baldacci, Toni Plummer, Matt Shear, and Anne Bensson. And a special, long-overdue thanks to the art department for continuing to come up with such great covers.

Ellen Geiger and the crew at the Frances Goldin Literary Agency and Dave Barbor at Curtis Brown.

My friends, both writers and readers, who brainstorm with me, critique with me, or just help keep me sane while I'm writing: N. Renee Brown, Erin Bush, Carla Coupe, Chris Cowan, Meriah Crawford, Ellen Crosby, Kathy Deligianis, Laura Durham, Suzanne Frisbee, John Gilstrap, Barb Goffman, Peggy Hanson, C. Ellett Logan, David Niemi, Alan Orloff, Valerie Patterson, Art Taylor, Dina Willner, Sandi Wilson, and all the Teabuds.

Many thanks to my family—Mom, Stuart, Elke, Aidan, and Liam—for being only a little like Meg's family.

And above all, thanks to all the readers who continue to welcome Meg and her family into their reading lives.

The Real Macaw

Chapter 1

"Stop!" I hissed. "Bad dog! Don't you dare bite me!"

Spike, aka the Small Evil One, froze with his tiny, sharp teeth a few inches from my ankle. He looked up and growled slightly.

From one of the cribs across the room I heard another of the faint, cranky whimpers I'd detected over the baby monitor. Jamie always woke up slowly and fussed softly for a few minutes, which gave us a fighting chance of getting to the nursery to feed him before he revved up to cry so loudly that he woke his twin brother. Josh never bothered with any kind of warning, going from fast asleep to wailing like a banshee in two seconds or less.

"I mean it," I said to Spike. "No more treats. No more sleeping in your basket here in the nursery. If you bite me again, you're out of here. Back to the barn."

Do animals understand our words or do they just pick up meaning from our tone of voice? Either way, Spike got the message.

He sniffed at my ankle. Pretending to recognize my scent, he wagged his tail perfunctorily. Then he trotted back to his basket, turned around the regulation three times, curled up, and appeared to fall asleep.

I tiptoed over to Jamie's crib in time to pick him up and

shove the bottle in his mouth a split second before he began shrieking.

I settled down in the recliner and leaned back slightly. Not for the first time, I felt a surge of gratitude to my grandfather, who had given us the recliner and helped me fight off all Mother's attempts to banish it as an eyesore from the nursery she had decorated so elegantly in soft tones of lavender and moss green.

Eventually, Jamie finished his milk and fell asleep. I gazed down at him with maternal affection—and maybe just a guilty hint of gratitude that he and his noisier brother were, for the moment, both fast asleep and not demanding anything of me.

I pondered whether to get up, put him in his crib, and go back to bed, or whether it would be just as efficient to doze here until Josh woke up for his next bottle. If I dozed here, I could turn off the baby monitor and make sure Michael got a full night's sleep, so he'd be well rested for teaching his Friday classes.

Or should I rouse myself to pump some milk for the boys' next meal? I glanced at the clock—a little after 2:00 A.M. Dozing was winning when an unfamiliar noise woke me up.

It was a dog barking. And not Spike's bark, either. At eight and a half pounds, Spike tried his best, but could never have produced the deep basso "woof!" I'd just heard.

Or had I just imagined it? I wriggled upright and stared over at Spike.

He was sitting up and looking at me.

"Did you hear anything?" I whispered.

He cocked his head, almost as if he understood.

We both listened in silence for a moment. Well, almost silence. I could still hear the faint, almost restful sounds of the white noise machine we ran at night to minimize the chances of some stray sound waking up the boys.

Just as I was about to relax back into the recliner, I heard another noise. This time it sounded more like a cat meowing.

Spike lifted his head and growled slightly.

"Shush," I said.

There was a time when shushing Spike would have egged him on. But almost as soon as we'd brought the twins home, he had appointed himself their watchdog and guardian. His self-assigned duties—barking whenever he thought they needed anything, and then biting anyone who showed up to take care of their needs—were made all the more strenuous by the fact that in spite of our efforts, the boys maintained completely opposite sleep schedules, so there was nearly always at least one twin awake and requiring Spike's attention. After four months, like Michael and me, he'd learned to grab every second of sleep he could.

He curled back up on the lavender and moss-green cushion in his bed and appeared to doze off. He looked so innocent when asleep. An adorable eight-and-a-half-pound furball. What would happen when the boys started crawling, and mistook him for a stuffed animal?

I'd worry about that later.

I sat up carefully to avoid waking Jamie, and managed to deposit him, still sleeping, on the soft, lavender flannel sheet in his crib. I glanced over to make sure Josh was still snoozing in his own little moss-green nest. Then I tiptoed over to the nursery door, opened it, and listened.

I could hear rustling sounds that weren't coming from the

white noise machine. Soft whines. An occasional bark. Meows. Cat hisses.

Probably only someone in the living room watching Animal Planet on the big-screen TV and being inconsiderate about the volume. Most likely my brother Rob, and it was just that sort of behavior that had inspired us to get the white noise machine.

But white noise wouldn't keep the growing commotion downstairs from waking Michael, who had to work tomorrow. Or five-year-old Timmy, our newly acquired long-term house-guest, who needed to be up early for kindergarten.

Unless of course Timmy was downstairs with Rob, watching television on a school night again.

"Woof!"

Definitely a dog, and not Spike, and it sounded a little too immediate to be coming from the television. Had Rob, miffed that Spike had deserted him for the twins, acquired a new four-legged friend? Or perhaps the local burglars were celebrating Bring Your Dog to Work Day.

I turned the monitor back on, slipped out of the nursery, and closed the door behind me. Now that I didn't have the white noise machine to mask it, I could hear rather a lot of animal noises. A few barks and yelps. And an occasional howl that sounded more like a cat. Definitely not burglars, unless they'd stopped in mid-crime to watch Animal Planet. Time to go downstairs and see what was up. I didn't exactly tiptoe, but I moved as quietly as possible. If someone had smuggled in a contraband menagerie, I wanted to catch them red-handed.

I stopped long enough to peek into the guest room that had become, for the time being, Timmy's room. He was fast asleep with his stuffed black cat clutched under one chubby arm. Under any other circumstances, I'd have been tempted to fetch the digital camera and take a photo I could e-mail to his mother to prove that yes, he'd settled in fine and was enjoying his stay. And maybe ask again if she knew just how long that stay would be. But that could wait. I shut his door to keep out the increasing din and crept downstairs to track the din to its source.

No dogs festooning the tall oak staircase or lurking in the front hall. I even glanced up at the double-height ceiling, because my first martial arts teacher had railed about how most people never looked up and were thus remarkably easy to ambush from above. No dogs or cats perched on the exposed beams, and no bats or ninjas hanging from the chandelier.

I stopped outside the wide archway to the living room, reached inside to flip on the light switch, and stepped into the room.

"Oh, my God!" I exclaimed.

The room was entirely filled with animals.

A dozen or so dogs, ranging in size from terriers to something not much smaller than a horse, were in the middle of the floor, lapping up water from several serving dishes from my best china set. Bevies of cats were perched on the oak mantel and on the tops of the bookshelves, some gobbling cat food from antique china dishes while others spit and hissed at the dogs and uttered unearthly howling noises. One irritable-faced Persian was hawking strenuously, apparently trying to launch a hairball at our wedding photo.

Several rows of crates and animal carriers were ranged up and down both sides of the room, some empty, while in others I could see eyes and noses of dogs and cats peering out at their liberated brethren and perhaps wondering when their turn for the food and drink would come.

A tiny black kitten was licking the oriental rug—had we spilled milk there or did he just like the taste of rug?

A Siamese cat had ventured down from the mantel and sat atop a leather photo album on our coffee table, fixedly eyeing a cage in which a small brown hamster was running frantically in his wheel, as if hoping that he could propel the cage away from the cat with enough effort. Several less anxious hamsters and guinea pigs gazed down from cages perched on other bits of furniture.

On our new sofa, an Afghan hound sprawled with careless elegance, like a model artfully posing for a photographer, its white fur vivid against the deep turquoise fabric.

"Hiya, babe! How's about it?"

A bright blue parrot was fluttering in a cage just inside the door. I eyed him sternly, and he responded with a wolf whistle.

"Meg! Uh . . . what are you doing awake at this hour?"

My father had popped up from behind the sofa. He was holding a small beagle puppy in each hand. The two puppies were struggling to get at each other, and from the soprano growling that erupted from behind the sofa, I suspected there were other juvenile beagles still on the floor, tussling.

"I was feeding the boys," I said. "What the hell are you and all these animals doing here?"

Dad looked uncomfortable. His eyes scanned the room as if seeking a safe place to set down the beagles, though I suspected he was merely avoiding meeting my eyes.

"We won't be here long," said a voice behind me.

The tall, lanky form of my grandfather appeared in the hall. He was carrying two Limoges soup tureens full of water.

"If you were thinking of giving those to the dogs, think

again," I said. "They belong to Mother, who will eviscerate you if you break them."

"Oh," he said. "They were just stuck on a high shelf in the pantry—I thought they were things you didn't use much."

"We don't use them much, mainly because they're expensive antiques that Mother lent us for that big christening party we threw last weekend," I said. "And they were on a high shelf in the pantry to keep them as safe as possible until we got a chance to return them. I can show you some crockery you can use, but first I want to know what all these animals are doing here."

"It's no use," came another voice. "The window's too small."

I turned to see the enormous leather-clad form of Clarence Rutledge, the local veterinarian. Since Grandfather was an avid animal welfare activist and Dad a sucker for anything on four legs, the menagerie in our living room was beginning to make a little more sense. But only a little.

"You were trying to break into the barn, I suppose." They all looked a little startled at what I assumed was a correct guess. "We keep it locked, since all my expensive blacksmithing equipment is out there. But I might be persuaded to unlock it, if somebody could just tell me what the hell is going on."

They all exchanged looks. One of the beagles Dad was still holding began peeing on him. He rushed to deposit the offender on a nest of newspapers in a corner.

I fixed my gaze on Grandfather.

"It's all Parker's fault," he said. "If he'd showed up on time, we never would have come here. I'm going to call him again."

As if that had explained everything, he stumped over to our living room phone.

"Want to use this?" My father held out his beloved iPhone.

"No, I want a real phone," Grandfather said. He began dialing a number from memory.

I looked at Clarence.

"It's a matter of life or death!" he exclaimed. He clasped his hands as if pleading for mercy, clenching them so hard that the tattooed ferrets on his burly forearms writhed.

I looked at Dad. The weather was mild, not warm, and yet his bald head glistened. Nerves, probably. A trickle of sweat began running down his face, and he dabbed at it absentmindedly with the puppy.

"Just why is our living room filled with dogs, cats, puppies, kittens, hamsters, guinea pigs, and parrots?"

"Only the one parrot," he said. "A macaw, actually—very interesting species."

"Hiya, babe!" the macaw said.

"Whatever," I said. "Why are they here?"

"It's because of that new county manager," Dad said.

"Horrible man," Clarence muttered.

"You mean Terence Mann?" I asked.

"Dammit, Parker, answer your bloody phone!" Grandfather snarled into the receiver.

"Hey, Clarence!" My brother, Rob, bounced into the room. "There's a window open on the second story of the barn! So if you can help me haul the ladder over, we can— Oh. Hi, Meg."

"Hi," I said. "What's your version?"

"My version?" Rob looked guilty for a moment. He fiddled with the black knit cap that concealed his shaggy blond hair, then his face cleared. "I was helping Dad and Granddad."

"Helping them do what?"

"Foil the new county manager," Dad repeated. "That Mann fellow. He's cutting the budget right and left."

"Probably because the town of Caerphilly will go bankrupt if he doesn't," I said.

"And most of his cuts we can understand, no matter how much we hate them," Clarence said. "Cutting back on the library hours."

"And the free clinic hours," Dad added.

"Postponing the teachers' raises," Rob said.

"But then he decided that the town animal shelter was too expensive," Grandfather said. "So he said the town could no longer afford for it to be a no-kill shelter."

"Can he do that?" I asked.

"Well, in the long run, probably not," Clarence said. "Public opinion is against it, about four to one. But we were afraid that some of the animals might be harmed before we could convince him to reverse his policy."

"So you adopted all of the animals from the shelter?" I asked.

"No, actually we burgled the place and stole them," Rob said.

"Wonderful," I said. "Our living room isn't just filled with animals. It's filled with stolen animals."

"Rescued animals," Grandfather said.

A burglary. Well, at least that explained why all four of them were dressed completely in black. Individually, none of them looked particularly odd, but anyone who saw the four of them skulking about together in their inky garb would be instantly suspicious.

"Did you really think you could get away with it?" I asked aloud.

"We don't care if we get away with it," Grandfather said, striking his noblest pose.

"Once the animals are safely out of his clutches, we don't care what happens to us," Dad said, following suit.

"And we knew Mann would quickly figure out that prosecuting us wouldn't do him much good in the eyes of the public," the more practical Clarence added.

I looked around. Okay, the animals were refugees. They might have been saved from an untimely death. Of course, that didn't make it any less annoying to see them lying on, shedding on, and in a few cases, chewing or peeing on our rugs and furniture. At least, thanks to the child gates we'd recently put up in all the doorways in case the boys started crawling early, the livestock weren't free to roam the whole house.

"The problem is that they're not safely out of his clutches," I said. "What now? Were you planning on hiding them in our barn until you change the county manager's mind?"

"We weren't going to bring them here at all." Dad plopped down on the sofa with a sigh. The Afghan hound scrambled over to put its head in his lap. The patch of upholstery it had vacated was covered with so much shed fur that it looked like tweed. "We'd arranged to have them taken to new permanent or foster homes outside the county," Dad went on.

"Outside the state, in fact," Grandfather said. "Parker Blair made the arrangements."

"He has that big truck he uses to make deliveries from his furniture store," Dad explained.

"We were going to meet Parker at midnight down by the haunted graveyard, load all the animals on his truck, and there you have it!" Rob exclaimed. "Like *The Great Escape,* with poodles."

"Unfortunately, Parker hasn't shown up," Grandfather said. "I've been leaving messages for nearly two hours now. Not sure what the holdup is, but as soon as he gets here, we can load the animals and have them out of your hair. But in the meantime—"

"Shhh!" Clarence hissed. He was peering out one of our front windows. "It's the cops!"

Everyone froze—even the animals, who seemed to sense danger.

I strolled over to the window and looked out.

"It's only Chief Burke," I said.

"Oh, no!" Dad wailed.

"We're lost," Clarence muttered.

"Get rid of him," my grandfather said.

The chief was getting out of his car. I hadn't heard a siren, but I could see that he had the little portable flashing light stuck on his dashboard.

"If he were just calling to see the babies, maybe I could." I glanced at my watch. "But the chief doesn't usually make social calls at two thirty in the morning."

"Then stall him while we move the animals," Dad said.

"Move them how?" Clarence asked. "All the pickups are out front where he's probably already seen them."

"Put the animals in the barn till Parker gets here," my grandfather said. "I'll call him again."

He grabbed our phone and began dialing. Dad leaped off the sofa, picked up a puppy in one hand, and grabbed the macaw's cage with the other.

"All gone!" the bird trilled.

"I wish," Clarence muttered.

The windows were cracked slightly, to let in a little of the mild April air—or possibly to prevent the smell of the animals from becoming overwhelming. I could hear the staccato sounds the chief's shoes made on our front walk.

"There is no way in the world I can stall the chief while you move all these animals to the barn," I said. "And even if I could, do you think they'd go quietly?"

As if to prove my point, one of the dogs uttered a mournful howl, and several others whimpered in sympathy. I even heard a faint bark from the porch.

"Besides," I added, "the chief has probably already spotted the dog you left outside."

"What dog?" Dad asked.

"I thought they were all accounted for." Clarence was fishing in his pockets for something. "We have an inventory."

"Dammit, Parker, pick up!" Grandfather muttered.

The dog on the porch barked again.

"Just let me handle it," I said. "The chief's an animal lover. He probably won't approve of your methods, but I'm sure he shares your concerns. Let me assess what kind of a mood he's in. Maybe we can work something out."

Clarence and my father looked at each other, then back at me.

"What else can we do?" Dad said.

The dog outside barked.

The doorbell rang.

Upstairs, Josh erupted into howls.

"Damn," I said, pausing halfway to the door. "I was trying to let Michael sleep."

"I'll take care of the baby," Clarence said, bolting for the stairs. "You deal with the chief."

"Why doesn't the bastard answer his phone?" Grandfather growled.

"Hiya, babe!" the macaw said.

"Put a lid on him," I said to Dad, as I turned back to the door.

He scrambled to pull a tarp over the cage.

Upstairs, Jamie joined the concert.

"I've got it," Michael called from upstairs.

"I'm almost there," Clarence called, from halfway up the stairs.

I opened the door. The dog outside barked again, but I pretended not to hear him and didn't look around to see where he was.

"Good morning, Chief," I said. "What are you doing up at this hour, and more important, what can we do for you?"

The chief held up a cell phone. I looked at it for a moment.

The cell phone barked. Clearly it belonged to a dog lover. No one else would choose such an annoying custom ring tone.

"I'm investigating a murder," Chief Burke said. "And I came over to ask why for the last couple of hours, you've been trying to call the dead guy's cell phone."

Chapter 2

I closed my eyes and counted to ten. Tried to, anyway.

Upstairs, the babies were wailing, and Michael had begun reciting "The Hunting of the Snark" to them. I hoped his trained actor's voice would have its usual calming effect.

"Ms. Langslow?" the chief said.

Ms. Langslow. As if I didn't already know this wasn't a social call. These days, the chief usually just called me Meg. Reverting to formality was his way of signaling that he was on a case.

Spike had begun to bark, and the dogs downstairs joined in, accompanied by frantic shushing noises.

"Dammit!" I heard my grandfather say. "Pick up, you damned fool."

I heard an unearthly howl and opened my eyes to see what had caused it. A gray tabby cat streaked out of the living room and toward the kitchen, caterwauling all the way, with two beagles in pursuit and Rob bringing up the rear, hissing, "Shh! Stop that! Come back here!"

The cell phone barked again.

I took a deep breath.

"It's Parker Blair, isn't it?" I asked. "Your murder victim with the barking cell phone."

"How do you know Parker?" the chief asked.

"I don't," I said. "Grandfather's the one who's been trying to call him. Though I have no idea how he could have been calling from our phone for two hours. I thought he just got here."

"I beg your pardon," the chief said. "You're correct. The calls were originally coming from Dr. Blake's cell phone. Apparently he switched to your home phone approximately twenty minutes ago. That's when we headed over here."

"Makes sense. I'll let Grandfather explain." The nosy part of my brain noted that the crime scene must be no more than twenty minutes' drive away and began trying to figure out where it was. I tried to squelch those thoughts. Odds were I'd find out soon enough. I stepped aside and gestured for the chief to enter.

I also squelched a pang of guilt at betraying the animal rescuers. This was a murder. Grandfather and his accomplices couldn't very well expect me to lie to the chief in the middle of a homicide investigation.

Maybe the chief would be too busy solving Parker's murder to worry about their raid on the animal shelter. Or if not, at least it sounded as if they'd all been trooping around together for the last several hours, and would be alibied for the murder. Not that I suspected them of murdering their wayward getaway driver but the chief couldn't be expected to share my confidence in them.

I followed the chief into the living room, where my grandfather was still muttering at the phone.

Grandfather looked up to see the chief holding the cell phone. It barked again.

"That's Parker's phone," Grandfather said. "How did you get his phone? Is he under arrest?"

"No," the chief said. "He's dead."

Grandfather slowly hung up the phone. His face fell, and for a moment he looked every one of his ninety-some years. The chief turned Parker's cell phone off and put it into an evidence bag. Grandfather heaved himself up and glared back at the chair he'd been sitting in. I'd had to negotiate with Mother for weeks when she decorated the living room, but except for that one chair, every piece of furniture was either comfortable or practical or both. I'd only allowed her to get away with the small, elegant, backbreaking side chair by the phone because I figured it would discourage visitors from settling in for long, leisurely calls.

"What the hell happened to Parker?" Grandfather sat on the sofa and thumped the Afghan hound on the rump a couple of times. "The fellow wasn't even forty. Healthy as a horse. Did he wreck that damned truck?"

The chief was stripping off the gloves he'd been wearing to handle the phone. He stuffed them into his pocket as he took a few steps toward the front door.

"Sammy!" he shouted.

"Yes, sir!" Heavy footsteps raced up our walk and clomped across the front porch. Deputy Sammy Wendell appeared in the foyer. Unlike the chief, who appeared perfectly normal and wide awake, Sammy had clearly been roused from a sound sleep and hadn't yet combed his hair, which was sticking out in all directions.

"Ms. Langslow," the chief said. "I gather you and Mr. Waterston have been home with the babies?"

I nodded.

"And your grandfather and his party arrived about twenty minutes ago?"

"No idea," I said. "We were all either asleep or upstairs feeding the kids with the white noise machine on. It was about fifteen or twenty minutes ago that the racket from the animals got loud enough for me to hear it."

"Who else is here?"

"Well, apart from Rob, I expect Dad is out in the barn," I said. "Clarence Rutledge is upstairs helping Michael with the babies. My cousin, Rose Noire, and our houseguest, Timmy Walker, are upstairs asleep, unless the noise woke them. That's all I know about."

I was assuming, of course, that "who else" didn't include four-legged visitors.

"Dr. Blake, Dr. Langslow, Dr. Rutledge, and Mr. Langslow." The chief had taken out his notepad and was scribbling in it. "Dr. Blake, was there anyone else with you?"

"No," Grandfather said. "Damn! I guess I should take back some of the harsh things I've been saying about Parker for the last couple of hours, when I thought he was just being feckless."

"Sammy," the chief said. "Round them up and keep them in the kitchen." He looked at me. "If that's acceptable."

I nodded.

"Or you can use the library, if you like," I said. "Or both."

"Keep them in the kitchen, Sammy." The chief glanced down at his notebook and appeared to be studying something. "I'll just talk to them here. Now, Dr. Blake. Where—"

He stopped and glanced down. One of the kittens was loose and had begun climbing the crisply pressed left leg of his uniform trousers as if it were a tree. He blinked, then forced his eyes back to Grandfather.

"Dr. Blake, where were you for the last couple of hours?"

"It wasn't just an accident, was it?" Grandfather asked. "Someone knocked him off."

The chief nodded. He winced as the kitten's razor-sharp little claws dug into his skin. The chief shook his leg slightly in an attempt to dislodge his attacker. The kitten thought this was fun, and scrambled a little higher.

"And you want to know if we have alibis," Grandfather said. He glowered for a moment. Clearly he was reluctant to admit what they'd been up to. Understandable, but this was not the time to clam up.

"Clarence, Rob, James, and I were all together," Grandfather said finally. He glared at the chief as if daring him to ask where.

I realized I'd been holding my breath. I let it out as quietly as I could.

"During what time period?" the chief asked.

Another kitten had joined its brother or sister in scaling the chief's pants leg.

"Since about ten o'clock," Grandfather said. "We were supposed to meet Parker at midnight at the intersection of Little Creek Road and the Clay County Road."

"By the old churchyard?"

Grandfather nodded.

"We got there about five minutes to midnight, and stayed until maybe one forty-five A.M."

The chief was trying to shoo the kittens—three of them by now—off his trouser legs without looking at them. I suddenly realized why. He was trying not to look at the kittens because if he took notice of them, he might have to deal with the whole shelter burglary thing. And right now he didn't want to do that. Maybe he was in sympathy with Grandfather's protest, or maybe he just felt the murder was more important and didn't want to be sidetracked.

I decided to help him.

"I'm sorry," I said. "Rose Noire's new kittens aren't very well trained yet."

"Trained?" Grandfather snorted at the thought. "You can't train cats."

"You can make sure they know that climbing on people is not acceptable," I said as I plucked one of the kittens off. "And you could help me with this. I've only got two hands."

We finished plucking the kittens off the chief and returned them to the large cardboard box where they belonged.

As I stood up from depositing the kittens, I jarred the macaw's cage. The tarp that had been partly covering it fell all the way off.

"Hiya, babe!" the macaw squawked. "How's about it? Just you and me."

"Put a lid on it, bird," I said.

The macaw responded with several rude remarks in language so blue they'd probably have bleeped the entire sentence on network television.

I stood staring at the macaw for a few moments, speechless.

When I looked around, everyone else in the room was also speechless and staring.

"Do that again, featherbrain, and I'll wash your beak out with soap," I said.

The bird responded with another string of off-color insults.

"No crackers for you, Polly." I pulled the cover over the macaw's cage. I could hear him muttering a few more four-letter words as he settled down for a nap. At least I hoped the cover would have that effect.

The chief—who always apologized if, under extreme provocation, he uttered the occasional "hell" or "damn" in front of a lady—was frowning severely at the shrouded cage.

"He's new here," I said. "And not staying."

"I should hope not." He glanced around the living room and shuddered. Mother would probably shudder, too, if she saw the room in its current state.

"I think I will take you up on that offer of the library," the chief said. "Assuming it's empty."

"Of animals? Yes," I said. "And it's going to stay that way," I added, looking pointedly at my grandfather.

"Could you send Clarence down to the kitchen when he's finished babysitting?" the chief asked.

I nodded.

"Now, if you don't mind, Dr. Blake."

Grandfather and the chief disappeared into the long hall that led to our library.

I tried to shove some of the cats and dogs into crates and cages but gave up after a few minutes.

"Let sleeping dogs lie," I said. "And sleeping cats, too."

At least until I could task someone else with waking them up to crate them. I went upstairs to the nursery.

I peered in to see a heartwarming domestic scene. Michael,

in boxer shorts and a tattered Caerphilly College T-shirt, was sprawled on the recliner, half-asleep, feeding Josh.

Heartwarming wasn't exactly what I'd call the vision of Clarence in his full leather and denim biker's outfit stretched out on the moss-green rug with Jamie sleeping on his well-padded stomach, but it was rather entertaining. I hoped Michael had captured the scene on the digital camera that he'd taken to carrying everywhere since the boys arrived. Yes, the camera was lying on the arm of the recliner.

Clarence looked up when I entered, his face anxious.

"The chief's not here about the animals," I said.

"It's Parker, isn't it?" he said. "Did he wreck the truck, or did some jealous husband catch up with him? Is he just injured or . . . ?"

"He's dead." I reached down to take Jamie. "You're very quick to assume that Parker met a violent end. Why is that?"

"Obviously you didn't know him." Clarence was trying to loosen the death grip Jamie had on one of the many chains dangling from his vest. "Parker was passionate about animal welfare. He'd never just blow off an animal rescue mission. So something serious must have happened. And the chief wouldn't be coming here in the middle of the night if he'd died in his sleep, or just had an accident."

Jamie woke up enough to release his grip, fussed a little, and dozed off again.

"Speaking of the chief," I said. "He'd like you to go down and wait in the kitchen with Dad and Rob and Deputy Sammy."

Clarence nodded.

I eased Jamie into his crib.

"If you could stop by the living room on your way and make sure all the animals are secured, I'd appreciate it," I said to Clarence. "I'd really like them out in the barn, but just having them caged or crated would do for now."

He nodded again and went downstairs.

"All the animals?" Michael said, opening one eye. "You mean there really is a herd of animals downstairs?"

"You couldn't hear them?"

"I was hoping maybe it was your grandfather watching some kind of animal video on the big-screen TV with the sound cranked up. How many dogs and cats?"

"I didn't count."

He winced.

"Only half a dozen guinea pigs and hamsters, though," I said. "And only one macaw."

"What did they do—rob a pet store?"

"Not a bad guess." I explained about the animal shelter.

He shook his head.

"I don't like the change in policy, either, but aren't they over-reacting a little?" he said. "They couldn't just picket the place?"

I shrugged. It was too late—or maybe too early—to get into a discussion about why my relatives did what they did.

"Well, I don't want to kick the animals out if there's no place else for them tonight, but we can't keep them here indefinitely," he said. "Not even out in our barn. You're going to want to get back to your blacksmithing eventually."

"I already want to get back to it," I said. "But I think it will still be a while before I have the time. And—"

I interrupted myself with a gigantic yawn.

"Go to bed," he said. "That's what I plan to do when I finish feeding Josh. If the animals aren't in the barn by breakfast time, I'll lay down the law to everyone. Meanwhile, let's both get some sleep."

"I will," I said. "As soon as I pump some more milk for the boys' next meal."

Unfortunately, by the time I finished that, Jamie was hungry again. And by the time I'd fed him, I was wide awake. Dog-tired, but wide awake.

It was 5:00 A.M. The smart thing to do would be to lie down, and rest even if I couldn't sleep.

Instead, I went downstairs to see what was happening.

Chapter 3

Dad, Clarence, and my cousin Rose Noire were in the living room, tending animals. Grandfather and the Afghan hound were sitting on the sofa, supervising. The others were sitting on the rug, either because their tasks required it or because all the chairs were already occupied by sleeping dogs and cats. No one appeared to have made much headway toward moving the animals to the barn.

Why wasn't Dad racing to the scene of the crime? He was an avid mystery buff with a two-book-a-day crime novel habit. Normally he'd be driving the chief crazy, trying to get involved in the investigation, instead of peacefully tending animals.

Maybe having someone he knew and liked as the victim made it more real and a lot less fun.

"How's it going?" I was leaning against the archway to the front hall, hoping to signal that I wasn't staying long enough to help.

"The chief should be finished questioning Rob soon," Dad said. "Come on, Tinkerbell." Tinkerbell? He was attaching a leash to the largest of the dogs. An Irish wolfhound, from the look of it. Was Dad taking it out for a walk or going for a ride? Both seemed possible. I winced as Tinkerbell's unclipped nails clicked on the oak floor on their way down the hallway to the kitchen. I loved the redecorating Mother had done for us, especially the living room and hall, which were filled with Arts and Crafts—style oak furniture, oriental rugs on the newly polished oak floors, and upholstery in a beautiful shade of turquoise that Mother insisted on calling cerulean. But if I was going to flinch every time a child or an animal threatened to mar the perfection of our decor, maybe we should have waited.

Or maybe having the animals here—briefly—would be a good thing. Maybe we'd feel better when we got the first nicks and stains over with. Like getting past the first scratch on a new car.

Of course, there was a difference between getting a scratch on your new car and driving it through a barbed-wire fence into a bramble bush.

"I've checked out all the animals," Clarence said. "None are any the worse for their ordeal." Clarence seemed to be applying an ointment to a dog with oozing skin sores. Or maybe it was the ointment that was oozing. Either way, I wished he'd do it someplace other than our living room. Or at least put down newspapers to protect the rug.

Rose Noire was flitting about, spritzing something from an atomizer. Probably a blend of essential oils custom-designed to soothe the animals' nerves and boost their immune systems. I only wished she'd find something to spritz that didn't make quite so many of the cats sneeze. Her normally exuberant mane of hair was pulled back into a loose braid. Was she adopting a new personal style, or had she merely decided that the braid was more practical for today's animal tending?

"I'm sure the animals will all be much happier and calmer once they've settled in," she said, with a final flourish of her atomizer.

Two of the cats sneezed again, violently. One sprayed the mirror over the mantel, which could easily be washed. The other aimed at a nearby patch of the wall that Mother's crew had painted four times before she decided "dove wing" was the perfect color. I had a feeling "dove wing with accents of cat snot" wouldn't be allowed to stay.

"I'm sure they will." I stepped into the room and began looking for a carrier for the sneezing cats. "The problem is that they shouldn't be settling in here in the living room. Couldn't you find the key to the barn?"

They all looked crestfallen—except Grandfather, who simply shrugged, and brushed another handful of Afghan fur off his shirt and onto the rug.

"I'm sorry," Rose Noire said. "We have the key, but there just always seems to be something else more urgent." Her urgent task of the moment seemed to be teaching several kittens to chase a bit of string.

"You need more help," I said. I was vastly proud of myself for having said "you" instead of "we."

"We're bringing in more Corsicans to help," Grandfather said, waving his hand grandly, as if he had an infinite number of Corsicans at his disposal, along with Sardinians, Sicilians, and perhaps even a few surviving Etruscans.

"Corsicans?" I echoed. "What do you need Corsicans for? Do they have some kind of national expertise at fostering animals?" I probably sounded a bit hostile, but I had good reason. We'd only recently gotten rid of a Spanish houseguest who'd come for a few days to see a college drama production and ended up staying nearly four months. I wasn't eager to see any more European visitors showing up in need of lodging.

"No, that's what we call ourselves," Dad announced. "Corsicans. Members of the Committee Opposed to the Ruthless Slaughter of Innocent Captive Animals. CORSICA."

"It's a new organization," Clarence explained. "Formed in the wake of the town manager's inhumane new policy."

I was willing to bet they'd spent at least as much time working on their catchy acronym as they had on formulating their plan to combat the new shelter policy. Possibly more, if burgling the shelter was all they'd come up with.

"Invite as many Corsicans as you want, then," I said. "As long as they're not expecting bed and board."

The doorbell rang.

"That's probably one of them now," Rose Noire said, leaping up to race to the door. "And about time, too. I started calling over an hour ago!"

I glanced at my watch. No, I hadn't been mistaken earlier. It was only a little past five in the morning.

"You were calling people at four A.M.?" I exclaimed. "How many of them blessed you out for waking them?"

"They were all thrilled at the chance to be of use," Dad said. "Everyone wanted to help with the mission, of course, but we had to keep the numbers down. For security."

"And now that the word is getting out, I'm sure we'll be simply flooded with volunteers," Rose Noire called from the hallway.

"Swell," I muttered. And when the volunteers grew thirsty, hungry, or needed a bathroom?

"Caroline!" Rose Noire exclaimed. "Come in! You're the first one here!"

My spirits rose a little. I liked Caroline Willner, the elderly owner of a wildlife refuge a few counties away. Even better, she had more common sense than anyone in the room—possibly more than everyone in the room combined—and was one of the few people in the world who could give my grandfather orders and actually get him to follow them.

"Welcome," I said, as Caroline sailed into the room like a small, plump, gray-haired whirlwind.

"Meg! I can't believe these idiots brought all those animals here—and you so busy with the twins. But we'll take them off your hands, no problem. Monty! You old goat! What are you doing sitting on your duff goofing off when there's work to be done?"

"I am not goofing off!" Grandfather said, holding his head high with wounded dignity. "I am endeavoring to come up with a plan of action."

"Well, any plan has to start with getting the livestock out of Meg's living room," Caroline said. "Let's get cracking on that, and then you can do your endeavoring out in the barn."

Under Caroline's direction, things started moving, and the pace picked up rapidly, as other Corsican volunteers trickled in. By 7:00 A.M., we had fifteen volunteers out in the barn, working with the animals.

Well, actually only twelve working with the animals. I took my big coffeemaker out to the barn and showed Thirteen how to use it, then gave Fourteen and Fifteen some cash and sent them to town for provisions, human and animal.

"This would be a lot easier if you'd left all the stalls here," Grandfather complained as he surveyed the interior of the barn.

"No, it wouldn't," I said. "The old stalls were literally falling down from neglect. They wouldn't have been safe for the animals."

"I suppose it will have to do." He strode off and began giving orders that contradicted everything Caroline had planned. I decided to stay out of the ensuing verbal donnybrook.

Instead, I drifted over to my workspace. Mother might be proud of the redecorating she'd done in the house, but I thought I'd done a rather nice job on the renovation of the barn—with help from the Shiffley Construction Company, of course. The former tack room was now my office, and right outside we'd torn down some ramshackle stalls to create a storage room for supplies on one side and a forge area on the other. I twined my fingers through the metal grate that separated me from the forge—an ingenious suggestion from Randall Shiffley, that allowed me to spread out into the main part of the barn if I wanted to, and then lock up my expensive work tools safely when I was finished.

Evidently today would not be the day I unlocked the grate and fired up my forge. Though I should do that soon. The longer my pregnancy-induced sabbatical lasted, the more I fretted that my muscles would atrophy and I'd lose all those skills and instincts I'd built up over fifteen years of blacksmithing.

I gazed wistfully at my anvil and imagined myself working at it. Actually, I imagined myself hammering fiercely at a stubborn bit of metal that gradually yielded to the force of my blows.

Always a bad sign when I started fantasizing about smashing things with my hammer instead of envisioning new designs. I sighed, and turned away from the grate.

We'd left a few stalls at the other end of the barn, with the idea that eventually we might want a few cows, or even horses for the boys. The rest of the space had been roughly finished into a huge open area that had already proven invaluable for rained-out family picnics, the annual plant sale held by Mother's garden club, and rehearsals of plays that Michael and his drama department students were directing.

Unfortunately, it was also perfect for housing the refugee animals. I hoped the Corsicans didn't use that as an excuse to procrastinate about finding them permanent homes.

I couldn't help eyeing the Corsicans suspiciously. Most of them were probably harmless animal lovers—well-meaning people who were doing their best to help out in a difficult situation. But from conversations I overheard, I got the impression that the plan to burgle the animal shelter was pretty widely known among the group. Which meant that any number of them would have known Parker Blair would be making that dramatic midnight rendezvous in the graveyard.

If I were the chief, I'd consider the Corsicans prime suspects.

Assuming he knew they all had advance knowledge of the burglary. Did he? Should I tell him?

I felt a sudden qualm. Why was I plotting ways to rat out the Corsicans? Was I just feeling resentment because they'd filled my house with animals and animal by-products?

No. The burglary plot could easily have something to do with the murder. And odds were they wouldn't be very forthcoming with the chief about it, and that meant he might not get some vital piece of information that would solve Parker's murder.

So I'd keep my eyes and ears open. Try to figure out what the chief knew, and what the Corsicans ought to be telling him and weren't.

I'd have to do it carefully. The chief could be touchy if he thought anyone was trying to tell him how to do his job. And rightfully so, since he had nearly two decades of experience solving homicides with the Baltimore police department. But he also got very touchy if he thought you knew some critical piece of information and didn't tell him.

Besides, I didn't want to get the Corsicans in any more trouble than I had to. Their hearts were in the right place, even if their brains appeared to have gone AWOL.

So since it would be a lot easier to suggest that he investigate the Corsicans if one of them actually did something suspicious—and a lot easier on my conscience—I tried to keep a careful eye on them. And I was beginning to notice a curious dynamic among the volunteers.

None of the Corsicans seemed particularly cheerful, which was understandable under the circumstances. One of their own had fallen, and the fate of the rescued animals was up in the air.

But there was a woman sitting at one end of the barn, near the stalls, whom they all seemed to treat with special deference, as if recognizing that she had a superior claim to grief.

And at the other end of the barn, right outside my forge, another woman was receiving the same tender, kid-glove handling.

Were they Parker's relatives? Particular friends? Or might Parker's life contain a love triangle that had a great deal more to do with his murder than the animal shelter?

I needed to ask someone who knew Parker. Someone trustworthy, or at least someone whose foibles and biases I knew. I looked around for Grandfather and the other ringleaders. They weren't anywhere to be seen. Had they gone away and deserted their fellow Corsicans? Then I noticed that the door to my office was ajar. I could have sworn I'd asked Caroline and Rose Noire to keep both the forge and the office locked, at least as long as so many people were coming and going.

I peered in. Rob, Clarence, and Caroline were all there, tending some of the orphaned puppies in the relative comfort of my office chairs.

"What's with all the kittens and puppies?" Caroline was saying. "Where are the mothers?"

"According to the shelter records, they've had a rash of litters being dumped on them," Clarence said. "Litters of kittens and puppies that haven't even been weaned yet. What kind of person does that to poor, helpless creatures?"

"Same people who can't be bothered to spay or neuter." Caroline glanced up and saw me. "Meg! How are the twins?"

"They're fine," I said. "They're upstairs with Michael." I decided not to mention that thanks to the middle-of-the-night interruption, both the twins and their parents had slept far less than we needed and would be cranky today. I'd save that bit of information until I needed to induce guilt.

"So tell me about Parker Blair," I said. "I know he owned Caerphilly Fine Furniture, but that's about all I know."

"He's a founding member of CORSICA," Rob said.

"And a big supporter of a lot of environmental and animal welfare causes," Clarence added.

The two of them returned to the puppies as if this were all anyone needed to know about Parker.

"He arrived on the local scene about five years ago," Caroline said. "His aunt Emmaline died and left him the furniture store. I don't know what he did before, but I suspect it was something in sales or business. The shop was pretty moribund when he arrived, and he's revived it considerably."

I nodded. Clearly Caroline had a better idea of what constituted a biography. I hadn't met Parker, and I usually left my furniture shopping to Mother, who had started a small decorating business, and now actually had a few clients who weren't also relatives. But I knew where Parker's store was. So far Mother hadn't found much to like in it, but lately she had begun doing an occasional tour of inspection, which probably meant he was successfully appealing to a more affluent market.

"Was he married?" I asked.

"Parker?" Rob fell back into his chair and dissolved with laughter. The puppy he was holding seemed to think he had caused this, and began wriggling, wagging his tail, and yipping with joy as he jumped up to lick Rob's face.

"Seriously involved with anyone?" I asked. Rob's laughter continued, and Clarence was visibly suppressing a smile.

"Involved with a lot of women, but none of it all that serious," Clarence said. "Not on his part, anyway. He was a free spirit."

"He was a no-good letch with the morals of a tomcat," Caroline said. "Damn! Give me that towel—this one's piddling on me again."

"But very kind to animals," Clarence said, handing Caroline a towel. Not one of our towels, I was relieved to see.

"And the jerk used it to the hilt," Caroline said. "I don't mean that he wasn't kind to animals. He was, and he did a lot of good work. But let a pretty girl walk into the room, and suddenly he's Mother Teresa and Dr. Doolittle, all rolled into one, bending tenderly over a sick kitten as if only he could save it."

"Yeah, he was a little sleazy with women," Clarence said. "But I've seen him stay up all night with a sick dog. He even let himself get stuck with taking care of any iguanas that got turned in to the shelter, which is definitely above and beyond."

"Why above and beyond?" Rob asked. "Iguanas are cool—I've been thinking about getting one."

"Don't," Clarence said. "They're too much work. There's no such thing as iguana chow—you have to chop just the right mixture of fresh fruits and vegetables for them every day, and make sure they get enough sunlight and mist their skin to keep it healthy or they don't thrive."

"What happens when they don't thrive?" Rob asked.

"Getting back to Parker," I said. "He was good at feeding and misting iguanas? Is that important?"

I thought I was asking if iguana husbandry could possibly have had anything to do with Parker's murder. But Clarence took my question at face value.

"Not only good at it," Clarence said. "He was willing to do it, in spite of the fact that iguanas are the most unrewarding creatures on earth to foster. The ones turned in to the shelter can get up to five or six feet long, aggressive as hell, and like most reptiles, about as affectionate as the rocks they're sitting on."

"Yes, Parker was a good volunteer," Caroline said. "I'll give him that. He never shirked when there was something that needed doing with the animals. I just wish the bastard had learned to keep his pants zipped, that's all. Sorry—I hate to speak ill of the dead, especially someone who's not even cold in his grave yet—"

"Not even *in* his grave yet," Rob put in. "Probably just down at the morgue."

"But if you want the honest truth," Caroline went on, "he was a letch."

"So it wouldn't surprise you to know that two of the Corsican volunteers are carrying on a dueling widow act?" I asked.

The three of them looked at me and blinked.

"Good Lord," Caroline said. "Which two?"

"I bet Vivian is one of them," Clarence said.

"That's just a rumor," Rob said. "I don't actually believe it."

"I do," Clarence said.

"Is Vivian a tall, willowy redhead?" I asked.

"Yes," Clarence said. "Vivian Forrest. She's a nurse at Caerphilly hospital. They met when Parker got badly bitten by a dog he was rescuing."

"That doesn't mean she was seeing him," Rob said.

Clarence glanced over at me, rolled his eyes, and shrugged. Yes, I got it. Apparently Rob was also interested in the attractive Vivian. Thank goodness he was alibied for the time of the murder.

"Well, she's not going to be seeing him anymore, is she?" Caroline said. "Who's the other one?"

"Petite blonde, not as elegantly dressed as Vivian," I said.

They all looked blank.

"Beats me," Caroline said. "Rob, go check it out."

I went back out into the main barn. Rob followed me, and I pointed out the two women.

"Yes, that's Vivian." He shook his head as if only now detecting some profound character flaw in the lovely redhead. "And the other one? Good grief! Louise Dietz? Who'd have guessed her?"

"What does Louise do when she's not volunteering for CORSICA?" I asked.

"Works down at the courthouse as an administrative assistant." He glanced around to see if anyone was within earshot and lowered his voice. "She's kind of like our mole inside the mayor's office. Parker recruited her—but I hadn't realized before just how. Damn! I need my video camera for this."

He shook his head as he went back into my office. Clearly the late Parker's romantic triumphs had earned Rob's respect—and possibility his resentment. I continued to watch Vivian and Louise.

They had completely opposite notions of how to carry off their self-appointed roles of chief mourner.

Vivian was dressed entirely in black and gray, and her tailored black wool pants were certainly not what I would have put on for tending dozens of animals. She was impeccably groomed and made-up. She strode about with her head held bravely high, looking quite dignified when she wasn't tripping over the furniture or the animals. Occasionally she would sweep up one of the animals, sigh, and clutch it to her chest, as if its presence brought back bittersweet memories of Parker. The abundance of animal hair of every conceivable color on her black mohair sweater seemed to indicate she'd been clutching quite a lot of animals. But clearly not a single tear was going to be allowed to sully the perfection of her makeup. I hadn't yet spotted her doing anything useful, like feeding, walking, or cleaning up after the animals, but perhaps making the animals feel wanted was also an important task.

I liked Louise's style better. She was wearing ragged jeans and a faded sweatshirt, and didn't appear to have combed her hair before she came over. She was a lot more efficient with the animals in spite of the fact that tears were running down her cheeks all the while. Never more than one or two tears at a time, which gave the impression that instead of actively sobbing she was bravely holding her sorrow in check, making what we saw merely the accidental spillover from a vast reservoir of tears. It certainly made you want to avoid upsetting her.

Which was probably why she was doing one of the prime jobs: feeding baby animals. She looked like a modern-day Pietà, bending dolefully over each kitten or puppy in her lap. Some of the other Corsicans watched over her and kept her supplied with baby animals to feed. I hoped they had a plan for what to do with her when all the baby animals were full. Or were there enough puppies and kittens that the first ones would be hungry again by the time she finished with the last? Looking around, I didn't discount the possibility.

What worried me was the fact that neither Vivian nor Louise seemed to take the slightest notice of what the other was doing. Were both aware of having a rival and studiously ignoring her? Or was some kind of confrontation brewing? I hoped not. Or if it was, I hoped I could be far, far away when it happened.

Rob, on the other hand, appeared eager to capture any fireworks on the little pocket video camera he'd gotten for Christmas. He moved among the volunteers, ostensibly filming them all, but he seemed to pay particular attention to Vivian and Louise.

Or maybe just Vivian. Was he interested in her as a woman, or only as the most likely source of drama that he could film? I could probably figure it out if I stayed around a little while. But if Rob was trying to capture Vivian on the rebound, I'd find out soon enough.

I decided it was high time I checked on the boys. Or at least used them as an excuse to get away from the barn, where any minute now someone might suggest that I use my newfound maternal skills on an orphaned beagle. I waved farewell to the Corsicans and headed back to the house, where I ran into the chief packing up to leave.

"Thank you for your hospitality," he said, as courteously as if I'd served him a gourmet dinner instead of merely staying out of his way while he interviewed a few witnesses.

"You're welcome," I said. "I hope the investigation goes well."

He peered at me over his glasses for a few moments, frowning slightly.

"Something wrong?" I asked.

"Get some rest, Meg," he said. "You look done in."

I nodded. He frowned at me for a few more moments, then shook his head, as if doubting I'd follow his advice, wished me a good morning, and left.

Perhaps I should have reassured him that I had every intention of following his advice.

I detoured through the kitchen and stayed long enough to restore it to some semblance of order. Rob had accused me of becoming a neatnik since the babies were born, which was ridiculous. If anything my housekeeping standards had plummeted. But I'd also quickly learned that it was much easier to *keep up* than to *catch up*. The dirty diapers alone would bury us in a few days if we didn't keep after them. So I made time for a little triage in the kitchen, lulled by the peaceful silence I could hear over the nursery monitor.

I got carried away, and it was nearly eight before I finished in the kitchen. For once, I'd done more than triage. The pale gray countertops and white-painted cabinets gleamed and the countertops and the heavy oak table contained only the things that were supposed to live there. I took a long, satisfied look. I even thought of running upstairs for my camera to take a few shots. It might be weeks before the room looked this good again.

I was pushing the button to start the dishwasher when Rob sidled in.

"Um . . . Meg? Could you help us with something? Just for a minute?"

Chapter 4

"Help you with what?" I turned around and tried not to frown as I waited to hear more. Evidently I failed.

"See!" he exclaimed. "That's exactly what you need to do to him. Give him that stern, maternal look."

I wasn't sure I liked that thought.

"Who are we talking about?"

"The guy who's here to take the animals away," he said.

"Rob, you're a lawyer. Can't you deal with him?"

"He's got an official order and everything."

I was opening my mouth to say something harsh—something that would probably have included the words "grow up." But I reminded myself that there was a reason Rob made his living as a designer of bizarre computer games rather than in the legal system.

"I told him he needed to talk to the owner of the property first," Rob said. "I've set the stage—all you have to do is waltz in and squelch him."

"Okay," I said. "I'll see what I can do."

Rob raced out. I followed at a more sedate pace, putting on my sternest, most businesslike manner.

"I still don't see why the Corsicans can't fend him off themselves," I muttered.

A small panel truck had backed up to the barn door. Its back doors were open and a ramp led up from the ground to the body of the truck.

But nothing was being loaded. The barn doors were closed, and I could see Corsicans peering from most of the barn windows. Rob stood in front of the barn door, arms folded, looking very stern now that he had me to back him up.

The driver of the truck was sitting on the truck bed beside the ramp. He was a lanky young man who looked barely old enough to drive, in a uniform clearly intended for someone several inches shorter and at least a hundred pounds heavier. He looked up when I approached, and scrambled to his feet.

My appearance on the scene was greeted with cheers from the Corsicans.

"Are you the owner?" the driver asked.

"Of this property, yes," I said. "What can I do for you?"

"I have this paper," he said.

The Corsicans had begun chanting, "Hell, no! We won't go!"

I turned to Rob.

"Please ask your fellow members of the committee to refrain from any action that would exacerbate the situation," I told him.

"Um . . . okay." He took a few steps closer to the barn, and then stage whispered, "Hey! Meg says shut up."

Not precisely what I had in mind for him to do. I could have done that myself.

I turned back to the kid in uniform. He handed me a sheet of paper.

It was on stationery from the mayor's office. The heading read "EXECUTIVE ORDER!!!"—not only in all caps but in boldface, in type several sizes larger than the body of the document.

It was barely light, and yet already the mayor had not only

found out about the animal shelter burglary, but had presumably rousted several hapless civil servants out of their beds—one to fetch the animals and one to type this document. He hadn't done it himself. The lack of typos and spelling and grammar errors was a dead giveaway. But whoever had typed it could do nothing about his ghastly style.

I had to read the text two times to realize that underneath all the bombast and persiflage was an order directing that the animals should return to the shelter. I had a brief, improbable vision of the animals gathering around to read the proclamation, and then forming an orderly procession to march back to town and surrender themselves. Under other circumstances, I might have found the whole thing funny. Of course, presumably the mayor was aware that even if the animals could read his order, they weren't likely to comply, so he'd sent this kid to collect them. I recognized the uniform he was wearing now—the little logo on the pocket said, "Caerphilly County Solid Waste Department."

"You work at the county dump," I said. "You're not taking the animals to the dump, are you?"

"No, ma'am," he said. "Back to the animal shelter. All three of the shelter employees quit this morning, so the mayor sent me."

"Quit or got fired?" I asked.

"Quit," the kid said, with the ghost of a grin. "He called them up before dawn and told them to come out here to collect the animals or he'd fire them, and they all up and quit before he could do it."

Interesting. The animal shelter was technically owned by the county, but the county board allowed the town council to handle day-to-day operations. They did that with most of the county facilities located within the town limits because otherwise the council members had almost nothing to do, and spent way too much energy tweaking town parking zone restrictions and speed limits. But the county ran the dump directly.

So the mayor was giving orders to county employees. Did that mean he and the county manager were working together on the animal shelter problem? Or had the mayor simply given an order whose authority the kid hadn't thought to question. I could see either happening. Not something I could find out from the kid, who looked as if doing anything more complicated than loading trash might be an intellectual leap. No sense giving him a hard time. But I couldn't let him take the animals. Inspiration struck.

"Well, this seems to be in order," I said.

Shouts of "No! No!" "Traitor!" and a few more rounds of "Hell, no! We won't go!" from the barn.

"Just one more thing," I said. Why not? It worked for Colombo; why not for me? "I have to call someone to clear this. Won't take long."

The kid had clearly learned to exercise patience in the face of bureaucracy. He leaned against the side of his truck and folded his arms to wait. Realizing that I might be up to something useful, the Corsicans in the barn shut up again.

I walked around to the side of the house to a point where I could see the front yard. As I'd suspected, the chief's car was no longer parked on the road near our front walk.

So I called the police station. The nonemergency number. Debbie Anne, the stalwart police dispatcher, answered both, so it wasn't as if I'd get a slower response than on 911. And even in an emergency, I often called the regular number. Less stressful for Debbie Anne.

"Hey, Meg," she said. "How are you holding up with that whole menagerie in your barn?"

"Reasonably well," I said. "The Corsicans are here in force to take care of them. The animals are the reason I'm calling. Could I talk to the chief?"

"Is it urgent?" she asked. "Because you know how he gets when he's on a case."

"This could be related to his case," I said. "I don't know yet. And while I'm not positive he'd find it urgent, it's definitely time-sensitive."

"Okay," she said.

"I should be getting back to town with those animals," the kid called out. It was a token protest, with no real sense of urgency behind it. I returned to the barn door. He was slumped back onto the tailgate of the truck.

"This won't take long," I told him.

He sighed as if he'd heard that before.

"Ms. Langslow?" The chief. "Is there something I can do for you?"

"Thanks for taking my call," I said. "I just wanted you to know that the mayor sent someone down here to collect the animals and take them back to the shelter."

"Poor creatures," he said.

"And before I let him take them, I thought I'd check to see if you still wanted them held as evidence."

"The animals? Evidence in the murder? Or in some other crime that certain people are blasted lucky we don't have the time to investigate right now?"

"If you're finished with the animals, he can take them back to the shelter. I think they have some itchy trigger fingers down there. Or itchy lethal injection fingers. But if you still want them held as evidence . . ."

The chief finally got it.

"Oh, I see," he said. "No, you mustn't let him take the animals. They're evidence, all right."

"Let me put you on speaker." I punched the correct button and walked over until the kid was within earshot.

"To repeat," the chief said, his voice loud and distinct. "I do not want those animals moved! They are material evidence in at least one felony, and I want them to stay right where they are until I release them. If anyone really wants to incur a charge of interfering with a police investigation—"

"No, no," the kid said, sitting up straight for the first time since I'd seen him. "We're good. I'll go back and tell them. No rush."

He was backing away as if afraid the chief would come through the phone at him. The chief tended to have that effect on people. Even people who didn't know him. The kid began fumbling to load the ramp back into the truck, and Rob jumped to help him.

"Ms. Langslow?"

I turned the speaker off.

"Was there anything else?" the chief asked.

The kid had started his truck, and was lurching down our dirt driveway back to the road. I waved at the Corsicans and headed back for the house.

"Thanks," I said to the chief. "You've got him on the run."

"Sooner or later, you're going to have to figure out what to do with those confounded animals," he said. "I don't like the idea of killing them either, but do you realize how hard it's going to be finding homes for all of them?"

"I'll get the Corsicans to start working on that." I glanced back, decided I was safely out of earshot of anyone at the barn, and continued. "That's the Committee Opposed to the Ruthless Slaughter of Innocent Captive Animals."

"Yes, I'm aware of them," the chief said. "Were they all involved in planning the shelter burglary, do you think, or was that your grandfather's pet project?"

I winced.

"No idea," I said. "Since I'm not a Corsican."

"A pity you're not," the chief said. "I expect you'd have talked them out of this nonsense. Well, with any luck, by the time I have resources to divert to the burglary, some of the saner county board members will have persuaded the mayor and the county manager that pressing charges would be a PR disaster. Right now I'm focusing on Parker Blair's murder. So how many of these so-called Corsicans knew about the plans for the burglary, do you think? Apart from the actual burglars, who alibi each other rather convincingly."

"No idea," I said. "From what I've overheard, I think the burglary plan was an open secret throughout the organization."

"Drat," he said.

"Of course, a lot of them could be just pretending," I said. "To look like they're part of the inner circle. And I doubt if too many people knew exactly where they were planning to meet Parker."

"Which would be relevant if he'd been killed at the rendezvous spot, but he wasn't."

"Where was he killed? And how? I haven't—"

I stopped myself. On the other end of the call, the chief was silent. I mentally kicked myself. Clearly that question had crossed some kind of boundary.

Then the chief sighed.

"It'll be in the papers tomorrow," he said. "He was shot at relatively close range, apparently through the open driver's side window of his truck. Which was still parked behind his furniture store. He might not have been found till morning, except that the truck's lights were on, and one of the neighbors called to complain that they were shining in her windows."

"And that location doesn't help your investigation one little bit, does it?" I said. "All the Corsicans would have expected him to be involved in the burglary, because he's one of the few members with a truck big enough to haul away all the animals. And anyone who guessed he was involved could also guess that sometime that evening he'd show up in the parking lot behind his store to pick up his truck."

"It's also possible that his murder had nothing to do with the Corsicans," the chief said. "His store's only two blocks from the bus station, you know."

"Ah," I said. To an outsider, of course, the chief's words would have made no sense, but locals all knew——and newly arrived students soon figured out——that the few blocks around the bus station were the closest thing Caerphilly had to a high-crime, low-rent district. During his years on the Baltimore PD, the chief had seen plenty of neighborhoods that made Caerphilly's worst look like Beverly Hills, so it was amusing that he'd started referring to places near the bus station with the same vague dismay as the rest of the town.

"Of course you're right," he said. "The Corsicans are prime

suspects. Which is unfortunate, since now I have to check alibis on every single blessed one of them. Doing one alibi is time consuming; can you imagine how much work it's going to be doing dozens?"

I made a sympathetic noise.

"Speaking of dozens," he went on. "It was nice of you to figure out a way to save the animals, but you do realize that now you're stuck with the whole kit and caboodle for the time being?"

"I don't see a way out of that," I said, with a sigh. "Do you?"

A small pause.

"I hereby authorize you to deputize additional concerned citizens to assist you in preserving the evidence from the animal shelter." Did I detect a note of amusement in his voice?

"Will that hold up in court?" I asked.

"Shouldn't need to," he said. "I grant you, there probably are wretches who'd try to take kittens and puppies away from decent homes on a point of law and put 'em back in a shelter. And if you wanted to suggest a certain local elected official is curiously indifferent to the welfare of those kittens and puppies, I wouldn't give you much of an argument. But even Mayor Pruitt's not stupid enough to try and take the animals back once someone's adopted them. Makes for bad campaign publicity, crying children asking why he took away Fluffy or Fido. So if you and the Corsicans can get those animals into loving homes, for heaven's sake, do it, quick."

"Roger," I said. "And thanks."

"You know those kittens that were trying to climb my trousers? They spoken for?"

I blinked in surprise.

"Not that I know of. Do you want one?"

"No, but our pastor's wife lost her cat to old age a few months ago. One of those little rascals put me in mind of him. White, with a black spot over one eye like a patch. Spitting image of old Pirate."

"I know the kitten you mean. Shall I hold it for you?"

"Well, I wouldn't put it that way—but let me get my wife on it. Maybe she can bring the pastor's wife over to help, and you could haul out the kittens and let her see Pirate the second."

"It's a plan."

I felt better when I hung up. The massive job of finding homes for all the animals was underway. Okay, it was only one animal. One down—maybe—and who knew how many to go. But still—a start.

I stuck my phone in my pocket and headed for the house.

The kitchen had already begun to revert to its usual state of entropy. Rose Noire was there, making sandwiches by the dozens. Which made sense. The Corsicans had crawled out of bed before dawn to come down here and help with the animals. No one could reasonably expect them to have packed lunches while they were at it, and even though it was only eight thirty, lunchtime would come all too soon.

But seeing the sandwiches piling up made me feel more tired than ever. Or was it the thought that in an hour or so, even I would have a hard time believing that the kitchen had once been tidy.

Rose Noire looked up, saw my face, and jumped to a conclusion.

"Don't worry," she said. "CORSICA will reimburse you for the food and—"

"Don't worry about it," I said. "There's just one thing."

"Yes?"

She was standing with a ham and cheese sandwich half made, clasping the mustard knife with both hands.

"I don't suppose we could ask any of the Corsicans to do a little cleaning in the living room," I said. "Just the animal fur and whatever."

"I think everyone's pretty much got their hands full with the animals," Rose Noire said. "But don't worry. I'll try to come back in and help you later."

Help me? Help *me*? That wasn't exactly what I expected to hear. What I thought I had a right to hear. I wanted to hear, "Don't worry; I'll make sure it's taken care of." The Corsicans had brought the animals here without asking our permission. If they'd checked with me first, I probably would have said yes, but I'd have steered them to the barn, not the living room. Much as I sympathized with the plight of the animals, I didn't think cleaning out the mess they'd made in our living room was exactly my responsibility.

Of course, fat chance getting Rose Noire to understand that. She was clearly in her Joan of Arc mode, head held high, eyes blazing, passionately sharing the suffering of the lost and abandoned animals of the world. Cleaning dung and fur out of our living room was low on her priority list.

I understood. But I also knew that I'd been up since about 2:00 A.M. and I was already at the ragged edge of exhaustion. I counted to ten and choked back several biting things that I'd probably regret later.

"Maybe you could talk to the rest of the Corsicans and see if anyone would like to take a break from tending the animals to do a bit of cleaning," I said finally. "Because I don't have the time or energy to do it anytime soon, and the longer it waits, the nastier it's going to get. God help us if Mother sees it like that."

I strode out of the kitchen and headed upstairs to check on the twins. If neither of them needed feeding or changing, maybe now would be a good time to pump their next meal. And then start a load of diapers. And then—

"Meg?"

I paused halfway up the stairs and glanced down to see Rose Noire staring up at me with an astonished look on her face and her mouth hanging open.

"Yes?" I said.

I watched as a series of expressions flitted across her face. Shock, outrage, and then a look of intense sympathy and compassion.

"Of course," she said. "You do look exhausted. You should get some rest."

"Thank you." I turned to continue up the stairs.

"After all," she called after me, "we have a murder to deal with. I'm sure that's going to take a lot of your time."

I paused for a second. I considered saying that with two infants on my hands, not to mention assorted family members and guests underfoot, it was extremely unlikely that I was going to get involved in any murder investigation, especially not a murder at the other side of the county of someone I hardly knew.

But that would only start an argument. I murmured thanks and continued upstairs.

After all, before I disavowed any interest in the murder, I should make triple sure none of my family or friends was involved. I couldn't imagine anyone I knew knocking off someone who was in the middle of committing an animal rescue, however bizarre and misguided. Then again, I didn't know that much about Parker, apart from the fact that he had a reputation as a small-town Romeo. What else did he do when he wasn't rescuing animals? Maybe I'd try to find out tomorrow.

Or maybe I should just mind my own business.

So should I go back to nap on the recliner in the boys' room, or collapse into my own bed for a change?

I had just reached the top of the stairs and was hovering between the two alternatives when the nursery door opened and Michael stepped out with a twin on each shoulder.

"You're already up!" Michael exclaimed. "Here, if you can take one of the boys, I'll go downstairs and start breakfast."

So much for catching up on my sleep.

Chapter 5

"More blueberry pancakes?"

I shook my head. More pancakes was an impossibility, because so far I hadn't had any. I couldn't quite face breakfast yet. I envied Josh and Jamie, who were happily playing in their crib across the kitchen and could eat and sleep on their own schedules.

I gulped more of my coffee. Decaf coffee, of course, since I didn't want to caffeinate the twins, so any effect it had would be purely psychological.

"More blueberry pancakes, Timmy?" Michael asked.

Timmy, our five-year-old houseguest, nodded enthusiastically.

"What's he doing here?" my grandfather asked, pointing a fork dripping with maple syrup at Timmy.

"Eating breakfast," Michael said. "Don't mind him," he added to Timmy, who was looking suddenly anxious. "He's just cranky before he's had enough coffee."

"Am not," Grandfather growled.

"Are too." Michael grabbed the coffeepot and refilled Grandfather's cup with the real stuff. I tried not to drool.

"You didn't answer my question," Grandfather said. "What's he doing here? Don't you two have enough on your hands already?"

"Timmy's mother's in the army," I began.

"Drafting women now, are they?" Grandfather muttered. "What's the world coming to?"

"She joined up to take advantage of the educational benefits," I said. "Try the coffee."

I hoped he'd drop the subject. Too much talk about his absent mother's whereabouts upset Timmy. For that matter, her absence wasn't a happy subject with me. I had sympathized when my friend Karen decided to leave her job in Caerphilly College's Human Resources department—a dead-end job with a miserably controlling boss. In fact, I'd encouraged her to quit. But her decision to join the army came as rather a shock. Hadn't it occurred to her that she might be deployed somewhere where she couldn't easily take her son?

"She doesn't have family?" Grandfather asked.

"No," I said. "And not a lot of friends who could care for a five-year-old."

"And Timmy likes it here," Michael said. "And we like him."

Timmy's anxious expression gave way to his usual sunny smile.

"Which reminds me," Michael added, looking at me. "Timmy has a T-Ball game today."

"On a Friday? I thought they were always on Saturdays."

"Yes, but it's rained the last two Saturdays, so they're trying to catch up by holding one today. Can you . . . ?"

"Sure," I said. I took out my notebook-that-tells-me-when-to-breathe and flipped to today's page.

"One P.M. at Peter Pruitt Park," Michael said.

I nodded and scribbled.

"What about the animals?" Grandfather asked.

"The Corsicans are looking after the animals, remember?" I said. "I have Timmy and the twins."

"Where is the mother, anyway? Off in the desert somewhere, I suppose, or some remote mountainous part of Afghanistan."

"Germany," I said. "Wiesbaden. Lovely, safe place. On the Rhine. They have wine festivals there."

At least Karen wasn't in a combat zone. Not at the moment, anyway. We were hoping to get word soon that her posting in Germany would be fairly long term, which would mean Timmy could join her. In the meantime, thanks to my brother, Rob, she wasn't going to miss too many of those precious childhood moments.

"Look this way, Timmy!" Rob said. He was once again wielding his new little video camera—a marvelous bit of technology, simple enough for a mechanical klutz like Rob to use and small enough to fit in his pocket. Which meant no one was safe from his quest to capture every single significant or picturesque moment in all our lives.

Timmy grinned, displaying three very large blueberries stuck, with suspicious regularity, in his front teeth. He and Rob both dissolved with laughter.

Timmy was currently Rob's favorite video subject. He had days of footage of the boys, of course, separately, together, and with every willing member of the family. But since at four months the boys' repertoire consisted of eating, sleeping, crying, having their diapers changed, making cute faces, and being played with by family members, even as doting an uncle as Rob eventually became restless for new subjects. Timmy's arrival several weeks ago had been a godsend.

"Come on, Timmy," Rob said. "Let's go film some of the animals."

"Let's talk to the macaw," Timmy said. "He's funny."

"Not the macaw," Michael said. "He's sleeping."

"Can't we wake him up?" Timmy asked.

"Maybe later," Michael said.

"We need to document the animals in the barn anyway," Rob said.

They dashed out, followed more slowly by my grandfather.

"Macaws need a lot of sleep?" I could sympathize.

"This one does," Michael said. "The more he sleeps the better. When he's awake, he has a vocabulary that would make Lenny Bruce blush."

"I know," I said. "I met the macaw last night, remember?"

"I don't want Timmy picking up any bad habits from the damned bird." Michael was already working to reform his own vocabulary, not that he'd ever been as bad as the macaw.

"For that matter, we don't want the boys to hear too much of him," I said.

"No way the macaw is staying long enough for the boys to be influenced," Michael said. "Or any of the other animals."

"I agree," I said. "No matter what Dad and Grandfather may think."

But I was relieved to hear that Michael was so adamant, since he was a sucker for stray animals himself. Only a month ago he'd brought home a half-blind elderly rescue llama that brought our herd to four. Of course the llamas stayed out in their pasture, and throwing out feed for four wasn't that much more work than feeding three, but still.

"So," I said. "What's our schedule for the day? Apart from T-Ball at one?"

I flourished my notebook. Michael reached into his pocket, pulled out his small Day-Timer notebook and flipped it open.

"My Friday afternoon class ends at two thirty," he said. "Do you want me to come back home and pitch in with the child-care, or do the grocery shopping?"

"I'd love to do the grocery shopping," I said. "And I freely warn you that I feel that way because with all these animals underfoot, things will be crazy around here."

"My plan is to use the animals to keep Timmy amused, and guilt-trip a few of the Corsicans into giving me a hand with the twins," Michael said.

I thought of pointing out how difficult it would be, sticking to a plan with the twins on your hands, an ancillary kindergar-tener underfoot, the barn filled with stolen animals, and a mur-der investigation underway. But he already knew that.

And for the moment, the Corsicans did seem to have the animal care well in hand. During the interval between break-fast and my departure for Timmy's ball game, they only inter-rupted me about four or five times an hour, which meant that I had more than enough time to handle my few chores: feeding, burping, washing, and dressing the twins; gathering up four times as many dishes as usual and putting as many of them as possible into the dishwasher; dumping all the towels and other washable linens soiled by the animals by the washer; rolling up a small piddled-on area rug so I could drop it at the carpet cleaners, chivvying Timmy into his uniform and then loading him, his T-Ball gear, the babies, and all their accoutrements into the Twinmobile, as Michael and I called the used minivan we'd acquired to handle our suddenly expanded family.

On my way to the ballfield I passed more than the usual number of cars heading out toward our house on our relatively peaceful country road. More Corsicans volunteering to help out, I hoped. Or maybe even aspiring pet owners coming to view the selection.

"Meg," Timmy asked. "Where did all those puppies come from?"

He wasn't really asking *that* question, was he? I decided to answer him more literally.

"From the animal shelter."

"But how did they all fit?" he asked. "It's not that big."

"They didn't fit very well," I said. "So—"

"Is that why the nasty mayor was going to kill them all?"

Glancing in the rearview mirror, I could see that his normally cheerful face was frowning thunderously. Mayor Pruitt had lost another future voter.

And I saw no reason not to tell him the truth.

"That's pretty much the reason," I said. "Not enough space, and also feeding all those animals costs a lot of money."

"But they're safe now with you and Michael, right? You won't let him have them back."

I winced.

"Yes," I said. "They're safe. The Corsicans will take care of them until they find permanent homes."

But what would the Corsicans do if the crisis turned into a siege?

Not something I could solve right now. We turned into the parking lot and my worry over the future was pushed aside by the immediate challenge of getting all three small boys safely to the field.

I made sure that Timmy's uniform was on properly and that he had all his equipment, and released him in the direction of the rest of his team. Then I wheeled the double baby carriage over to a place beside the bleachers and parked myself and my well-stocked, two-ton diaper bag on the metal bench. I nodded to several mothers I knew slightly, but in the few weeks Timmy had been with us, I'd been too busy with the twins to spend much time getting to know the parents of his classmates and teammates. I started to feel guilty about that, and squelched the impulse mercilessly. Feeling guilty about letting down Timmy was Karen's job. My job was feeling guilty about letting down the twins.

Out on the field, the coach and various parents who'd volunteered or been drafted as assistant coaches were herding the Caerphilly Red Sox toward their bench. Someone had applied generous daubs of eye black to all the players' cheeks, making them look more than ever like a small but savage tribe about to go on the warpath.

I peered down at my own small savages. Josh was fast asleep. Jamie was awake, and happily watching a small, faceted toy, rather like a miniature disco ball, that hung from the roof of the carriage, twirling and glittering in the slightest breeze. Rob's contribution. Clearly I should pay more attention to Rob's notions of how to amuse the twins.

Odds were both boys would want something soon, and probably simultaneously, but for now, I could bask in the pleasantly warm April air and relax.

Or maybe not. Over on the Red Sox bench, Timmy and one

of his teammates had begun hitting each other on the helmet with their bats and giggling uproariously. Where was the bench coach? And for that matter, where was the other kid's mother?

I should do something. But the bench was a good ten feet away from the bleachers. I looked around and spotted someone I knew from the pediatrician's office.

"Could you keep an eye on my twins for a second?" I asked her.

She nodded, and I strode over to the bench and grabbed the end of the other kid's bat just as he was about to pound Timmy's helmet.

"Stop that," I said.

"We're wearing helmets," the other kid said. "It's not going to hurt anything."

He pulled at the bat, trying free it.

"Bats against the fence unless you're actually batting." I was quoting one of the few T-Ball rules I'd learned so far. I pulled a little harder and gained possession of the bat. "You, too," I said, holding out my hand to Timmy, who promptly surrendered his blunt instrument. He wasn't a bad child, just a little easily misled.

I hooked the bats into the chain-link fence behind home plate and returned to my seat by the baby carriage.

"Thanks," I said to my temporary babysitter.

"You're welcome," she said. "You saved me the trouble of walking over there. That was one of my monsters trying to bludgeon your kid."

I wasn't quite sure how to respond, but fortunately I didn't have to. She was soon immersed in a conversation with two other mothers about logistics for a birthday party. A birthday party to which Timmy hadn't been invited. Maybe I should start working to improve his social life.

The Caerphilly Red Sox took the field. Timmy was playing the pitcher's position. Of course since in T-Ball the kids whacked a stationary ball set atop an overgrown golf tee, "pitcher" was a purely honorary title for an additional infielder. I smiled and waved, in case he was watching. The Clay County Yankees' coach hauled out the tee, placed a ball on it, and began coaxing the first batter to take his place at the plate.

"Hello, Meg."

I turned and smiled.

"Hello, Francine," I said. I tried to make my smile warmer than usual, since I was looking at the one parent on the bleachers who probably felt even more out of it than I did. Francine Mann, wife of our new and unloved county manager, was so shy and self-effacing that she hadn't had much luck making friends in her six months in Caerphilly. It didn't help that she had a New England accent so strong it sounded like someone trying to parody one of the Kennedy clan. Many locals had a hard time accepting anyone whose southern accent revealed that they came from a different corner of Dixie. A strong Yankee accent could be the kiss of death with them. And Francine's husband's decision on the animal shelter was probably the last nail in the coffin of her social aspirations. I could bet she wasn't getting a lot of friendly looks from the locals these days.

I'd been on the receiving end of "not from around here" my-self when I'd first moved to Caerphilly, even though I'd grown up only an hour's drive away. I felt a sort of kinship with her. Or was it just pity?

"Nice to see you," I said. "How have you been?"

"Fine." She didn't look fine. Her shoulders were hunched as if she expected a blow from somewhere. Then again, she was tall—almost a match for my five feet ten. Perhaps she merely had an extreme case of the bad posture many tall women adopt in a vain attempt to minimize their size.

"How are the babies?" she asked.

I reported their latest stats and accomplishments, and she oohed and aahed. Thank goodness for the twins, who provided a neutral topic of conversation. I liked Francine well enough. She'd been very kind to me when I was in the hospital, where she held some sort of administrative job. But I had no idea what her interests were and I suspected we had little in common.

Except babies. Clearly they were an interest. Quite possibly an obsession. I'd heard enough town gossip to know that she and her husband had no children of their own, and that the six-year-old she chauffeured to practices and games was her husband's son by a brief first marriage.

As she cooed over the twins, I found myself suspecting the lack of additional children wasn't her choice. Her husband's maybe, or Mother Nature's, but not hers.

"They're dahling." Her accent was, as usual, particularly pronounced on the *ar* and *er* sounds.

I heard some muttering behind me. Did I detect the word "Yankee"? I focused on Francine.

"And you're so lucky," she was saying. "Didn't I hear you've found a live-in nanny?"

"No," I said. "We do have one of my cousins living with us. The house is enormous, and you know how tight the housing market is in Caerphilly. And luckily Rose Noire likes helping with the children."

Actually, although Rose Noire loved the boys dearly, I suspected her motive for helping out was her fear that, left to our own devices, Michael and I probably wouldn't feed the boys entirely on wholesome, organic food, much less raise them to be self-aware, environmentally responsible little vegetarians.

"Oh, no," someone behind me said. "They're swarming again."

Swarming? I looked around, expecting to see a cloud of some kind of insect and ready to throw myself between it and the twins. But no one else seemed alarmed, and I realized that the speaker was pointing to the ball field. One of the Clay County Yankees had gotten a decent hit, and several of our Red Sox were competing to see who could reach it first.

In fact, the first, second and third basemen, the left and right shortstops, and the left and center fielders were all running madly in the direction of the ball. I understood what the other mother meant by swarming. The only players not involved were the right fielder, who appeared to be taking a nap; the catcher, who was so weighed down by his protective gear that he could barely walk; and Timmy, who was watching a bug crawl up his arm.

"Play your positions! Play your positions!" the coach was shouting.

"Jason! Get back on first base!" one mother shouted. "Jason, I mean it! Now!"

Other mothers and a few fathers shrieked equally futile instructions. The kids were ignoring them, and had ended up in a small, writhing heap in the general vicinity of where we'd last seen the ball.

The Yankee runner had reached first base and was watching the action, perhaps wondering if she should try for another base. In a real ball game, she'd have been crazy not to. By this time, three of the Red Sox were wrestling for the ball, while the coach and one of the fathers tried to separate them, and the rest of the team stood watching and cheering them on. The Yankee batter could probably have made two or three circuits of the bases by the time one Red Sox player emerged holding the ball.

But in T-Ball, there was either a rule or a longstanding tradition that you only got one base when you hit the ball, so after looking longingly at second, the runner sat down on first base to untie and retie her shoelaces half a dozen times.

"Positions!" the Red Sox coach shouted, giving various players gentle shoves in the right directions. "Positions!"

But it took a while for the game to resume, because one of the players who had not won the fight for the ball ran off the field to be comforted by his mother, and another sat down in the outfield and refused to get up. And when the Red Sox coach finally got all his players upright and back where they belonged, someone finally noticed that there were two Yankee runners on second base. It took several minutes to sort out which one belonged there and which one should have continued on to third when the batter got her hit.

"Coach really needs Sammy," one of the mothers behind us said when the game finally resumed. "Keeping those kids in line is tough enough without being shorthanded."

"Well, don't count on seeing Sammy for a while," another mother said. "Chief's got him pretty busy with this murder investigation."

"He'd be here if this wasn't the very first day of the investigation," the first one said.

"I hope you're right," said the other. "Because if the chief kept him on overtime until they could check out everyone Parker Blair ever fooled around with, the season would be over before we saw him again."

"The season?" The other mother snorted. "Are you kidding? Our kids would be in college before we saw him again!"

The two of them cackled together.

I glanced at Francine. She was frowning, lips pursed. Evidently she shared my feeling that too much hilarity at the expense of a murdered man was in poor taste.

"Good God," one of the mothers at the top of the bleachers stage-whispered, pointing at the field. "What do you suppose *those* two are up to?"

"No good, that's for sure," another muttered.

Chapter 6

I looked to see what the two mothers were talking about and winced. Terence Mann, Francine's husband, was the third-base coach. But he wasn't watching the game at the moment. He was talking intently to Mayor Pruitt.

I studied Mann. He was tall, a little over six feet, but gave the impression of being taller—partly because he was rail thin and narrow shouldered, and partly because he had a slight, habitual stoop, as if he spent far too much time courteously bending down to listen attentively to much shorter people. He had the sort of face most people called handsome mainly because it was symmetrical and you couldn't put your finger on anything in particular that was wrong with any of the features.

He was stooping even more than usual to reach down to Mayor Pruitt's level. Why, I have no idea—considering how red the mayor's face was, and how wildly he was waving his arms, he was probably shouting loud enough for Mann to hear him without stooping. In fact, stooping probably put Mann much closer to the mayor's bellows than I'd care to be.

And even from the bleachers I could tell that the mayor wasn't using language you'd want five- and six-year-olds to hear. Someone should go over and tell him to clean it up in front of the kids.

I was standing up to do it myself when the Red Sox coach dashed over and shooed them off the field. The mayor ignored him, but Mann began loping off the field almost before the coach arrived. To keep haranguing him, the mayor had to scurry in his wake, like a ping-pong ball chasing a praying mantis.

"Good riddance to bad rubbish," one of the mothers said. Several others tittered.

Francine shot a quick glance in their direction and then fixed her eyes on the field. Her face looked grim, but I had to admire her presence of mind. I'd have been tempted to confront the two gossiping mothers if they'd said something like that about my husband.

Then again, maybe she wasn't angry at them. Maybe she was at least a little upset with her husband. I had a feeling she wasn't just annoyed because his inattentiveness had contributed to the melee on the field.

I patted her arm.

"Don't let it get to you," I said, softly enough that the others wouldn't hear.

She glanced up and smiled, briefly.

"I'm used to it," she said, in a similarly quiet tone. "Of course, this whole shelter thing is making it worse than ever." She pronounced shelter more like "shelteh," causing me to mishear it, just for a second, as "sheltie," and spend a few anxious moments racking my brain to recall if we had a sheltie at the house, or if there had been some kind of sheltie-related incident in town. Clearly I had dogs and cats on the brain.

"It'll blow over," I said.

"I doubt it," she said. "I've even thought of taking some kind of speech lessons so I blend in more. Do you think maybe your husband would know someone at the drama department who could teach me how to speak more like the locals?"

"Probably," I said. "But why would you want to? A lot of people pay good money to get rid of southern accents—why would you want to learn one? Especially since in a year or two—"

I was about to say that in a year or two, they'd probably move someplace else when her husband took another job. Probably not a tactful thing to say. What if she was hoping they'd settle down and lead the rest of their lives in Caerphilly? Or what if she was thinking, like many of the locals, that her husband might not last a few more months in his job, let alone another year or two?

"In a year or two, people will stop noticing your accent so much," I went on, changing my course. "They won't pretend to think of you as a native—I've lived in Caerphilly for years now, and they have yet to forget that I'm not from around here. To some locals, you're an outsider for life if all four of your grandparents weren't born in Caerphilly County. Don't sweat it."

"I just wish—" she began.

But whatever she was intending to say was drowned out by an abrupt howl from Josh. I began digging through the diaper bag.

"Hell of a set of lungs on that kid," one of the mothers said. She sounded cross and superior, as if to imply that as infants, her darlings had always asked softly and politely for their meals.

"Just stop your ears for a second," I said. "I'll take care of him." Jamie joined in.

"Can you handle both at once?" Francine asked.

"Not easily," I said. "Would you mind doing one?"

"I'd love to!"

I handed her Josh and a bottle, and picked up Jamie to do the honors with him.

"You're not breastfeeding!" one of the mothers exclaimed.

"Don't you realize how important breast milk is for babies' health! You should—"

"I completely understand the importance of breast milk," I said. "That's why I pump as much of it as I can, divide it in half so each boy gets his fair share, and top it off with enough formula to fill them up, since by now they're *each* drinking slightly more in a day than I can produce."

"Well, that's all right then." The woman pulled back slightly. Had I snapped at her? My tone had sounded perfectly civil to me, but I was running on even less sleep than usual, so I wasn't necessarily a good judge of the finer points of human interaction.

"Sorry if I snapped," I said. "My dad's a doctor, you know, so I get rather a lot of free medical advice from him."

"I'm sure," she said.

"He and my cousin Rose Noire are in complete support of what I'm doing," I said. Although Dad and Mother were only part-time residents of Caerphilly, he commanded a certain amount of respect in the county. So did Rose Noire, though in somewhat different circles—but if any of these women shared my cousin's interests in alternative medicine, organic nutrition, and holistic child-rearing, they'd probably feel reassured.

"Oh, well that's great, then," the mother said. She was edging farther away from me.

Had I made things better or worse? I couldn't tell. Either way, if I'd made her wary of publicly reproaching bottle-feeding mothers, maybe that wasn't a bad thing. Not everyone had a choice about how to feed their babies. What if I was one of those mothers who couldn't produce milk at all, or whose babies couldn't easily feed? Or an adoptive mother? Couldn't she imagine how someone in one of those situations would feel? Her words stung me a little, even though my only problem was that my kids outnumbered me and had healthy appetites.

And why did I feel so compelled to defend myself to these women I hardly knew? When had motherhood become so damned competitive?

At my side, Francine was shaking her head and chuckling slightly.

"Honestly," she whispered, rolling her eyes. "Some people."

I felt reassured. I settled Jamie in a comfortable position and checked on the game. The Red Sox were at bat now. Timmy and his teammates were having a competition to see who could pull his batting helmet down the farthest over his eyes.

"How many innings do these games run?" I asked.

"Only three," Francine said. "Feels like nine, though."

"That's because it takes about as long as nine in the majors." I sighed and tried to find a more comfortable position on the unpadded metal bench. I was probably in for a lot of hours on these bleachers. Both Michael and my father adored baseball, so if either or both of the boys showed the slightest shred of athletic ability, they'd undoubtedly be playing T-Ball in another five years.

So I'd get a head start planning how I was going to cope. For example, figuring out how to volunteer for a cushy job before getting assigned an impossible one. I didn't want to be bench coach, for example. It was like playing a game of whack-a-mole with live preschoolers. Not an assignment I should take on.

But the mother who was sitting beside a grocery bag of snacks and a cooler full of cold treats, guarding them lest the team begin pigging out prematurely—now that was the job to have. Snack Mom.

Or perhaps even better, the job of the woman who came up and exchanged a few words with the snack mom before scribbling a few things on the paper on her clipboard. Snack Coordinator.

"I hope she brought something my monster will eat," one mother muttered behind us.

"I think it's more important that the snack be healthy," another mother announced.

As I listened to the ensuing debate over the relative merits of organic trail mix and Cheetos, I decided that any job connected to the snacks was too controversial.

Base coach. You stood out in the field, you made sure the runner ran when the ball was hit, and in the right direction, and you tried to keep the baseman awake and pointed toward the game. And you stood far away from the bleachers and their gossiping occupants. My kind of job.

A job Terence Mann seemed to have given up on. He and the mayor had retreated to a more private place near the edge of the woods that surrounded the athletic field and were still having a visibly heated conversation. Mann seemed to be getting the worst of it—most people did when they argued with the mayor. But the mayor didn't look happy either.

What were they up to?

The thought continued to nag at me for the rest of the game and all the way home. Michael was out in the barn helping with the animals, so I dropped Timmy and the boys with him and went back to the house to grab what I needed to run my errands.

And maybe one of my errands should be stopping somewhere to learn a little more information about what was going on in town. But where? Bothering the chief for information was definitely out, but if I ran into Horace, I could probably get a few tidbits about the murder investigation. Ms. Ellie, at the library, kept her finger on the pulse of local politics, and could probably hazard a guess at what Mayor Pruitt and Terence Mann had been arguing about. But I wasn't sure anyone could answer the most nagging question—whether Parker Blair's murder had anything to do with any of this. For that—

"Earth to Meg?"

Chapter 7

I glanced up to see Caroline Willner looking at me with a concerned frown on her face. No wonder. I was standing in the pantry doorway with my stack of fabric grocery bags in my hand, staring into space.

"Sorry," I said. "I was just thinking. Sleep deprivation meets information overload. How's everything out in the barn?"

"Fine, as long as someone sensible's there to keep them organized." Clearly from her tone, Caroline considered herself the number one if not the only person to fill the sensible post. "Can I ask you a question or two? About something I can't seem to get a straight answer on from any of the Corsicans?"

"Sure." I dumped my empty bags on one of the kitchen chairs and sat down myself. Even if Caroline's question was a short and simple one, my feet were tired.

"You could use some tea," she said. She grabbed two cups from the cupboard.

"You don't have to bother," I said. "I could do that."

"Sit," she said. "And give me the straight scoop on this Mayor Pruitt."

"I'd call him a weasel, if that wasn't an insult to any self-respecting mustelid. What about him?"

Caroline popped two cups of cold water into the microwave and punched a few buttons before answering.

"I've been talking to Randall Shiffley today," she said finally.

"What's Randall doing here?" Since Randall owned and ran the Shiffley Construction Company, we usually only saw him when something needed repairing or renovating. Just hearing his name made me want to go and make sure the family checkbook was still safely stowed in my desk, and that the stubs didn't show any more five-figure bites out of our savings.

"Doing a few repairs that your father thought we needed for the safety and comfort of the animals," Caroline said. "Don't worry," she added, seeing from my expression that I already was. "I think you'll find they're all improvements, and if you don't agree, Randall can undo them."

I took a deep breath. I didn't trust Dad's judgment, but if Caroline and Randall thought these were improvements, they probably were. And then Caroline added the final note of reassurance.

"And CORSICA's paying, of course. Anyway, since he got here this morning, Randall Shiffley's been telling me some pretty shocking things about Mayor Pruitt. Should I take them with a grain of salt?"

I sighed.

"Yes, but only a grain," I said. "Randall's a Shiffley, and the mayor's a Pruitt. Randall would almost rather cut out his tongue than say something nice about a Pruitt. Not that I can imagine the mayor doing anything worth praising. Keep in mind, of course, that I'm not precisely a neutral observer. I've had a few run-ins with the Pruitts myself."

"The Pruitts and Shiffleys are feuding then?" Caroline looked as if she would enjoy a nice, juicy bit of gossip. "Kind of a Montague and Capulet thing?"

"I'd have said Hatfields and McCoys, but you get the general idea," I said. "The Shiffleys are old Caerphilly. Their ancestors settled the area, and some of them are living on and farming land that's been in their family since before the Revolution. The Pruitts were carpetbaggers—came in just after the Civil War and built factories and mansions. In some places, a hundred and fifty years would qualify you as a native, but not in this part of Virginia. To the Shiffleys, the Pruitts are still Not from Around Here."

The microwave dinged.

"And yet a Pruitt got elected mayor," she said, as she popped tea bags into our steaming cups.

"Of the town," I said. "Half the town council are Pruitts, if it comes to that. Pruitts or political allies of the Pruitts. Town politics are dominated by the Pruitts and the college, which was founded by a Pruitt. It's different in the county. That's dominated by farmers."

"Ah," she said. "That explains why the town's so progrowth while the county's doggedly against it."

"We here in the county prefer to think of ourselves as pro-preservation," I said.

"Makes it hard for the two to work together, I should think," she said.

"Almost impossible," I said. "The town's governed by an elected town council headed by the mayor. They don't really have much jurisdiction over anything except town ordinances, but they meet at least twice a week and issue no end of press releases and proclamations that everyone generally ignores. The county is governed by an elected county board, most of them working farmers or people who come from farm families. They meet once or twice a month, make all the important decisions pretty efficiently, and delegate carrying them out to the county manager."

"This county manager," she said.

"Terence Mann," I said. "He's new. Here about six months. And even before the animal shelter fiasco broke, I wouldn't have bet on his staying around much longer."

"You can't blame him for the financial problems," she said. "Not something he had any control over."

"And not limited to Caerphilly," I said. "I don't think people blame him for the problem, however unhappy they are about some of his proposed solutions. No, what's got people in the county grumbling is that he seems to be getting along way too well with the Pruitts. And in case you hadn't already figured it out, in the same way that the town council is dominated by the Pruitts and their friends, the county board is mainly the Shiffleys and their friends."

"Okay," she said. "Now I understand what Clarence was suggesting at our last Corsican meeting."

"Was this the meeting when you finalized your plans for the burglary?" I asked. "I'm still wondering why you didn't help out."

"Had a fund-raiser in Charlottesville that night," she said. "Or I would have. According to Clarence, the animal shelter belongs to the county?"

"I assume it does," I said. "Given how small a population the town and county have, it doesn't make sense to have separate facilities. There's one school system, one library system. The chief is both chief of the town police and the deputy sheriff of the county, since the elected sheriff is older than Grandfather and a lot less active."

"So if it's a county shelter, why's the town running it?"

"The county lets the town run most of the facilities that fall within the town limits," I said. "Keeps the town council busy and out of mischief."

"Okay, it's making more sense," she said. "Right now, we have to deal with both the mayor and the county manager because the shelter belongs to the county but it's in the town. And we could cut the mayor out entirely if we found new premises for the shelter. Premises outside the town limits."

"Our barn is not a viable option for that," I said.

"No, it's not," she said. "I was thinking of someplace out at your grandfather's zoo. But don't mention that to him yet. I will, when I have all my ducks in a row."

"Of course not." The thought of Caroline railroading my grandfather into turning a part of his beloved zoo into an animal shelter charmed me.

"Of course, we want to get the county board to issue a strong no-kill policy before we let them have the animals back," Caroline said. "What's the best way to get that done?"

"Talk to Randall Shiffley," I suggested. "He could enlist the rest of his family."

"Hmm." Caroline's eyes showed a familiar fund-raiser's gleam. "Big animal lovers, are they?"

I pondered the question. I rather thought the Shiffleys did love animals, but with a love that was tempered by the pragmatic realism of the working farmer. A love that couldn't afford to get too sentimental about turkeys who'd be going to market for Thanksgiving. That could appreciate the beauty of a Virginia whitetail deer without losing a taste for venison. Left to their own devices, I wasn't at all sure that the men and women of the county board would stand fast on the no-kill shelter policy. Too many of them had had to sell off their herds in lean years or put down ailing animals when they could no longer afford even Clarence's low fees and lenient terms. I could see them, however reluctantly, agreeing to the change in shelter policy.

But having the town try to ram the policy change down their throats? Properly handled, that was exactly the thing that would make the board members dig in their heels like so many mules.

"Some of them are big animal lovers," I finally said aloud. "But all of them are big Pruitt haters. Get Randall to talk to them, and make sure he knows this is a chance to spite the mayor and his family. That should do the trick."

"Excellent," Caroline said. "As always, you're more help than any three normal people put together."

She drained her teacup and strode briskly out the back door.

"What do you mean by 'normal people'?" I asked, but she was out of earshot.

Still brooding over her comment, I finished my own tea and put both mugs on the counter at the base of the mountain of dirty dishes that wouldn't yet fit into the dishwasher. I realized it was four o'clock, and I needed to hurry if I wanted to beat the Friday after-work shoppers to the grocery store. I grabbed my purse and the stack of totes and headed for the front door.

Which was standing open to allow Rob and several other Corsicans to carry the macaw's enormous cage through it. I was waiting with reasonable patience for the path to be clear when I realized something was wrong.

"I think you've got that backwards," I said. "The cage should be going out to the barn, not coming into our living room."

Chapter 8

My objection had no effect on the Corsicans lugging the cage.

"Dad says we need to bring the macaw back inside the house," Rob said. He seemed to welcome an excuse to abandon his comrades to struggle with their burden. "He's a bad influence."

"Dad? I wouldn't say that. Just a little obsessive sometimes."

"The bird," Rob said. "He's picking up bad habits."

"I've heard his current vocabulary," I said. "I can't imagine anything he'd pick up from the Corsicans that wouldn't be an improvement."

"He's learning to bark, growl, hiss, caterwaul, and howl," Rob said. "Gets the other animals riled up. We had to move two Persian cats and a Pekingese into one of the sheds before they had a nervous breakdown. And every time he makes a noise like an animal in agony, all the Corsicans have to come running to check it out. He's driving every other creature in the barn crazy, two- and four-legged alike. So Dad said bring him back into the house for a little bit, until we can find another place to keep him."

"Why not move him to one of the sheds?"

"Dunno." Rob shrugged. "Dad's back; ask him."

He followed the cage into the living room. I went outside and looked around for Dad.

I spotted him in the backyard. He and Randall Shiffley were standing by one of the larger and more dilapidated of our dozen or so sheds, apparently discussing some renovations. I strolled over to join them.

"Please tell me you don't have to do much work to make this shed macaw-worthy," I said.

"Needs a new roof." Randall thumped the lowest part of the roof. Several shingles and a lot of little wood splinters rattled down as if in emphasis.

"It needs a lot more than that," I replied. "We're not even sure we want to keep that one."

"No, it's not the best of your sheds," Randall said. "You're probably eventually going to want to tear it down, but for right now, it only needs a new roof for you to keep the macaw in it."

"And if after that you still don't want it, Randall can put it on his big truck and move it to our farm," Dad said.

"Move it anywhere you like." Was Randall just being accommodating, or did he, like me, have some idea of exactly how Mother would greet the arrival of a dilapidated shed on the grounds of the farm she was trying to transform into a picture perfect weekend haven?

"Okay, if that's what it takes to get the macaw out of our living room, then do it," I said. "How soon can you start?"

"Heading out to get the supplies now," Randall said. "If they have everything I need in stock at the hardware store, maybe today. If they have to order anything, it'll be Monday before they can get it in."

Not what I wanted to hear, but then another night or two with the macaw in the living room wouldn't kill us. Especially if we kept the cover on his cage.

"Keep me posted." I nodded to Randall and headed back to the house. Dad trotted along after me.

"So how was your day?" he asked.

"Busy," I said. "And not over yet. But okay." And then, since he was obviously dying for me to ask, I added, "How was yours?"

"Difficult," he said. "This is going to be a tough case to solve."

"I'm sure the chief is up to it," I said.

"And poor Horace." Dad shook his head. "He had to go all over that grisly crime scene, and he hardly found any usable evidence."

Dad sounded remarkable cheerful about Horace's ordeal.

"I thought Parker was shot at close range in the cab of his truck," I said. "You're not saying it left no traces?"

"More than traces," Dad said. "The cab was horrible. But the range wasn't quite that close. Not close enough to guarantee blood spatter on the suspect's clothing. Not that we've got enough evidence against anyone to make it worth testing their clothing."

I winced at the "we" and hoped he wasn't annoying the chief too badly.

"How do you know?" I said. "About the range?"

"Well, Smoot is out of town, you know," Dad said.

I shook my head. Dr. Smoot, the acting medical examiner, was already on thin ice with the chief. And this wasn't the first time he'd been out of town when needed.

"No, I didn't know. Was the chief irritated or relieved?"

"A little of both, I think," he said. "So the chief had me do a preliminary examination of the body. And a good thing, too, since I discovered something important."

Apparently he and Horace were feeling competitive today,

which at least partially explained his glee over Horace's supposed failure to uncover any evidence.

"Congratulations," I said.

Dad frowned, and glanced around to make sure no one was within earshot. The yard was peaceful and empty, except for a border collie chivvying three sheep around the corner of the house.

"Of course I shouldn't be telling you this," he began.

And, of course, he would, if I just waited.

"The shot may have been fired from a slight distance," he said finally. "Making Horace's life difficult. But before his death, Parker appears to have struggled with his killer in some fashion. Or possibly quarreled. Because— Remember, you have to keep this to yourself."

I nodded. I was watching the border collie, which appeared to be herding the sheep toward our barn. He didn't seem to be accompanied by a human shepherd.

"The killer appears to have taken a trophy!" Dad announced.

He seemed to find this fascinating. I didn't.

"Yuck," I said. "I do not want to know about missing body parts, if that's what you mean."

"Oh, no!" he said. "Nothing like that. You know how Parker always wore an earring in one ear?"

"I hardly knew the man." I mentally applauded as the border collie deftly steered the sheep away from our rosebushes. "So I'll have to take your word for it."

"Well, he did. It was a ruby. Or maybe just a sparkly red stone that looked like a ruby. I suppose that's trendy, earrings on men?"

"It was at one time." I shifted position so I could continue watching the border collie, which had succeeded in driving the sheep through the barn door. "It still could be. I'm not exactly up on trendy. Dad, were there sheep at the animal shelter?"

"No, only domestic animals. Why?"

"Then what's he doing?" I pointed to the border collie, which had popped out of the barn door, minus his flock. "He just herded three sheep into our barn."

"Yes, I saw that," Dad said. "Good technique. They look like Seth's sheep. Maybe the Corsicans borrowed some to keep the border collie happy."

"Maybe," I said. He was probably right that the sheep belonged to Seth Early, our across-the-street neighbor. But I wasn't sure I believed that Seth would willingly lend a trio of his prized Lincoln sheep just to keep a rescue dog happy. I suspected the border collie was doing a little unauthorized herding.

But that was the Corsicans' problem, not mine.

"Getting back to Parker," I said. "So he normally wore an earring. Is this important?"

"I suppose he thought the earring made him look rather piratical," Dad said. "And of course he could never have foreseen that it would be a clue in his murder!"

"No," I agreed. "I don't suppose he was expecting to be murdered. Most people aren't. But even if the earring's missing, it isn't necessarily a clue. They fall off, you know, and sometimes people forget to put them on."

"It's not just missing—it was ripped out with enough force to tear the earlobe!"

I winced and had to consciously stop myself from touching my own earlobes. In the last several months I'd given up wearing earrings except on special occasions, to avoid the very real danger that the boys would innocently do the same thing to me.

"Poor guy," I said.

"Of course, word will get out once we have the funeral," Dad said. "Maudie Morton can make the ear look fine, of course, but people will notice that his earring's missing."

"The chief probably won't release the body for a few days," I said. "Maybe they'll find the earring by then."

"If they do, it'll be evidence," Dad said.

"Buy another one," I said. "Or tell people he couldn't be buried with it because he was leaving it to someone in his will."

"He was only in his late thirties," Dad said. "With no dependents. I'd be surprised if he had a will."

"Then get Clarence to say Parker told him he wanted his earring sent to his elderly mother in Dubuque, or wherever he's from."

Was he trying to make this difficult?

"He grew up here, and his mother died years ago."

"Or that he wanted it sold so the proceeds could be donated to some animal welfare organization," I went on.

"That might work," Dad said.

"Of course, there's always the option of having a closed casket," I suggested. "If he was shot in the head—"

"The neck, actually."

"If he was shot anywhere that Maudie would have to cover up a bullet hole for the viewing, maybe you should go for the closed casket."

"You don't think people will be disappointed, not being able to say good-bye?" Dad asked.

"I think they'll manage to say good-bye without a viewing," I said. "And think of the enjoyment everyone will have, looking solemn and intoning 'Of course, it *had* to be a closed casket.'"

"Good point," he said. "And it really would be easier."

I turned toward my car again.

"Of course," he added, to my back, "it would be even better if the earring were found."

And clearly he thought I was the one to do it.

"I'll keep my eyes open," I said. "Speaking of keeping eyes open—here comes the border collie with four more sheep. He's got to be getting them from Seth Early's pasture. Could you check it out? See if anyone knows he's doing it?"

"Can do!" Dad said. "Happy hunting!" He sounded cheerful again.

As he bustled off toward the barn, I found myself thinking that people were taking Parker's death quite philosophically. With the exception of the two ex-girlfriends, I hadn't seen anyone genuinely overcome with grief—and who knew how well the ex-girlfriends' grief would survive the discovery of each other's existence? Everyone said what a shame about poor Parker and how much he'd done for animals. A few people were honest enough to call him a letch. I hadn't yet met anyone whose reaction was anything like "You know, some people didn't approve of him, but damn! I'm going to miss him!"

"Poor guy," I said aloud.

And then I, too, forgot about him for the next several hours. By the time I reached the grocery store it was jammed with shoppers. When I finally got home, I grabbed provisions from Rose Noire's sandwich mountain and retreated to the nursery to spend some time with the twins. Downstairs, I could hear people coming and going, calling for Dad, Clarence, Grandfather, Rose Noire. Calling for me, occasionally, and I hope being told that I had a few other things on my plate.

I kept track of what was going on out in the barn through the nursery windows. I'm not really good at staying uninvolved, but I was trying.

Over the course of the afternoon, the border collie escorted ninety-seven sheep from Seth Early's pasture into our barn before they figured out how to secure the barn door and the pasture gate so he couldn't open them. Probably not ninety-seven unique sheep. The Corsicans took them back in batches when they had a chance, and as the day wore on the newly arriving sheep began looking distinctly cross and footsore. On the positive side, Seth was so impressed with the dog's skill and initiative that he put in a bid to adopt him when the chief's embargo was lifted. I made use of the chief's permission to deputize, and sent a very tired but happy border collie across the road to his new permanent home.

By bedtime things were remarkably quiet.

"In fact, it's too quiet," I told Michael as we were feeding the twins at about 8:00 P.M. In what had become a regular Friday night ritual, we had brought the boys to our room and were playing Mozart as we fed them. Rose Noire assured us that this would stimulate their intelligence and creativity. If it did that, fine; for now all I cared about was that it seemed to make them calmer and happier, though I was more than half convinced that their good humor during the weekly concert was a direct result of our more relaxed mood.

"Too quiet—you mean the Mozart? I can turn the volume up a bit if you like. Or are you suggesting we shouldn't have sent Spike off to your parents' house while the animals are here?"

"I think giving Spike a break from the animals was a brilliant idea, and talking Mother and Father into taking him in was a masterful stroke of diplomacy," I said. "I meant everything's too quiet. The animals. The Corsicans. Dad hasn't dropped by for hours to share his latest theory of the crime and nag me into helping him solve it."

"Maybe the chief has solved it."

"We'd have heard."

"Well, then it looks as if Mommy's going to have to help the chief crack the case," Michael said to Jamie. He followed this up by blowing a gentle raspberry on Jamie's stomach, a trick both boys adored. Jamie crowed, and waved his hands and legs furiously.

"See?" Michael said. "Jamie approves."

"He probably doesn't realize that by trying to solve the murder, Mommy would be making herself a target for a killer who might still have possession of the murder weapon," I said.

Michael's face fell.

"You're right, of course," he said. "You shouldn't do anything that might put you in harm's way."

Now if I could just get Dad to see it that way.

Around midnight, when I was up feeding Josh, I heard a noise from the backyard. Or maybe from the barn. I couldn't see anything from the side windows, so I hefted Josh to one shoulder and ventured downstairs.

My first thought was to go out and check on the barn myself. But by the time I got downstairs, I'd remembered what I'd said to Michael a few hours before. Someone had shot Parker, with a gun that had yet to be recovered. I hadn't known Parker well and hadn't seen the crime scene, but my imagination was perfectly able to invent a gruesome image of the blood-spattered windshield Dad had mentioned. As I stood there in the kitchen, with the sleeping baby on my shoulder, that image kept flashing into my mind and made me draw my hand back from the doorknob.

So I flipped on all the outdoor lights instead. We'd had them installed as a security measure, a series of floodlights mounted all around the house and the barn. With them on, the yard might be brighter at high noon, but only a little. I stood in the darkened kitchen, peering out at the barn, trying to catch a glimpse of a prowler, two- or four-legged.

After about five minutes, the barn door opened and Clarence peered out, shading his eyes against the glare from the spotlights.

"Hello?" he called. "Anyone there?"

I moved to the back door and opened it, still staying in the shadows.

"It's me," I called, as softly as I could and still be heard across the barnyard.

Clarence opened the door a little more and trudged across the yard, fighting yawns.

"What's up?" he asked, when he reached the back steps.

"I heard some noise," I said. "Was that what woke you?"

"No," he said. "I can sleep through the animal noise pretty easily. It was that spotlight shining through the window that woke me."

"Sorry," I said. "I thought there might be something wrong. A prowler, maybe."

"I'll check the perimeter," he said, suddenly sounding a lot less sleepy.

I pulled up a chair and sat just inside the doorway, keeping an eye on the barn door as Clarence disappeared around one corner of the barn. It seemed to take forever, but by the clock it was only ten minutes before he reappeared around the other side. He marched back in front of the barn door and lifted his arms and shoulders in an exaggerated shrug, as if to ask, "What next?"

I opened the back door.

"Thanks for checking," I called. "Probably nothing. Good night. And lock the barn door."

Clarence trudged back to the kitchen door. Now that the danger of a prowler seemed past, he was yawning again.

"I can't," he said. "Some of the Corsicans are coming early tomorrow morning to help with the animals."

"More like later this morning," I said. "Can't they just knock?"

"I'm a heavy sleeper," he said. "But I'll put my sleeping bag right in front of the door, where a prowler can't help but wake me."

As dragged out as he looked, I wasn't sure a herd of elephants would wake him. But at least I could make sure all the house doors were locked. Just because Clarence didn't find anything didn't mean there hadn't been someone or something prowling around the barn. Or even in the barn, if Clarence truly was a heavy sleeper.

I made my rounds, checking all the doors and windows. Then I carried Josh upstairs. I peeked in on Timmy, who appeared to have more stuffed animals than he'd had the night before. Closer inspection showed that the new additions were real, not stuffed. And what looked like a fur rug beside his bed would probably turn out to be Tinkerbell, the Irish wolfhound.

I would worry about that in the morning. I made my way quietly to the nursery and carefully settled Josh in his crib—although I figured my care was overkill, since he'd slept through his entire trip downstairs, my conversation with Clarence, my examination of all the ground floor doors and windows, the return trip upstairs, and my stop in Timmy's room.

The second his body touched the crib sheet, he woke up and began screaming bloody murder, awakening Michael and Jamie, who had been fast asleep in the recliner. It was a while before any of us got back to sleep.

Chapter 9

Saturday dawned crisp and clear—the sort of perfect spring morning that makes most people eager to leap out of bed and greet the day.

Of course most people hadn't spent several predawn hours pacing the nursery floor with wailing infants, and eventually driving doggedly up and down the road hoping the kids would fall asleep before their chauffeur did.

"Dad tells me some babies go through a phase when they won't sleep unless you're not just holding them but walking around with them," I reported over breakfast.

"Or driving them around the neighborhood," Michael added, with a yawn. "How long a phase?"

"I didn't ask. I wasn't sure we wanted to know."

Michael nodded.

"But he'll check them out today, just to make sure they're okay," I added.

Most of the time it was a blessing to have a highly qualified doctor willing and even eager to make a house call whenever I was worried about the boys' health. And the boys' arrival had reenergized Dad's interest in keeping up with new developments in pediatrics. I did hope the boys would take Dad's zeal in stride, as my sister, Pam, and I had, and not react as Rob had, by complaining that growing up he felt like a guinea pig.

"When did he have in mind?" Michael asked. "Remember, I'm taking the boys to Timmy's baseball game today."

"I thought his game was yesterday," I said. "I'm sure I remember taking him to participate in something that vaguely resembled baseball."

"Makeup game, remember?" Michael said.

"Oh, right," I said. "So today's the regularly scheduled game."

"Yes, so if your father's coming over specifically to see the boys—"

"He'll be out in the barn with the animals all day," I said. "Unless he gets sucked into the murder investigation again, but I doubt that. I gather there's not a lot of medical uncertainty about how Parker Blair died. So you can just take them out to the barn when convenient. And if you're cool with minding the boys, I'm going to catch up on all those overdue tasks from my notebook. Anything else on our agenda?"

"Only that your mother wanted to invite a few people to dinner, since Caroline and your grandfather are here."

"Our house or theirs?"

"She was a bit vague on the subject—"

"Which means she's planning to have it here." I winced at the thought.

"That's what I figured. So I convinced her that it was better to have it at their house, to avoid the possibility that your father and the other Corsicans would badger the dinner guests to adopt some of the animals."

"You are a genius," I said.

"Are we going now?" Timmy appeared in the doorway, dressed in his Red Sox uniform.

I'd let Michael deal with the fact that Timmy had put on his pants inside out and was wearing his cleats on the wrong feet.

"Shall I get Josh and Jamie ready?" I asked.

"I got them dressed while you were in the shower," he said. "And the diaper bag is waiting in the foyer."

Not for the first time, I gave thanks that Michael was not only capable of taking care of small children but absolutely matter-of-fact about doing it.

And we'd made it to another Saturday morning. Our usual weekend routine was for Michael to spend lots of time with the boys so I could have a little of what he liked to call "me time." I didn't always tell Michael what I did with my me time. He seemed to enjoy imagining me having massages, manicures, and facials before settling in the sunroom to eat bonbons and read a mystery cover to cover. And maybe one of these days I'd do a few of those things. To date, I'd spent my me time doing errands, catching up on neglected household chores, and napping. It was heavenly.

"Great," I said. "Call me if you need me."

I headed for my office in the barn. I had a few phone calls to make and e-mails to send before I started my errands.

Sending the e-mails took twice as long as it should, due to the distractions of a litter of puppies playing at my feet while a trio of kittens attempted to attack my fingers whenever I typed. I decided that unless I wanted people to think I was calling from the animal shelter—which come to think of it, I was—it would be easier to make the phone calls somewhere else. Anywhere else.

I left the barn, declining half a dozen requests for assistance as tactfully as possible, and strode outside.

I was just in time to wave good-bye as Michael finished stashing all three boys in the Twinmobile and drove off to Timmy's T-Ball game. I felt a brief pang of guilt that I'd left him to do it all by myself. But Michael made it look so easy that I sometimes forgot to volunteer help.

I'd pitch in later. Right now, I was running on too little sleep, and too many people were demanding things from me. I was beyond cranky and ready to take it out on someone. Not the boys, who were, as Rob was fond of saying, functioning as designed. But everyone else—

A walk. That was what I needed. It was a beautiful, mild day, perfect for a nice, calming walk. Once I felt better, I could stop somewhere out of sight and hearing of the barn and make my calls with the cell phone before starting my errands.

I set off at a brisk pace.

Ever since Michael and I had moved into our house, I realized that the surrounding countryside was an incredible source of stress relief.

Not our yard. That was part of the stress. Our several acres were pocked with tiny, ramshackle sheds and outbuildings that would eventually have to be removed at great expense or repaired at even greater expense. Seeing Randall's workmen beginning to prepare the roof of the future macaw shed for reshingling didn't improve my mood, especially after one of them stared at the shed, shook his head and muttered, "Lipstick on a pig."

And the landscaping consisted mostly of overgrown shrubbery that had been there when we bought the house, plus a few bare, weedy areas where we'd succeeded in hacking away moribund bushes but hadn't yet filled the space with anything better. Rose Noire had started off with great plans for beautiful, maintenance-free plantings of deer-resistant native plants—which was why we'd hacked out the old bushes in the first place. But by the time we'd finished our first round of machete work, she was too immersed in her organic herb business to carry through with her plans.

Why couldn't Mother turn her attention to the exterior of the house instead of nagging us to redecorate inside? Even the pool, which had been such a delight last summer, was a source of stress at the moment—when I looked at it, I didn't see a relaxing haven or a convenient source of the exercise I needed to finish regaining my old shape. All I could think of was the need to fence it in before the twins began crawling.

But long-distance walks calmed me. Through Seth Early's pasture across the road, to the top of the hill where, surrounded by his placid, friendly sheep I could sit on a familiar rock outcropping and gaze down at our house. The distance seemed to soften the edges and help me forget all the chores that swarmed into my mind up close. Or down to Caerphilly Creek, to listen to the water babble and check on the eagles' nest.

Or when time was short, as it was now, I could walk just over the hill to commune with our llamas and gaze down on the edge of my parents' farm. Dad was letting Rose Noire use the field next to our property for her herbs, and had leased the rest of the fields to an organic farmer who was raising buffalo, belted Galloway cows, and free-range chickens. My spirits always rose when I gazed across the gently waving fields of herbs and saw the majestic bison peacefully grazing, or ambling slowly toward the creek. And it was April already, which meant that any day now we'd start seeing the buffalo calves. And surely by now some of Rose Noire's herbs would be beginning to bloom and perfume the hillside.

I reached the hilltop, closed my eyes, and took a deep breath.

Then I opened my eyes, and instead of the majestic bison, I saw a pair of surveyors. One, wearing an orange safety vest and an orange hard hat, was holding up the stick while the other, in khaki with a white hard hat, was bending over and peering through the scope. The llamas, who were always fascinated by human activity, hovered nearby, two at each surveyor's elbow. Not for the first time, I wondered if we could possibly train the llamas to deal with trespassers. Not to hurt them, of course, just to loom menacingly and spit at them a few times until they left the premises.

I strode toward the trespassers.

"What are you doing here?" I said, when I got close enough. I cringed when I realized how much like my mother I sounded. Then again, sounding like Mother had its uses. Both men snapped to attention.

"You must be Ms. Harrison from corporate," Orange Hat said.

I wasn't about to tell a direct lie, but it occurred to me that they might be more forthcoming if they thought I was this Ms. Harrison. So I did my best to look corporate.

"I said, what are you doing here?" Faint accent on the "here," as if I had expected to find them somewhere else. And I tapped my foot in irritation. I didn't have to fake the irritation—they were trespassing.

"We already finished surveying the condo site down by the river," White Hat said. "We thought we'd get a head start on the golf course location."

"Golf course location?"

"See that run-down old farmhouse up there?" White Hat was pointing at our house. "That's the proposed clubhouse location."

I closed my eyes and counted to ten. I wasn't sure which made me angrier, the fact that they'd just applied the word "run-down" to the house we'd spent so much money renovating, or that some corporation thought they could tear it down to build a clubhouse.

And you couldn't have a clubhouse without a golf course surrounding it, of course. I had no idea how large a golf course was, but I figured you'd probably need at least a hundred acres, and that meant they also had designs either on Mother and Dad's farm behind us or Seth Early's across the road. Maybe both. And I didn't think either property owner would take kindly to the idea of turning those acres of rich, prime farmland into a golf course.

"Ma'am? Are you all right?"

I'd counted well past ten and it hadn't helped much, so I opened my eyes and glared at the two of them.

"Get off my property," I said. I didn't raise my voice, but something in my tone made the surveyors flinch, and all the llamas took a step or two back.

"Ma'am?"

"That run-down old farmhouse is my home, and this is my land, and I want you to get the hell off my property," I said.

"Go back and tell whoever sent you that they're wasting your time and their money. There's no way in hell we're selling our land to build a golf course, and they have a lot of nerve sending someone to survey the land before even asking us if we were interested in selling."

"But ma'am——" White Hat began.

"You are trespassing." I spoke as loudly and distinctly as I could.

"Hey, Meg!"

It was Rob, approaching rather more rapidly than his usual pace, no doubt because he was being pulled along by Tinkerbell, the wolfhound. I frowned at the interruption. I turned back to the two surveyors and was irritated to see that they looked relieved. I glared at them until Rob drew near.

"Hey!" Rob said, a little out of breath. "What's up?"

"You're just in time, counselor," I said.

Rob's eyes bugged out at the word "counselor," but he was smart enough not to say anything. Or maybe just too surprised to speak.

"These two gentlemen appear to be lost," I went on. "They're trying to survey some land where their employer is planning to build a golf course, and they wound up here by mistake. And they were just leaving."

"Look, lady——" White Hat began.

"Because they really don't want me to call the police and report them as trespassers," I said. "Much less set my dog on them."

I glanced at Tinkerbell, who was staring fixedly at them. Which probably meant one of them had some food in his pocket, or perhaps had wiped greasy hands on his work clothes at lunchtime—I'd already observed that Tinkerbell was a chowhound, not a watchdog. But the two of them didn't know her. They both looked anxious, and one of them took a half step backward.

"Look, lady, we're sorry." White Hat again. I pegged him for the senior member of their team. "We thought you knew about the project. That's what my boss said—that the mayor had informed the landowners whose property was affected, and we should go ahead and survey. But if that's wrong, we can come back later."

"Just how—" I began. And then I stopped. If the mayor was involved, then something sneaky was afoot.

I noticed that the llamas were creeping closer again. Apparently Tinkerbell's presence didn't bother them. Given her size, they probably just thought she was a new, rather odd-smelling llama.

"It's called eminent domain," Orange Hat said.

White Hat glared, as if he wished Orange Hat had kept quiet.

"I've heard of that," Rob said.

We all looked at him. From the looks on the surveyors' faces, they clearly didn't think much of my attorney's expertise.

"That's nice," I said. I wanted to add that I was relieved to know Dad hadn't paid all that money to a law school that would let him graduate without taking a single class in property law, but I held my tongue. No use showing the enemy that we had dissension in our ranks.

"I meant I heard a rumor the mayor was thinking of using it," Rob said. "I didn't hear where," he added quickly, with a glance at me.

"But eminent domain is the government seizing private property if it's in the public interest, right?" I asked.

Rob and the surveyors all nodded.

"Just how do condos and a golf course serve the public interest?" I said. "I thought eminent domain was mostly used to build roads and dams and such."

"Kelo v. City of New London," Rob blurted out. He had a look of pleased surprise on his face, as if he wasn't quite sure where the reference came from. "Went to the Supreme Court. They upheld taking someone's property for redevelopment that would increase the city revenues."

"Economic development," White Hat said. "Lot of jurisdictions are using eminent domain for that these days. Sorry, ma'am. Can we get on with our work?"

"No," I said. "Just because the mayor's thinking about doing something doesn't mean it's done. For one thing, we're not in town—we're in the county, and the town and the county don't always see eye to eye on everything."

In fact, the town and county were almost sure to disagree when it came to the subject of development.

But the mayor knew that. If he had some kind of sneaky plan to get around the county voters' longstanding passion for protecting the farmlands . . .

"My boss isn't going to be happy about this," one of the surveyors said. "Can I have him call you to discuss this?"

"No," I said. "If he needs to discuss it with anyone, he can call my attorney."

They both glanced over at Rob.

"Not me," he said. "I'm just her brother. And not actively engaged in legal practice at the moment," he added hastily.

I had pulled my notebook out of my pocket and was scanning the pages where I kept useful names and numbers—specifically the several pages of lawyers who were either members of the Hollingsworths, Mother's vast extended family, or had gone to school with Mother, or were otherwise indebted to her. I found the name and number I was looking for and scribbled on a slip of paper.

"Here." I handed him the paper, and was gratified to see his eyes widen. Yes, someone who worked for a property development company might well have heard of Cousin Festus Hollingsworth.

"And just who shall I say will be calling him?" I asked.

White Hat fished in several pockets before finding a battered business card, and he had to borrow my pen to cross out his own name and add that of his boss.

"I guess we'll be going now," he said.

Rob, Tinkerbell, and I watched as the two surveyors trooped back to an SUV parked far enough down the road that I'd never have seen it from our house. Maybe there wasn't anything sinister in that. Maybe it was simply the most convenient spot to where they wanted to survey.

Then again . . .

Tinkerbell whined slightly as they went and strained a little at the leash, causing the surveyors to glance back nervously over their shoulders. The llamas were following them, and to my great delight, just before they reached the fence, Groucho, the largest of the llamas, nailed White Hat with a gob of smelly green llama spit. Maybe they weren't such bad watch animals after all.

"Tinkerbell wouldn't really have attacked them, you know," Rob said when they were out of earshot.

"I didn't say she would," I said. "I said I'd sic my dog on them. You know Spike would jump at the chance."

"Yeah." He sighed, then patted Tinkerbell as if appreciating her more mellow temperament. I winced. I was resigned to the possibility that Rob might emerge from this whole adventure with a dog of his own, but did he have to pick the largest one possible?

"I think in Virginia these days you have to have blight," he said.

I waited for some explanation that would make this remark comprehensible. Rob just beamed at me.

"What do you mean, 'you have to have blight'?" I asked finally. "Because I'd really rather not if it's all the same."

"For eminent domain. I think the new law says that you can't seize property for economic development unless it's blighted."

"Well, we should be fine, then," I said. "Does our property look blighted?"

"No, no," he said, a little too hastily. "It's looking better all the time."

Great. My own brother thought our house looked blighted. Who knew what someone with real standards would think?

I'd worry about that later.

"Did you need me for something?" I asked.

"Not really," he said. I sighed. I knew Rob well enough to translate. "Not really," probably meant, "Yes, but I don't want to admit it, so I'm going to make you drag it out of me with pliers."

"Just spit it out," I said. "You made points, helping with the surveyors. You're in my good books right now. As long as you don't make me play twenty questions."

He visibly braced himself.

"Should I tell the chief that I'm not completely alibied for all of Thursday night?" he asked.

I closed my eyes and said nothing for a few moments, mainly because the only words that sprang to mind were ones I was trying to expunge from my vocabulary long before the boys began talking.

"Meg?"

"Yes." I opened my eyes. "You should definitely tell the chief. Better for you to tell him than for him to find out from someone else. Just how did you happen not to have an alibi? I thought you were all together for hours."

"We were," he said. "Most of the time. But Clarence and I went to the shelter early, around nine thirty, so he could get the animals crated before Dad and Grandpa got there. And pretty soon we realized we didn't have enough crates. There were like a dozen or so more animals than there were the day before. Clarence thinks maybe someone tipped off the Clay County Animal Shelter and they dumped most of their animals on us at the last minute."

I winced. Neighboring Clay County's budget crisis was even worse than ours, so it made sense, both that the animal lovers would leak news of the planned burglary and that Clay County would seize the chance to find new homes for their unwanted animals. But it would further expand the chief's list of people who knew Parker might be in his truck Thursday night.

"Interesting," I said. "But what does it have to do with you not having a complete alibi?"

"Clarence sent me back to his office to get more crates," Rob said. "It took a while to find them and load them. I didn't get back till a quarter of eleven, just before Dad and Grandpa got there. So for the first hour or so that Grandpa said we were all together, actually we weren't. He and Dad were, and he probably thinks Clarence and I were, too. But we weren't, so I don't have an alibi for all of that time."

"And neither does Clarence," I pointed out. "And I expect nine thirty to ten thirty won't be the critical part of the alibi. After all, Parker was supposed to meet you at midnight, maybe a quarter hour's drive away. Why would he go to his truck before eleven thirty or so?"

"You're right!" Relief washed over Rob's face. "So I don't have to tell the chief!"

"No, you should still tell the chief," I said. "He's unlikely to suspect you, but the more he knows about what happened the night of the murder, the better his chance of solving it. While we're on the subject of what happened that night, why the melodramatic midnight rendezvous at the graveyard?"

"Parker said he couldn't meet us any earlier," Rob said. "And of course once we set the meeting for midnight, Dad insisted on the graveyard."

"Of course," I said. "What I meant was, why the rendezvous in the first place? Why not just drive Parker's truck up to the shelter and load the animals directly? Wouldn't that have saved a lot of fuss and bother?"

"Beats me," Rob said, with his characteristic shrug. "Maybe everyone was afraid people would start to wonder if they saw that big furniture store truck backed up to the shelter loading dock."

"No, not a lot of fine furniture deliveries to the shelter," I said. "Of course, there were a bunch of smaller trucks there."

"Two pickups and a van," Rob said. "I bet every other vehicle in the county's either a pickup or a van. Maybe Parker wanted a buffer between him and the actual burglary."

"Maybe," I said. "Still—meeting at midnight to load the truck. Maybe you and Clarence are night owls, but it's hard on Dad and Grandfather. Did he give a reason why he couldn't meet you earlier?"

"No." Rob snickered slightly. "He was a little secretive about it. We all figured he had a date or something."

"A pity he was secretive," I said. "If he'd boasted a bit, maybe you'd know who killed him."

Rob nodded.

"So tell the chief," I said.

"Okay," he said. "First chance I get."

He began loping off, half following Tinkerbell and half pulled by her.

Should I tell the chief myself?

Probably best to give Rob a few more hours.

And what if I was wrong about when Parker went to his truck? What if the time of death fell within the window of time when neither Rob nor Clarence was alibied?

No matter how unlikely I found the idea of either of them killing Parker, if their alibis failed, the chief would have to consider them suspects. The chief would know that Rob had been interested in a woman romantically involved with the victim—he'd have to wonder if the murder was the result of a lethal love triangle. And I had no idea what Clarence's relationship with Parker had been.

Damn.

I looked around to see if I could spot any of the bison. No such luck. And even if I had spotted any, I wasn't sure they'd work their usual magic on my mood.

Though I did rejoice to see that the llamas had clustered by the fence and were spitting vigorously, using the surveyor's SUV as their target. I made a mental note to reward them each with an apple or two for an evening snack.

I called Cousin Festus's cell phone number and left a message on his voice mail. Then I turned and strode back toward the house.

Chapter 10

I was still fuming as I threaded my way through the sheds and the shrubbery that cluttered our yard.

Chill, I told myself. I needed to find something to distract me until Cousin Festus called back. I made a quick stab at seeing the place through the surveyors' eyes. The house, I decided, didn't look bad. It was all the sheds, plus the general lack of anything even beginning to approach landscaping. All the more irritating that Randall Shiffley and his two workmen were busily making repairs on one of the largest and most ramshackle of the sheds. We were already having a hard time deciding if that particular shed should go or stay. Now we'd probably feel obliged to renovate it to go with the new roof. Far better to tear it down altogether. It blocked the best view. If it were out of the way I might occasionally catch a glimpse of the bison from the kitchen window. It was time to thin the shed herd.

I spent the next hour cleaning as if spit and polish alone could save the house. By the time I had the nursery and several of the bedrooms tidy and gleaming again, I felt much calmer. Especially after Cousin Festus called and promised he wouldn't wait for Monday to start finding out exactly who had designs on our property.

"As it happens, I'm down in Yorktown right now, visiting

Mom and Dad. Would you like me to run up to Caerphilly to-morrow to strategize about this?"

"That would be excellent," I said.

I strode downstairs feeling reinvigorated and determined. Mother was sitting at the kitchen table, looking poised and elegant as usual. She was supervising as Rose Noire and one of the other Corsicans made more sandwiches.

"But the barn is so . . . dirty," Mother was saying. "Should the boys really be spending so much time out there?"

"It's all right," Rose Noire said over one shoulder. "Studies have shown that children raised in an environment with at least one animal have better immune systems and a lower incidence of asthma."

"Great," I said. "The boys will grow up healthy as horses with this menagerie around. Even in the short term," I added, lest anyone think I was volunteering our barn for long-term animal shelter duty.

"What's wrong, dear?" Mother asked. "You look pale. Do you need an aspirin?"

"I'm fine," I said. "Hungry, but fine."

Rose Noire took the hint and handed me a ham sandwich.

"Thanks." I took an enormous bite and closed my eyes to savor it.

"You still look stressed," Mother said.

Luckily chewing allowed me time to think about my answer. Should I tell her about the surveyors? Perhaps better to wait until I heard what Cousin Festus could learn. Ask her if she thought the place looked blighted? She'd probably use my question as an excuse to foist off some new furniture on us.

But then an idea struck me.

"Mother," I said. "I have a decorating project for you."

She blinked slightly and peered at me as if suddenly unsure who I was.

"You're not interested?" I asked.

"Of course I'm interested, dear," she said. "I'm just rather surprised. Normally I have to nag you to take an interest in your home."

"Well, I'm taking an interest now. Let me show you."

I led her out onto the back porch. It was large for a back porch, six feet by twelve feet, and largely empty.

"Yes," she said, recovering enough to look around with something more resembling her usual critical eye. "Yes, there's a lot we need to—er, could do here. You want me to tackle the deck?"

I glanced around. I wouldn't have called it a deck. It was a plain slab of concrete. I'd just have said stoop instead of porch if it hadn't been so large. But if Mother thought "deck" a more elegant term, who was I to argue?

"Yes, the deck to start with," I said. "But why stop there? We need to do something about the whole yard."

I spread my arms wide as if embracing the space, then strode toward the side yard.

"The yard? But that's really landscaping."

"Outdoor decorating," I said, as I rounded the corner of the house and headed for the front yard. I was trying to see my surroundings through unfriendly eyes and finding more and more to wince at. "You're always saying how important the foyer is, that it gives your guests their first view of the house. Well, that's not quite accurate. Before they get to the foyer, they have to walk down the front walk, through the yard. And look at it!"

I was striding through the front yard by now, with Mother close behind. I stopped to survey my surroundings. So did she. She was still a little taken aback.

"When you come down to it, it's the largest space of all," I said. "And it's virtually untouched. We need to deal with those overgrown hedges in the front yard. Plant something along the front walk. Maybe replace the front walk with something nicer. And don't forget the backyard. All these sheds and outbuildings look so junky. We need to spruce them up or get rid of them! Move some of them to better locations so they don't block the view."

"We could do that." She still sounded dubious.

"We need an outdoor foyer in the front yard! An outdoor dining room there!" I gestured toward the side yard. "An outdoor living room . . . somewhere! An outdoor playroom for the boys! And the pool—it needs to be an outdoor party space. A safe, kid-friendly outdoor party space."

"Yes," she said. The word "room" seemed to revive her spirits. "Yes. This should be interesting. My first real venture into outdoor decorating!"

"And Dad can help with the plants," I said. "What he doesn't know about plants isn't worth knowing."

Mother nodded, absently.

"So you'll draw up some plans?"

"Yes." Her voice sounded absent. Clearly she was already hard at work. She turned and went back inside.

Maybe it didn't make sense, revving Mother up to decorate something we might be in grave danger of losing. But it made sense to me. By the time Mother finished with it, there was no way anyone could possibly call our yard blighted. Over the top, maybe, but not blighted. I felt a surge of power, as if I'd just put a stake in the ground to tell the encircling forces of development, "Not here!"

"Hey, Meg!"

It was Randall, waving at me from atop the macaw shed. I strolled over to see what he wanted. As I did, it occurred to me that maybe I should have him give me an estimate on painting the house. Better yet, I should ask him what repairs he thought we needed to make the house look first rate.

And I also remembered that half the county board was made up of Randall's family, and the rest was mostly people whose grandparents had gone to school with his. Surely if the developers wanted to seize our land through eminent domain, they'd have to go to the county board, not the town council. And the county board wouldn't do that—would they?

By the time I reached the shed, Randall had climbed down from the roof and was standing with crossed arms, supervising a cousin who was continuing the work.

"You still working on figuring out how Parker was murdered?" he asked.

Okay, I hadn't been, but if that was what Randall wanted to talk about, I didn't mind. I was curious, and maybe it would give me an opening to work the conversation around to see what Randall knew about the surveyors and which way he thought his relatives on the board would jump.

"I'm not trying to do the chief's job," I said aloud.

"'Course not." He sounded amused, as if he didn't really believe me.

"But I am curious," I said. "Someone suggested Parker was killed by one of his former girlfriends. Or possibly one of their husbands or boyfriends."

Randall chuckled softly.

"It's possible," he said. "More than possible. The man got around, I'll give him that. But I'm wondering if maybe they want us to think that."

"They? You mean whoever did it?"

"I mean the powers that be in town," he said. "I have a feeling maybe someone doesn't want the chief to look past Parker's love life."

"I think the chief's smart enough and stubborn enough to keep looking till he finds the truth," I said. "And what do you think he's going to find?"

"I think Parker was about to be a whistle-blower."

"A whistle-blower about what?"

"Remember that whole town beautification project?" he said. "The one that was supposed to turn Caerphilly into a major tourist destination?"

"The one where they went around putting down cobblestones in streets that weren't built until long after cobblestones went out of style?"

"The cobblestones, the gas streetlights, the miles of split-rail fence." He snorted and shook his head. "Maybe if they'd picked one historical era and tried to stay authentic to it."

"I didn't realize they were trying for historical authenticity," I said. "I thought they were just trying to pretty everything up. A lot of that work was done over in the ritzy part of town, and it's pretty hard to make the houses over there look like anything but McMansions with pools and tennis courts."

"They wanted to go for historical accuracy," he said. "But that plan ran aground on the fact that up until the late eighteen hundreds, there wasn't really anything here. Maybe twelve houses surrounded by a few thousand acres of cow pasture. So they went in for prettifying the town center. And I guess they succeeded."

"Succeeded in prettifying all the character out of it," I said. "Looks like hundreds of gentrified town centers all across the country."

"Maybe that's why the tourist traffic they were expecting never materialized."

"Yes, we Virginians are reasonably picky about our history," I said. "We've got too much of the real thing to be fooled by some developer's plastic imitation. But fascinating as this all is, what does it have to do with Parker's murder?"

"We tried to raise a red flag when that project went through," Randall said. "Me and some of my cousins. But no one wanted to believe us. Mayor Pruitt made it look like sour grapes because they brought in an outside firm for the construction work instead of hiring us. Nothing came of it. No one believed us. Then Parker started poking around."

"Why?" I asked. "Is he a Shiffley relative?"

Randall shook his head.

"Parker's people are all gone now," he said. "They came here and opened that furniture store right after the war."

"The Civil War?" I asked.

"World War II," Randall said, giving me an odd look.

"You never know around here," I said. "So if he's not a Shiffley, what was his interest in the beautification project?"

Randall smiled and leaned back against the shed.

"He started out wanting one of those beautified buildings," he said. "He figured the only way to keep his store going was to go upscale. No way he could do that a couple blocks from the bus station. So he made a list of the buildings that would do for his fancy new store, and then he started digging into who owned them. And the more he dug, the less he liked what he found. Nearly every one of those buildings in the beautified section of town is owned by a Pruitt or someone who's thick as thieves with the Pruitts."

"And that surprises you?" I asked.

"No, but it surprised Parker, and he was going to blow the whistle on the low-down scam Mayor Pruitt pulled—putting the county up to its eyeballs in debt for a bunch of expensive civic improvements that never benefited anyone except for a few dozen property owners that he happens to share a family tree with."

"Wait a minute—up to its eyeballs in debt? I thought the beautification project was done with federal funds and private donations. That's what he said in that newspaper article last year."

"And he wasn't completely lying. He did get a small federal grant or two, and a few rich locals kicked in a few hundred dollars here and there. *With* federal funds and private donations, yes—but not entirely with. Not by a long shot. Most of the money came from borrowing. And they lied to the county board about it, or they wouldn't have gotten approval. That's what Parker figured out."

A lot of what had been happening in recent weeks was all starting to make more sense. Caerphilly wasn't an impoverished area. In addition to the college, the town had a small but thriving high-tech industry, with Mutant Wizards, my brother's computer gaming company, as its centerpiece. The county was full of farmers who had adapted very successfully to the world of modern agriculture, mainly by providing organic or boutique meat and produce to the high-end restaurants and markets in the nearby cities. Like everyone, I'd assumed that a little belt-tightening would get the town and the county through the current financial hard times. The news of Terence Mann's draconian service cuts had taken everyone by surprise, and most of us were still alternating between wondering if he was overreacting and fretting over how it could possibly have gotten so bad so fast.

"So that's why the county financial situation suddenly got so dire?" I asked aloud.

"Yeah, we probably could have trimmed our sails a bit and weathered the recession," Randall said. "It's Pruitt stupidity and Pruitt greed that's bringing us down. And maybe a little old-fashioned Pruitt profiteering. I know construction costs, and in my opinion we should have gotten a hell of a lot more for our money than we did."

"So what happens now?" I asked.

"What usually happens when someone doesn't pay a debt?" Randall said. "Swarms of lawyers should start showing up soon. And if the county can't pay, the lenders are going to want their collateral."

"Collateral? What collateral?" I asked. "You think they're going to repossess all those overpriced cobblestones and wrought-iron streetlamps?"

"The collateral's all the government buildings in town," Randall said. "The courthouse. The library. Even the police station and the jail."

I was stunned.

"It's okay," Randall said. "Odds are they won't actually take over the property. After all, what's a New York bank going to do with a Reconstruction-era courthouse, a beat-up Carnegie library, and a small-town jailhouse? Parker said they'd probably just rent them back to us."

"They might," I said. "Or they might try to cut a deal with the mayor. What if they offered to trade all the town buildings back if he got the county to seize some property that the bank really wants—some waterfront property and a few hundred acres of prime farmland. A tract of land one of their other customers might find useful—say a real-estate developer who's been hankering to build fancy condominiums and a golf course in Caerphilly County and has been beating its head for years against the county's antidevelopment stance."

Randall frowned and pondered for a few moments.

"Can they do that?" he asked finally. "Seize private property to give it to a developer. Seems . . . un . . . un . . ."

"Unconstitutional?"

"I was thinking just plain un-American. Can they really do it?"

"I don't know," I said. "It has worked in some places. And even if it doesn't work, you can bet fighting it will cost the moon and take forever."

"And the whole time that sneaky bastard of a mayor will be doing everything he can to help out his developer buddies. Okay, the first thing we have to do is figure out what land they're targeting and make sure the owners are ready to fight."

"I already know that," I said. "I found the surveyors working on Michael's and my land and Mother and Dad's farm."

"I reckon you aren't interested in selling, as much money as you've put into the place."

"You're right." Randall, of course, had a very good idea how much we'd spent, since Shiffley Construction had done most of the work. "They probably want Seth Early's sheep farm, too, and I hope the surveyors steer clear of him, or they're likely to see the business end of his shotgun. And they're talking about waterfront condos. I can't remember who owns the farms on either side of the road between us and the creek, but they're very nice farms, and I doubt the owners want to sell."

"That would be my cousins, Orville and Renfrew on the east side of the road," he said. "And you're right. Likely as not they'd join Seth's shotgun brigade at the mere mention of building condos and a golf course on their land. And the farm on the west side of the road belongs to Deacon Washington of the New Life Baptist Church. Just try to pry him off that land—I think his family's been there since just after the war—and this time I do mean the Civil War. Okay, we know who the developers are after—now we need a lawyer."

"I already called one," I said. "Festus Hollingsworth. One of Mother's cousins."

"No offense, but we probably need a pretty high-caliber lawyer," Randall said. "You think your mother's cousin is up to it?"

"Cousin Festus is pretty high caliber," I said. "He specializes in making life miserable for sleazy developers and their corrupt friends in local governments. Makes a very good living at it. Wait till you see this year's Jaguar. If anyone's up to it, he is."

"You have a useful kind of family." His cell phone rang, and he reached for it automatically. "Now what we need to do is— Hang on a minute. I need to take this. Yes, ma'am?"

I watched Randall's face as he listened to his caller. His expression went from one of cheerful respect to shock.

And clearly whoever had called him had a lot to say. Randall did a lot of listening, interjecting an occasional "Yes, ma'am" or "No, ma'am."

"I'll have them there as soon as possible," he said finally. "Yes, ma'am. You bet!"

He hung up and stared at the phone for a few seconds.

"It's starting," he said. "That was my aunt Jane."

"Judge Jane?" I asked.

"The same. She just called up and ordered me to bring as many of my trucks as possible down to the courthouse. That financial company gave notice that they're seizing their collateral Monday morning and kicking everyone out."

"And she's going?"

"She's hopping mad, but she says so far she can't see a clear legal way around it, and she's damned if she's going to give them grounds to cause trouble, so she's moving. Looks like anyone who wants a warrant or needs to pay a traffic ticket will have to go out to her farm for the time being."

"Are they starting with the courts, or have they given everybody notice?"

"Everybody," he said. "Whole town's in a tizzy. Aunt Jane called to make sure she and the courts had first dibs on our trucks. I'd better get moving."

"By the way, on this developer thing—"

He turned and tilted his head as if asking a question. Probably whether my question was important enough to keep his aunt waiting.

"Rob's looking it up, but he thinks in Virginia you can't

seize land for economic development unless it's blighted. Michael and I might need you to do a little work around the place to make damned sure no one in their right mind could call it blighted."

"Good call," he said. "And once we're sure where else they're targeting, we can make sure they're all showplaces."

"One more thing," I said. "When did you find out about all this? I didn't know anything until just now, when I ran into the surveyors."

He frowned and clenched his jaw.

"I first heard about it Thursday," he said, finally. "Parker told me. But it sounded so loony I thought he had to be wrong. Then yesterday, after I heard someone had killed him I began to think about it, and it didn't sound nearly as loony. And then I started asking a few people some questions, and the more I asked, the saner Parker seemed."

"Where were you when he told you?"

"On the sidewalk outside Geraldine's bakery," he said. "And before you ask, I have no idea if anyone was listening in. It was just past eight A.M. Thursday, and lots of people were coming and going, getting coffee and pastries. I suppose any one of them could have heard what he was saying. I didn't get the idea he was trying to keep it a deep dark secret. Sorry; I know that's no help."

He turned and strode off, dialing his cell phone as he went. Rallying the family troops? Shiffley trucks from all over the county would soon be converging on the courthouse.

I wondered what the other three judges were doing. Two of them were Pruitts, and the other was a long-time business partner and golfing buddy of the mayor, so I wouldn't want to bet on their chances of finding anyone willing to haul their stuff.

Then again, if the lender was one of mayor's buddies, maybe the other three judges weren't being evicted.

And how many other offices would be affected? And was it just offices? What other services would have to close down or relocate? We had well water and could get along without trash collection for a while, but what about the people in town?

At least Timmy would have a classroom to go to on Monday. Back in the fifties, Mayor Pruitt's grandfather had closed Caerphilly's schools rather than integrate them, never expecting that the county would rebel and build a new central school system just outside the town limits.

And what should I do about Randall's theory? I'd forgotten to ask Randall if he'd already shared it with the chief.

I pulled out my cell phone and called the nonemergency number for the police station.

Chapter 11

"What's up, Meg?" Debbie Anne.

"I know the chief is pretty busy," I began.

"You have no idea."

"Ask him if he's heard Randall Shiffley's theory of why Parker Blair was murdered," I said.

"Is it a good theory?" she asked.

"Beats me," I said. "I'll leave that to the chief. But it was news to me, and I just wanted to make sure Randall had told him. Gotta run!"

I didn't particularly have to run, but now, with any luck, Debbie Anne's curiosity would be roused, and she'd nag the chief till he interviewed Randall.

And I should tell Cousin Festus about what I'd learned from Randall. I called his number and got voice mail. I hung up. I didn't want to leave as long and convoluted a message as this would take. E-mail would be better. I hung up and headed for the barn to use the computer in my office.

The barn was quiet. A little too quiet. I saw no one—no humans, anyway—on the way into my office, and when I came out again, I saw only Clarence, feeding a bottle to one of the beagle puppies.

"Meg!" he exclaimed. "Great! I could use the help."

I glanced around. Still no other Corsicans in evidence. I didn't like the looks of this. Less than forty-eight hours and already they were deserting the ship.

"Could you possibly keep an eye on things here, just for a little while?" Clarence asked. "I need to go figure out a proper outfit for the funeral."

"The funeral? You mean Parker's? They can't possibly be having it already."

"Not yet, but the chief says they'll be releasing the body before long, and once he does, there's no use waiting around, is there?"

"Won't that depend on Parker's family?"

"He doesn't have any." Clarence shook his head as if the lack of family to bury him was as much a tragedy as Parker's death. "And I'm his executor, so I guess it's up to me, and I say the sooner the better. The longer we leave him unburied, the more time people have to gawk and gossip."

I wasn't sure about the gawking part, which made it sound as if Parker's unburied body would be on display in the town square instead of safely ensconced at Morton's Funeral Home. And if he thought burying Parker would cut off the gossip, he was more naïve than I thought.

But I guessed from the uncharacteristic frown on his face that the weight of his executor's responsibilities weighed heavily on him.

"So you need to go clothes shopping," I said. "Does it have to be right now?"

"I don't mean for me," Clarence said. "I have a dark suit. Or I could wear my uniform."

"Uniform?" I was eyeing the battered biking leathers that

were his usual daily wear. I couldn't remember seeing him in anything else. Was that what he meant by a uniform? If so, I hoped he had a newer set at home that he kept for funerals. One that hadn't yet encountered quite so many sick cats, piddling puppies, and incontinent macaws.

"I was a Marine, you know," Clarence said, drawing himself up to his full six feet six. "I could wear my dress blues. Out of respect. Of course it's been a few years since I've had them on."

More like twenty years, I suspected. He was eyeing his belly dubiously. I had a feeling it wasn't the years so much as the beers, along with quite a few pizzas, that might prevent him from squeezing into the uniform.

"But I can worry about that later," he went on. "What I meant is that I just got another call from Maudie down at the funeral home."

"Ah," I said. Clarence's curious haste to select Parker's burial clothes suddenly became more understandable. "She's fretting?"

"I told her the funeral can't be for a few days, but she keeps saying we need to settle what they're going to put him in for the services."

"You know Maudie," I said. "Only woman in town who finishes her Christmas shopping by Valentine's Day."

"I think she wraps it up by Twelfth Night," Clarence said. "So I went over this morning after the chief released the house and took Maudie some of Parker's clothes, but she says they won't do and she wants something else."

"What did you take?" I asked.

"Some new jeans, and a nice Hawaiian shirt," he said.

"I can see Maudie's point," I said. "You can't have Parker wearing a Hawaiian shirt and blue jeans to his own funeral."

"I don't see why not," Clarence said. "I can't remember Parker wearing anything else the whole time I knew him."

"Not suitable," I said. Perhaps I should bring up the closed-casket idea. Although that probably wouldn't placate Maudie, who fretted horribly if she had to send any of her customers to their reward in less than perfect fashion.

"I picked the most somber Hawaiian shirt in his closet," Clarence said. "Black and white flowers. And black jeans."

I shook my head and frowned at him. I was struggling not to laugh, imagining how Maudie Morton had reacted at being handed a Hawaiian shirt and a pair of jeans to put on one of her charges.

"It's just not done," I said.

"So Maudie tells me," Clarence said, with a sigh. "Which means someone has to drop everything to go over there and get a suit, if he has one. Or figure out what size he wears so we can borrow one."

"Borrow?" I said. "You think he's coming back to return it?"

"Buy, then," Clarence said. "Anyway, it looks as if I'm the one who has to take care of all that. So could you make sure the beagle puppies get their next feeding? And I need for you to pill a couple of the cats. And——"

"You take care of the animals." I held out my hand. "Give me the key and I'll work on Parker's funeral clothes."

"Are you sure?" He sounded uncertain, but I saw he was already fumbling in his pockets, presumably for Parker's key.

"Do you really want to face Maudie if you show up with another unsuitable outfit?" I countered. "I probably have a lot better chance of picking out something she'll approve of."

"Thanks." He plucked out an enormous key ring, fumbled with it for a few seconds, and then began sliding one key off.

Interesting. Clarence was Parker's executor, and had a key to his house, and yet he didn't exactly seem heartbroken over his friend's murder. Did that make him a more plausible suspect?

Not to me. And not to anyone who really knew Clarence.

Except, perhaps, the chief. After all, in his years of police work, he'd probably seen more than one friendship that had soured into homicide.

Perhaps that was the reason for the curious formality with which the chief treated everyone when he was in the midst of an investigation. Perhaps it was his way of reminding everyone—including himself—that we were, for the time being, not his friends and neighbors but so many witness and suspects.

Sad that anyone ever had to do that. Sad, but necessary.

I shoved these thoughts aside and took the key from Clarence.

"Back soon," I said.

But as I turned to go I realized I was about to do something sneaky, and maybe I didn't have to.

"I gather you and Parker were good friends?" I leaned against the barn door as casually as I could.

"You mean, because he made me executor?" Clarence said. "Surprised me when he asked. We mostly knew each other from our animal welfare work. Of course, once he asked, I realized I probably knew him better than anyone else in town."

"So you didn't know what else he was interested in?"

"Animal welfare, and his store and . . . well, his social life was pretty active." Clarence was blushing slightly. And he was no prude, which meant Parker's social life really must have been very active indeed.

"Randall seems to think Parker was investigating some kind of Pruitt sneakiness related to the town beautification project," I said.

"Randall does have a bit of a bee in his bonnet about the Pruitts," Clarence said.

"This time he might be onto something," I said. "Apparently the mayor talked the county into backing a loan for the beautification project. And the payments on that loan are what's behind the whole county budget crisis."

"That's . . . ridiculous," he said.

"You think Randall's got it wrong?" I asked.

"No," Clarence said. The puppy finished with the bottle, and Clarence cradled it to him as if it needed protection from something. "Randall's probably right. To think that they were about to kill this little guy and his brothers and sisters, just to pay for a bunch of stupid cobblestones and pretentious gas lamps."

"So while I'm fetching a suit for Parker's funeral, do you mind if I poke around a bit to see if I can find any evidence of this investigation Randall thinks Parker was conducting?"

"Mind? I think it's a great idea. Poke all you like; we'll hold down the fort here."

"Thanks," I said. "I'm taking off now."

I didn't set off for another hour. First, I made a pit stop, pumped some milk, called Michael to check on the boys, and gathered some snooping equipment. Just because my visit was okay with Clarence didn't mean the chief would be happy about it. But I figured as long as I took him anything I found, he couldn't be that mad. And what would be the harm if I took a few photos of anything that might turn out to be useful in fighting the proposed golf course? So, in addition to a tote large enough to hold file folders, I took along my little digital camera and a couple of spare batteries. By a little past noon, I was on my way.

Chapter 12

Parker had lived in Goose Neck, a neighborhood Michael and I had kept a close eye on back when we were house hunting. The houses dated from the twenties and thirties, all relatively small but charming and set far back on fairly large lots full of mature trees and shrubs. They were originally built by people coming off the farm to work at the Pruitt mills and the other businesses in the town, and most of them were still owned by descendents of their original owners. Try as we might over several years, Michael and I never saw a single "for sale" sign in the whole neighborhood, or found even one listing in our Realtor's database. I finally realized that when people in Goose Neck wanted to sell their houses, they didn't put up a sign or call a real-estate agent. They put out the word among their family and friends. Mother would approve.

The house was hidden behind towering hedges and shaded by several enormous cherry and oak trees. It was a squat red-brick bungalow, fronted by a small but substantial brick-framed porch. English ivy was making a good try at covering up the house entirely, and the unkempt boxwood and azalea bushes crowding the outside walls probably kept out what little natural light got past the oaks. It looked as if it would be cool and shady in summer and snug enough to be warm in the winter.

And it had an unsettling air of familiarity. I had spent many childhood hours visiting a great-aunt who'd lived in just such a quiet, tree-shaded little brick bungalow back in Yorktown.

Not what I'd expected of Parker at all.

If the similarity to Great Aunt Felicity's house continued, I'd find that Parker's house had a cellar reachable only by an outside entrance, and that the dormers I could see peeking through the ivy gave light to a roomy, old-fashioned attic.

The ancient wooden screen door squeaked as I opened it. The porch was as serene a retreat as it looked from the outside, and the old-fashioned metal chairs and glider looked curiously familiar and inviting.

The porch opened into a small living room. To the left, an archway led into a dining room. Straight ahead of me, a hallway led back, no doubt to the bedrooms. Common sense told me I should go straight to the closets to carry out my primary mission.

I decided to check out the rest of the house first.

The uncanny sense of déjà vu continued. The house was furnished entirely in a pre-war style of furniture that probably had a high-falutin' name when antique shops sold it and decorators like Mother bought it. I just called it comfortable and old-fashioned.

And the more I looked around, the less I believed that Parker had bought any of it. I peeked behind the dining room sideboard to find, as I expected, that the old-fashioned flower-sprigged wallpaper was bright and unfaded behind it, in a shape that precisely matched the shape of the sideboard.

The books in the glass-fronted bookcases were new. One shelf held paperback thrillers, arranged by author, and the rest of the shelves housed a neatly alphabetized collection of books on zoology and ecology. And in spite of the vintage furniture, the general effect of the rooms wasn't old-fashioned, mainly because there wasn't a single knickknack or crochet-edged doily in sight.

I'd bet there had been, though. He'd probably inherited this house and moved in without doing any more redecorating than necessary. The knickknacks and doilies had probably gone to Goodwill or to other, more sentimental relatives. Unless Clarence was right and he didn't have any. I supposed there was an off chance they were boxed up and stored in the attic.

I felt a curious sense of betrayal. I could shrug off the image I'd had of Parker, the cynical womanizer who'd used the glamour of his animal welfare activities to seduce women. But the Parker who lived in this neat, old-fashioned bungalow—a Parker who was either indifferent to his surroundings or cherished a kind of hominess that so closely matched my own? For some reason the idea of that Parker being a sleazy tomcat bothered me.

But time was wasting.

Nothing unusual in the living room. Or in the dining room, except that there was a furniture-sized empty space in front of the sunniest window. Had he sold a piece of furniture or disposed of a large dead houseplant? It would have to have been rather recent. People tended to fill such large, empty spaces rather quickly, either deliberately, with another plant or piece of furniture, or unintentionally, with the kind of clutter we humans seemed to generate just by existing.

Though I had to admit Parker's house was as devoid of clutter as any I'd ever seen. What did that say about him?

For that matter, what did it say that a man who owned a

furniture store lived in a house filled with comfortably run-down vintage furniture?

The kitchen suggested that Parker didn't cook much, apart from grilling the occasional steak or microwaving frozen meals.

The first of the two bedrooms was set up as a neat, efficient home office. An old oak table served as the desk, with only a small tray of papers and a few accessories on top. The office equipment and several old wooden file cabinets were concealed in the closet. I sat down in a well-maintained vintage wooden swivel chair and browsed in his files. I envied him his orderly, neatly labeled filing system. Business records for the furniture store were separated from personal financial records and from the files on his animal rescue efforts. I felt a sudden surge of hope—maybe these meticulous files contained information on where he was planning to take all the animals. Maybe somewhere out there we'd find people anxiously fretting over Parker's failure to bring them a much-anticipated macaw, or Irish wolfhound, or even a litter or two of unweaned puppies or kittens.

Yes, here it was: a file marked "Animal Rescue: Caerphilly Shelter," with Friday's date printed beneath. It contained a list of the people to whom he was taking the various animals, complete with addresses, e-mails, and cell phones. The list matched the menagerie we had in the barn, more or less. The macaw and the beagle puppies weren't there—presumably they were relatively new arrivals to the shelter. But at the bottom of the list were the names of the people who'd agreed to take any un-allocated animals. One name for the cats, one for the dogs, and apparently the Willner Wildlife Sanctuary would be harboring any birds, reptiles, exotics, or miscellaneous creatures.

I put the file in my tote and continued searching.

Next I found a small section of files labeled "Pruitt Investigation." Detailed records on who owned what downtown buildings. If the preponderance of Pruitts in the list surprised him, he was much too naïve. A thick sheaf of articles from the *Caerphilly Clarion* about the beautification project. Not likely to contain state secrets.

The farther I got in his investigation files, the more my spirits lagged. They clearly showed he was obsessed, but gave no proof of the skullduggery he alleged.

Until the next-to-last file. It contained a thick copy of the loan contract between Caerphilly County and something called First Progressive Financial, LLC. It was a bad photocopy, slightly crooked on some pages—probably not acquired in any official way.

I flipped through it briefly. I wasn't a lawyer, and I didn't have time to try to decipher the whole document, but even a brief inspection convinced me that it was dynamite.

I looked around. No computer. A mouse, a set of speakers, and various other bits of hardware were scattered around the desk with their cords lying useless instead of being plugged into anything. No doubt the chief had confiscated Parker's computer.

But he did have a printer like mine, one of those all-in-one machines that also served as a copier, a scanner, and a fax machine. I could make a copy of the contract.

And maybe I should make a copy of the contents of the next file, too. Apparently Parker Blair had been working on an article on his findings.

He'd missed his calling; he'd have been a natural as an investigative reporter. It was all here. Chapter and verse of exactly what the Pruitts and their cronies had been up to, and all the more scathing because he hadn't used inflammatory language or tricks of rhetoric. He just laid it out, step by step, precise, organized . . . damning.

I didn't miss not getting to know Parker the womanizer. But I wouldn't have minded meeting the Parker who lived in this curiously appealing old-fashioned house, and I knew for sure that the Parker who'd written this article was a major loss to the whole town.

At the back of the file, he even had a page of notes on where to send his exposé. The *Caerphilly Clarion* was there, of course, but he'd also been researching which reporters on the Richmond and Washington papers would be most likely to take an interest in a juicy small-town scandal.

I definitely needed a copy of the article, too.

As I was mechanically feeding the pages into the copier, I spotted a framed photo on the desk—the only one I'd seen so far. Not surprising. If he was juggling multiple girlfriends, making it look as if he didn't care much for photos kept him from getting flack about not displaying theirs.

The desk photo turned out to be a group shot. At first I thought it was a group of big-game hunters standing over their latest kill. Then I realized that the hunters were Parker, Clarence, Grandfather, and Caroline Willner. They were standing over a lioness, each holding up a newborn cub.

I peered at Parker. He was wearing a gaudy Hawaiian shirt and tight, faded jeans. I still couldn't understand why so many women were chasing him. He was handsome enough, with nice features and a good head of dark curly hair. I wasn't a fan of earrings on men, but I supposed some women might be. His goatee made him look a little saturnine, but it wasn't unflattering. He could stand to lose five or ten pounds, but that put him way ahead of most people in their late thirties. Not my type, but I could understand someone finding him attractive. Just not quite so many someones—that was what puzzled me. He must have been a real charmer in person.

I made sure I had a decent copy of all the pages of the contract and the article and stuffed them into my tote. While I was at it, I made two copies of the animal rescue information. Then I returned his original files to the file cabinet.

As I was returning the "Animal Rescue" file to its hanging folder, a thought struck me. I went to the other end of the alphabet and found Parker's will. It was brief and to the point, leaving his entire estate to several animal welfare organizations. It didn't shed any light on his murder, but at least Clarence's job as executor would probably be relatively easy.

I realized that I'd been poking around Parker's house for some time and still hadn't completed my commission for Clarence. I moved on to the back bedroom, where Parker slept. The bed was a full bed with a vintage headboard that matched the bureau and dresser. Not a king-sized bed with satin sheets or whatever was considered the height of bachelor decor these days. The tops of the dresser and the bureau were almost bare, and the drawers were impeccably organized and not overfull.

Not at all the stereotypical playboy lair I'd been expecting. I apologized silently to Parker and opened the closet.

Where I quickly realized that Clarence was right about one thing. The black-and-white Hawaiian shirt probably was the closest thing in Parker's wardrobe to a somber funeral suit. He had loads of T-shirts, many of them for animal welfare organizations or liberal causes. He had enough jeans to outfit a regiment. The dozen or so brightly colored Hawaiian shirts were clearly a central piece of his wardrobe.

I found two sports jackets, neither of them suitable. One was pale blue seersucker that probably hadn't been all that presentable thirty or forty years ago when it was new. The other was a threadbare brown wool jacket that appeared to have had several dozen holes gnawed in it, ranging from pencil eraser up to golf-ball size. Moths or teething puppies? Possibly a little of both. I had the feeling he kept these jackets, along with the two astoundingly ugly ties slung over a hook on the back of his closet door, so when he went someplace that required a coat and tie he could comply while making the rule-makers feel very, very sorry they'd insisted.

Nothing here to gladden Maudie Morton's heart. I pulled out my notebook and began jotting down Parker's shirt, coat, and pants sizes.

Then an idea struck me. Clearly Parker had no use for coats and ties in his current life, but had that always been the case?

Back to the files. In a section labeled "Employment Records" I found a neat, chronological list of the jobs he'd held between his graduation from college and five years ago, when he'd inherited the furniture store from his aunt. Most of them were office jobs, in sales or marketing. He'd have had to wear a suit for those. But had he ditched the business clothes when he came into his inheritance?

I continued poking through the files until I came across a section I thought I remembered spotting—one marked "Household Inventory." The first folder in the section, marked "Attic," contained a three-page list of boxes and items he'd stored there.

I ran my fingers down the list. Business records. Camping gear. Christmas decorations. All neatly listed in alphabetical order, with notations like "A5" or "F1" that corresponded to the markings on a neat floor plan of the attic.

Strange. I didn't often meet people who made me feel unorganized. I was liking Parker more and more. If I'd gotten to know him, would I have seen past his rather louche exterior to the man who nurtured kittens and kept a perfect filing system?

I continued down the list. Aha. "Clothing, Business." According to this list, he had a garment bag containing business clothing in section F8, which would be the far corner, ahead and to my right after I climbed the attic stairs, which looked to be in the middle of the attic. Which probably meant . . .

Yes, back out in the hallway I looked up and saw a trapdoor in the ceiling, with a hanging cord that indicated that there was probably a set of pull-down stairs.

The ceilings were ten feet high, so I had to drag a chair in from the kitchen to reach the cord. But neither a gentle tug nor a couple of sharp ones worked. I could see that there was a latch holding the door closed.

Strange. Unless he was afraid of monsters creeping down from the attic, the latch would seem to serve no purpose.

Slightly irritated, I pulled the chair back into the kitchen and looked around until I found a four-foot stepping stool.

And when I flipped the latch, the pull-down stairs lurched down a foot or so, almost hitting me on the head.

Okay, so that explained the latch.

I felt strangely triumphant. My files might not be as perfect as Parker's, but in my world, as soon as the stairs malfunctioned, I'd have made an entry in my notebook: "Have attic stairs repaired/replaced." And, at least prechildren, the booby trap would have been fixed long before anyone got beaned by it. No way it would have been broken long enough to warrant the latch.

I pulled the stairs the rest of the way down, tucked my purse in my tote so I'd only have the one thing to carry, and marched up feeling much less intimidated by Parker.

The attic wasn't overcrowded, thank goodness. A modest number of boxes, bins, and bits of furniture, arranged in neat, orderly rows on plain pine floorboards. A single bulb hanging from the ceiling probably wouldn't have given much light, but I didn't bother to turn it on. Enough rich, golden, afternoon sunshine made it past the ivy around the two dormer windows to let me see quite well.

For an attic, it was downright charming. If I'd owned the bungalow, I'd have given serious thought to turning the attic into living space.

I spotted two garment bags at the far end of the attic and strolled toward them.

The first garment bag held a tuxedo. Mother, who was a connoisseur of formalwear, could probably have pinpointed its age within a year or two. Judging from the waist size, I suspected that Parker had been a beanpole when he wore it, probably to his high school prom.

The other bag held three reasonably presentable suits and two starched, laundered white dress shirts, all sized much more like the clothes in Parker's closet downstairs. The suit pants would probably be a little snug in the waist, but Parker was past minding, and doubtless Maudie could cope. I picked out the most subdued of the suits, a dark gray wool, and added both of the shirts.

Holding the hangers high, so the pants wouldn't trail on the floor—although it seemed commendably dust-free for an attic— I turned and headed for the stairs, stopping along the way to read the detailed labels on some of the boxes.

I paused by two boxes marked "Family Memorabilia." Should I peek in to see what I could learn about his family? I found a nail for the hangers and was kneeling beside the boxes when I heard a noise downstairs.

"Who's there?" I called. "Clarence?"

No answer. Odd.

I stood up and headed for the stairs. I couldn't remember if I'd left the front door open. If I had, perhaps some curiosity seeker had come by and was poking about downstairs.

Before I could reach the stairs, they slammed up into the ceiling with a bang. I raced over to them and tried to push them down again, without any luck. Clearly whoever had closed the stairs had also turned the latch.

I was trapped.

Chapter 13

"Hey! I'm still up here!" I called.

I could hear someone moving about downstairs. They had to have heard me.

I pulled out my cell phone and called 911. Debbie Anne answered almost immediately.

"I need help," I said, softly but distinctly. "Someone locked me in the attic of Parker Blair's house, and they're downstairs."

"Doing what?" she asked.

"I don't know," I said. "Rummaging around. Stealing something. How should I know—I'm locked up here. Just send someone, quick."

"Already on their way. Stay on the phone till someone gets there."

"Roger."

Still holding the phone, I lay down and put my ear to the floorboards. I heard a faint squeak, like a door opening, but I couldn't quite tell if it was coming from the office or the bedroom.

I suddenly found myself wondering if the intruder was planning more than just theft. If they set the house on fire, for example, I'd be in real trouble.

No, I wouldn't. I got up and walked, as silently as I could, to one of the dormer windows. If it opened, I could crawl out onto the roof. I could hang from the edge and let myself drop and one of the overgrown azaleas or boxwoods would break my fall. Even better, I could crawl down the ivy that was growing so thickly up the walls. I slipped the latch so I could try opening the window.

"Meg? Are you all right?" Debbie Anne.

"I'm fine," I said.

"Sammy's about two minutes away, and the chief's a minute or two behind him. They're coming without sirens, so they can catch the intruder if possible."

The window slid up easily. No danger of being trapped in the attic.

Through the open window I heard a familiar squeak.

"I think they're going to be too late," I said, picking up the phone again. "I just heard the screen door open."

A car started outside, and roared off almost immediately.

"They're leaving," I said.

"They? Are there more than one?"

"How do I know?" I said. "I can't even see the car for all the shrubbery. He, she, or they just drove off in a hurry."

"I'll tell the chief."

I returned to the stairway and occupied myself trying to see if I could stick something through the opening of the trapdoor and dislodge the latch. It didn't take long to realize that if I hadn't had my cell phone I'd have been stuck with crawling down the ivy.

And I was definitely stuck for the time being, I took out my camera and the pages I'd copied from Parker's files. It only took a few minutes to photograph the pages of the contract and the article and e-mail them off to Cousin Festus.

I was pondering whether to call Michael or wait until I could report that I'd been safely rescued when I heard footsteps downstairs.

"It's us, Meg," Sammy called. "Are you okay?"

"I'm fine," I said.

"We're searching the house first," he said.

"Okay."

I was sitting cross-legged beside the trapdoor, crossing off a few completed items in my notebook when the trapdoor lurched open slightly.

"Blast!" the chief exclaimed.

"Did it hit you?" I asked. I peered down. He was frowning at the stairway, but he didn't appear to be nursing any wounds.

"It would have if I didn't have good reflexes," he said. "Are you all right?"

"I'm fine. Annoyed, but fine."

He pulled the ladder the rest of the way down and came marching up. I collected the suit and shirts from the nail where I'd parked them.

"And just what were you doing up here?" he asked, when he reached the top of the stairs.

"Finding some burial clothes for Parker." I held up the hangers. "For some reason, Maudie objects to having one of her clients in a Hawaiian shirt at the viewing."

"I haven't even released the body yet," he said. "I probably won't for days."

"You know Maudie. So Clarence asked me to come over and see if I could find something more suitable."

"In the attic?"

"That's where I found these." I held up the clothes again.

"He only had more Hawaiian shirts in the closet. But his household inventory showed that he stored his old business clothes in the attic. I was about to bring these down when someone closed and latched the door."

"You have no idea who?"

I shook my head and pointed to the dormers. He picked his way through the boxes to stare out of each one.

"Drat," he said, after the second. "No, you can't see a thing from up here. And you heard nothing?"

"Random noises." I shook my head. "Nothing that gave me a clue to who was down here."

"Did you snoop through the whole house before coming up here?" he asked.

He'd probably have Horace fingerprinting the place before long. Honesty was probably the best policy.

"Yes," I said. "I asked Clarence, and he gave his okay. Though I didn't search the cellar, assuming there is one. I figured it was the last place to look for clothes."

"Good," he said. "Come down and tell me if you see anything missing or rearranged."

"Can you give me a minute?" I said. "I need to let Michael know I'll be late."

Michael probably wouldn't worry for hours yet, but I wanted to hear his voice. And look, just for a few seconds, at the picture of the boys that appeared whenever I turned on my cell phone.

Michael's phone went to voice mail immediately, so I left a brief message and hung up. Then I spent the next forty-five minutes inspecting all the rooms but to the chief's disappointment I couldn't identify any major changes. In fact, the only change I found at all was one that I'm not sure the chief even believed, much less saw as significant.

"Someone moved this," I said, pointing to a small wooden tray about four inches square that was one of the half-dozen items neatly arranged atop Parker's dresser.

"It wasn't on the dresser when you first came in?"

"It was on the dresser, but square with the edges," I said. "This is askew."

He looked up from his notebook and peered over his glasses at me.

"I'm serious," I said. "Everything is organized. The books are alphabetical. The Hawaiian shirts are arranged by color. The beers and sodas in the refrigerators are lined up by brand like soldiers on parade. The few prints on the wall are framed identically and they're all precisely the same size and the same distance from the ceiling. By the time I peeked in here, I was expecting patterns. So I noticed that the book on his nightstand, and that little square wooden thing were both perfectly aligned with the edges of the furniture they were on. He was maybe a little OCD. I could relate."

He nodded.

"And I could have sworn it had more earrings in it when I came in."

He paused and looked up from his notebook with a wary look on his face.

"Earrings?"

"He wore an earring, you know," I said. "And I guess he dropped them in that little tray when he wasn't wearing them. I have something similar on my dresser. Mine's an antique satin glass box Rose Noire gave me a few birthdays ago, but it serves the same purpose."

"His earrings." The chief's voice was flat, and he was staring at me. "Been talking to your father lately?"

"I talk to him often," I said, but I could tell right away that my innocent act wasn't fooling him. "I figured out from something he let slip that Parker's earring is a clue of some sort, if that's what you mean, but I haven't told anyone."

"Don't worry about it," he said. "One of the ambulance crew who took the body to the hospital spilled the beans before I could warn him off. Apparently the *Clarion* has picked up that tidbit, so the twelve or thirteen people in the county who haven't already heard about it will know by Monday."

"I'm sorry," I said. "It could have been useful. Speaking of useful—I took a copy of this for the Corsicans."

I handed him the second copy of the list of people who were to have received the animals.

"Ah," he said. "Thank you. Mr. Blair had a folded document in his pocket that's rather too stained to be easily readable. But this appears to be a clean copy."

"I figured it could be useful," I said. "Of course, I suppose it's a long shot that any of them are strong suspects."

"Yes," the chief said, as he studied the document. "If they didn't want to be saddled with a litter of puppies, they could just say no."

"I found something else that might have something to do with the murder," I said.

I led him to Parker's office, opened up the file cabinet, and handed him the file containing the contract and the article.

He began reading, or at least skimming. After a minute or so, he looked up at me.

"So Randall wasn't just having another attack of anti-Pruitt paranoia? There really is something to this mortgaging the town thing?"

"It looks that way,"

"Lord help us," he muttered. "I was hoping it was all a mix-up. Judge Shiffley's family are all downtown emptying the court-house and hauling everything out to her farm, while she's up in the mayor's office, yelling to beat the band. I'm starting to wonder if I should send a swat team up there to pull him out before she hauls off and kills him."

"Can't you hold off till she hurts him a little?" I asked.

He smiled faintly.

"I should get back and figure out what's going on," he said. "See if I'm going to have a police station to finish this case in or if I'm going to be working out of someone's barn like Judge Shiffley."

When I got out to my car, I took a deep breath and tried calling Michael.

"Hey," he answered the phone. "Where did you put the llamas?"

"Our llamas?" I asked.

"Of course, our llamas. Why—were there any llamas at the shelter?"

His voice had taken on an acquisitive tone that worried me. Weren't four llamas enough?

"No, and the last time I saw our llamas, they were down by the fence, spitting at some trespassers, with my blessing."

I explained, as briefly as I could, about the surveyors.

"Do you suppose they could have left the gate open?" Michael said. "Accidentally, if they were a little spooked by the llamas?"

"Or on purpose, just as likely. Yes, and I'll hurry home to look for the llamas." I figured an account of my afternoon's adventures could wait until the llamas were safe and I had his full attention.

And of course my cell phone rang when I was halfway home. Normally I just let it ring while I'm driving, but when I saw Cousin Festus's name on the caller ID, I pulled over into a neighbor's driveway and answered it.

"Is this what I think it is?" he exclaimed.

"If you think it's the smoking gun that might finally convince the town voters that Mayor Pruitt is a sleazy crook, then yes," I said.

One of the neighbor's horses ambled nearer and was stretching his neck over the fence, hoping for a treat.

"Where did you find this?" Festus asked.

"In the files of a guy who might have been murdered because of it," I said. I turned my back to the horses so they wouldn't get their hopes up.

"Do you have the originals?"

"No, the chief of police has the originals." I glanced over my shoulder. Now all three of the neighbors' horses were staring at me expectantly. I felt vaguely guilty. "I have a very clean photocopy. Shall I fax it to you?"

"No, just hold on to it for now," he said. "I'm not going to wait till tomorrow—I'll be down there in a couple of hours. This is fabulous! You just made my day."

"I'm happy that you're happy," I said. "See you later."

I waved at the horses and pulled out of the driveway. I was feeling happier myself. I had hated the idea that Parker might have been killed because of his involvement in the animal rescue mission. The notion that one of his ex-girlfriends had done him in was not an improvement, since it threatened to make CORSICA look less like a legitimate animal welfare organization and more like one of the steamier soap operas. I could imagine the hatchet job the media would do on it.

But if Parker had been killed because of his plans to become a whistle-blower, then his death seemed at once more heroic and more solvable. There were a limited number of people who had a vested interest in hiding the scam that the mayor was pulling, and most of them were far too stupid to be successful at concealing a murder.

It was nearly suppertime by the time I got back to our house. I noticed that the number of cars outside had increased. The backyard was abuzz with energy. Good; the Corsicans weren't deserting their posts, just getting off to a slow start.

Mother was in the side yard, ordering Rob and Rose Noire about. They appeared to be measuring various bits of the lawn and garden so I deduced that the redecoration of the great outdoors was underway. By the time Mother was through, no one would be able to claim our property was blighted. We'd probably have trouble fending off requests from the Garden Club to open the place for their spring tours. And Rob should be grateful. Normally Mother's tape measure marathons were followed by orgies of furniture moving, but even Mother couldn't expect anyone to dig up and replant the trees and shrubs "just to see how they'd look in a different arrangement."

I grabbed my tote and the hangers with Parker's clothes and

headed for the barn. Half a dozen people called out my name when I entered, but I waved at them and proceeded undeterred to my office.

Clarence was sitting at my computer, pecking away at something. He leaped up when I came in.

"I just wanted to type something up," he said.

"Type away. Here." I handed him the hangers.

"Wow." He turned the suit and shirts from side to side and examined them with a faint frown, as if inspecting the strange and slightly unseemly native garb of an extinct tribe. "Nobody will recognize him in this."

"I'd have dropped them off with Maudie, but I ran out of time," I said. "I forgot to get a tie, by the way, but I expect you can supply one."

"I'll put these in my truck."

While Clarence was loading the clothes, I went over to my own printer/copier. By the time he returned, I'd finished making several copies of the contract and Parker's article.

"Here." I handed him one set. "Just in case you were wondering, Randall was right. Parker was definitely on to something. I'll leave it to the chief to figure out if this was why he was murdered."

Clarence blinked, and began eagerly reading the document.

"Oh, and this is Parker's list of who was going to foster the animals," I said. "The chief would appreciate it if you'd give him twenty-four hours to check up on them before you contact them."

I set that down on the desk. I glanced back when I got to the door and saw that Clarence was glancing from one document to the other and then back again, as if he couldn't decide which to read first.

I was overdue for seeing the twins, to say nothing of pumping them some milk. So I tried to make my passage out of my barn as rapid as my entrance. But I couldn't exactly ignore Caroline when she called out to me and beckoned me over.

"How's everything here?" I asked.

"Busy," she said. "CORSICA's organizing a meeting to discuss this new problem—the whole thing about the mayor hocking the whole town and maybe trying to seize your land."

"Why CORSICA?" I asked. "It's not exactly an animal welfare issue."

"Oh, that's right," she said. "You haven't heard yet. CORSICA has broadened its focus. We're now the Committee Opposed to the Ruthless Seizure of an Innocent County's Assets."

"Awesome," I said. "Where do I join?"

"You just did." She handed me a small wad of flyers. "Pass these out wherever you can."

I looked at the top flyer.

"Town meeting, seven P.M. Saturday night," I said. "Wait a minute—that's tonight. You're having a meeting here tonight?"

"In the barn, not in your house," Caroline said. "Your father thought it would be okay. And Michael approved."

"It's okay with me, then," I said. "How big a meeting do you expect it will be?"

"We're hoping to rouse the whole damned county," she said. "And the mayor's helping, not that he's trying to. Been calling up every department in the town and county government and telling them to go in and collect their personal belongings sometime this weekend, because the lenders will be taking possession on Monday morning."

"The hell you say."

"No one's actually doing it," she said. "Opinion's split on whether the employees should haul in food and sleeping bags and prepare to occupy their offices, or whether they should move out every sheet of paper and stick of furniture and set up a kind of government in exile."

"I hear Judge Jane Shiffley's already picked option number two," I said.

"And that carries a lot of weight," she said. "But we'll see tonight. Of course, first we have to convince some people that there's even a problem."

"Show them this." I handed her a copy of the contract. "If anyone needs me, I'll be in the nursery."

I did my part for the meeting. As I was walking upstairs, I called Cousin Festus and told him about it.

"Excellent," he said. "If it's acceptable to you, I shall plan to attend. And who's in charge of the meeting?"

I gave him Caroline's cell phone number.

As I was in the bedroom, trading my shoes for slippers, I heard several brisk barks outside. I peered out the bathroom window and saw our llamas walking up the road four abreast, followed by the border collie and five cars.

"Good dog," I murmured.

Then again, he bypassed our driveway and began herding the llamas up Seth Early's lane. Well, at least they were safe and sound, and the llamas enjoyed hanging out with the sheep.

I went into the nursery, shut the door, and took a deep breath.

Michael was stretched out on the recliner, a sleeping twin cradled in each arm. He opened one eye when I came in.

"The boys are fine," he said, and closed his eye again. "And the chief has an APB out on our llamas."

"The llamas are safe at Seth's," I said. "His new border collie got a little carried away. We can fetch them later."

"That's a relief." He looked exhausted. I wondered how long he'd spent running around looking for the llamas. And whether the surveyors or the border collie was to blame for their disappearance.

I glanced at the clock. Two hours until the meeting. The Corsicans were probably going crazy getting ready for it.

I picked up the nearest twin—Josh, as it happened—and settled in the rocking chair with him. I felt a brief twinge of guilt. My notebook contained a long list of tasks, and thanks to all the time I'd spent at Parker's house, I'd barely crossed off a dozen items all day.

And then I shoved the guilt aside. List or no list, life would go on if I took the chance to cuddle one of my sons.

Chapter 14

I was back in Parker's attic trying to figure out what was missing. There was a gap in the rows of neatly labeled bins and boxes, and an outline in the dust where something had been. Only a faint outline, because he really had been a very tidy housekeeper and there wasn't all that much dust.

"Meg?"

And if people would stop calling my name and let me concentrate, I could probably figure out what used to be in that space.

"Meg?"

I'd figured out by now that I was dreaming, and someone was trying to wake me up, but even as the dream faded, I screwed my eyes shut and tried to hang on to it, because I was sure if I could just figure out the meaning of that clear space, the whole mystery of Parker's death would be solved.

"Meg? It's nearly seven P.M. Don't you want to go to the meeting?"

I woke up and found that Michael was leaning over me, holding Josh.

And I had a crick in my neck.

"Oh, bloody h— Oh bother," I said. Michael wasn't the only one trying to clean up his language before the twins started talking.

"What's wrong?"

"Just another napping injury." I massaged my stiff neck. "That's it. Mother will have a cow, but we need a second recliner."

"Funny you should say that," Michael said. "I had the same thought myself a couple of days ago. And I thought I'd order it and surprise you."

"And did you?" I hurried over to the nursery bathroom to throw some water on my face.

"I dropped into Caerphilly Fine Furniture," he said. "And the guy there took down the make and model number and said he would order it."

"Guy?" I stuck my head out of the bathroom. "Was it Parker Blair?"

"I assume it must have been." He was checking the contents of the diaper bag against the checklist I had posted on the wall by the changing table. Both boys were babbling happily in their cribs. "Which means, I suppose, that we'll have to find someplace to order it all over again."

"Don't be so sure," I said. I grabbed Jamie and headed for the door. "Parker was super organized. If he said he was going to order it, I bet he did. Check with Clarence, or whoever Clarence gets to take care of the store until the estate is settled. While you were there, did you notice anything else?"

"Like the name of his future killer written on the wall in blood?"

I glanced over to see that he was grinning at me.

"Good point," I said. "He didn't know he was about to be murdered."

"He was pleasant, efficient, and organized," Michael said as he lifted Josh onto his shoulder.

"Yeah." I picked up Jamie, who was happily babbling, as if trying to join in our conversation. "Very organized. I bet if he knew his life was in danger, we'll find that he left some kind of record. The chief should do some more searching in his papers."

"After checking the alibis of all his girlfriends?" Michael stopped on the landing, halfway down the stairs. "There was one funny thing that happened. He has one of those bells that rings whenever someone comes into the store. We were at the counter, looking through catalogs, and the bell rang. He looked up, said, 'Come in,' but I heard a little gasp, and when I looked over my shoulder the door was shutting again."

"As if someone didn't want to be seen entering his store?"

Michael nodded and resumed his careful descent of the tall stairway.

"I can't be sure, but the gasp sounded feminine," he said. "And it was silly to run away—I'd have assumed she was there for the same reason I was—to buy furniture. So maybe the chief should concentrate on any of Parker's girlfriends who happen to be married or otherwise involved."

"Of course, those are going to be the hardest to find," I said. "Have you told him about this?"

"I only just remembered it," he said. "But I will."

And he probably would, if he remembered. Maybe I should mention it to the chief. And find out if Rob had broken the news about his imperfect alibi.

Downstairs, as we were settling the twins in their double carriage for the trip to the barn, I kept thinking about the second recliner—not just about how much comfort it would add to our lives, but also that in a weird way it would be a posthumous present from Parker. Assuming he had ordered it, and I was willing to bet he had.

It would be nice if I could repay him by helping the chief catch his killer.

"Whoa," Michael said. He'd stuck his head out the back door to see if the twins needed jackets and stood gaping.

"What's wrong?" I asked.

"This is some crowd," he said. "Is the whole county coming to this meeting?"

Since both twins were awake and happy, I helped Michael lift the carriage down the steps and then left him to wheel the twins out to the barn while I roamed around a bit to check out what was happening in our backyard and barn. Caroline might have hoped to turn out the whole county for her meeting in our barn, but I'd envisioned a few dozen people tut-tutting for an hour or so before adjourning to help with the evening's animal-tending chores. To my surprise, both sides of our normally quiet country road were lined for at least half a mile in either direction with the cars, trucks, and SUVs of people coming for the event. Nearly the entire congregation of the New Life Baptist Church had come en masse. Apparently anticipating the parking problem, they'd all parked in the church lot and were ferried over in loads using the converted school bus normally reserved for taking their award-winning choir to performances.

They'd brought the supplies and equipment to set up coffee and tea service at one end of the barn, and one of the deacons was driving the bus up and down the road, fetching latecomers who'd had to park far away.

They'd even brought folding chairs for themselves. In fact, most of the people who came brought their own seating. A forest of folding chairs, wooden, metal, or webbed plastic, was growing up on the barn floor.

Randall and a bunch of his Shiffley cousins were also at work. They had knocked together a small stage at one end of the barn, just in front of my office door. A few of them were testing the microphone and speakers they'd set up while the rest were arranging the folding chairs in rows that would gladden the heart of the fire marshal if she showed up.

And she probably would. I saw a lot of county and town employees. Including the chief. I wasn't sure if he was here in his professional role or as a member in good standing of New Life Baptist Church.

Several Shiffleys and Baptists were helping unload hay bales that Seth Early was lending to hold the people who hadn't thought to bring their own chairs. I recognized a lot of Caerphilly faculty members on the bales.

The one part of the barn not filled with chairs was Spike's pen. We'd installed it so Spike could keep me company while I did my blacksmithing with no danger that he'd trip me when I was carrying pieces of metal heated to a bright red nine hundred degrees. The Corsicans had populated the pen with many of the cuter and more appealing animals. Clarence, Rose Noire, and several other Corsicans were showing the animals off to the crowd, bless their hearts. Clarence was holding a clipboard and scribbling things on it. With any luck, he was getting commitments to take the animals as soon as they could be released. Maybe they wouldn't even need to call on the foster homes Parker had arranged.

"Over here!" I saw Michael waving to me. He'd found us seats on a hay bale just behind the stage, and was sitting there supervising as a regular parade of women came by to inspect the twins in their double baby carriage.

I spotted Cousin Festus on the other side of the barn, talking with Caroline and Dad, and waved at him.

Festus would be the first to admit that he'd decided to become a lawyer at the age of thirteen, after watching Gregory Peck in *To Kill a Mockingbird*. And while Jimmy Stewart in *Anatomy of a Murder*, and Spencer Tracy in *Inherit the Wind* had helped cement his career choice, Festus remained largely true to his original hero worship of Atticus Finch. He wore old-fashioned, light-colored three-piece suits and thick-framed glasses similar to the ones Peck had worn in the movie and styled his hair in as close as he could come to Peck's habitual fashion, the better to allow an errant lock to fall over one eye at the climax of his closing statements. He cultivated Finch's calm, mild-mannered tone of voice and had even replaced his original Tidewater, Virginia accent with the rather more generic Hollywood-style southern accent Peck had adopted in the movie.

Immediately after his graduation from law school, a brief, unhappy stint as a public defender convinced him that the criminal justice system was unlikely to provide a steady supply of the kind of stoic, long-suffering innocent clients that he had been looking forward to defending. After a period of intense soul-searching he'd switched to a civil practice. He now specialized in, as he put it, "helping Davids fell Goliaths"—the Goliaths in question being usually corporations and governments.

Juries loved him, and rumor had it that during negotiations, more than one opposing legal team had hastily settled after

Festus shook his head sadly and uttered, in the mildest of tones, the fateful words, "Well, gentlemen, I do believe we will be obliged to settle this in a court of law."

He was standing to the left of the temporary stage, with his left thumb tucked in his vest pocket, sipping a cup of New Life Baptist coffee and surveying the crowd with great satisfaction.

Part of his satisfaction probably came from the fact that there were two television crews taking crowd footage. The one from the college TV station was no surprise—most of the students who ran it came from Michael's drama classes. But the crew from one of the Richmond stations—now that was an achievement. I wondered if Festus or Caroline had arranged it, or if news was slow enough in the big city that what passed for a crime wave in Caerphilly had caught their attention.

And I could tell from Festus's expression that he liked what the TV cameras were capturing. If they panned across the crowd they'd be showing everything from New Life choir matrons in their Sunday best hats and dresses to farmers in overalls; from county board members in well-worn suits to faculty members in corduroy jackets with elbow patches. And all of them at least temporarily in perfect harmony with each other, united by their outrage against the Pruitts and buoyed by the excitement of the meeting.

About the only people who didn't seem terribly thrilled to be here were those few county board members. Clearly they'd have some explaining to do, eventually. They'd probably claim that the mayor had pulled the wool over their eyes, and they'd probably be telling the truth.

Timmy was sitting with a group of kids from his kindergarten class. Their teacher was pointing to various people in the room and talking to her charges. Using the town meeting as a teaching moment, no doubt. I moved a little closer so I could overhear.

"No, the town can't just fire the mayor," she was saying, "because the town voters elected him. But if enough voters are unhappy and sign a petition, we can unelect him."

"Can I sign?" one kindergartener asked, raising his hand. Half a dozen others also began waving their hands to volunteer. I left her to break the news of their disenfranchisement to the eager little citizens.

It was a few minutes after seven when Caroline Willner stepped to the podium and adjusted the microphone down to where she could reach it. She had a large tortoiseshell cat draped over one shoulder. I doubted live cats would really catch on as fashion accessories, but I predicted that the tortoiseshell would not go unadopted. Several people were pointing at him, and I overheard several variations on "Isn't he sweet!"

"Ladies and gentlemen," Caroline said.

The crowd began shushing each other, and settled down in a remarkably short time.

"I've been asked to chair this meeting." Scattered applause greeted these words. "Although I'm deeply concerned with the fate of Caerphilly, I'm not actually a resident, so I probably have as good a chance as anyone at being impartial."

Murmurs of approval from the crowd. I couldn't help thinking what a smart choice she was. Of the Corsicans who had the confidence to tackle chairing a meeting, she was certainly the best choice. Dad would have been too gentle with the crowd and Grandfather too brusque.

"Before we get started," she said. "I'd like to ask Reverend Wilson from the New Life Baptist Church to start off tonight's proceedings with a blessing. Reverend?"

The reverend, a slightly hunched elderly man with close-cropped white hair and skin like polished mahogany, stepped briskly to the podium. A few people shifted uneasily. No one had ever called any of the reverend's sermons boring, but then no one had ever called any of them short, either.

They needn't have worried. The reverend was a man who knew how to read a crowd.

"Lord," he said. "We ask your blessing on this gathering."

A few amens rang out from various parts of the barn. I wasn't sure whether this was intended as the usual call-and-response the reverend's words would inspire in church, or whether some audience members were trying to hint that he'd already covered the topic sufficiently.

"There has been a great wickedness done in this town," he went on. More amens. "And we ask your assistance in smiting the doers of that wickedness. Amen!"

He sat down amid a frenzy of amens and applause. Surely one of the shortest blessings he'd given within living memory. I suspected the reverend was as eager as most of the audience to get on with the meeting.

Caroline retook the microphone.

"I don't know how many of you are up to speed on developments here in the county. Bear with me while I repeat a few things that might be old news to some of you. Early Friday morning, the police found Parker Blair murdered in the cab of his furniture store's truck. I'm sure most people assumed that

Parker's demise had something to do with his . . . active social life."

Snickers erupted in various parts of the audience, and the snickerers were hushed back into silence.

"But this morning Meg Langslow and Randall Shiffley uncovered information that indicates Parker was about to blow the whistle on a serious scandal here in Caerphilly. We'll leave it to Chief Burke to determine whether Parker's findings had anything to do with his death."

She bowed to the chief, who was sitting along one side of the stage, and he bowed back with reasonably good grace.

"Parker learned that the town beautification project was not paid for with federal funds and private donations, as Mayor Pruitt claimed, but with loans."

"But that was a town project," someone called out. "What does that have to do with the county?"

"Town didn't have anything worth using as collateral," Randall Shiffley called back. "So they hornswoggled the county board into letting them use all the county buildings as collateral."

I'd have expected the crowd to erupt at hearing that, but after a few moments of low murmuring—and more than a few angry or reproachful glances at the county board members who'd been brave enough to attend—the crowd settled down. Evidently most of them had already heard the news. Or perhaps they were cynical enough about their local government that it came as no surprise.

"Doubtless the mayor had a plan for repaying the borrowing." This generated a few sardonic laughs. "But even if his plan was a good one, it apparently failed, no doubt due to the present adverse economic conditions. We've now learned that the lender has been demanding payment for months—and is preparing to foreclose on the collateral."

A slightly angrier buzz greeted that statement, and died down when Caroline raised her hand to indicate that she had more to say.

Suddenly the tortoiseshell cat, which had been lying languidly on her shoulder the whole time, launched itself toward the audience with a howl, and began scrabbling around the base of the stage. Several people in the front rows leaped back and a few startled shrieks rang out.

The cat then leaped nimbly back onto the stage and marched back over to Caroline.

"Mrowr!" it said, its voice a little muffled by the field mouse in its mouth.

"What a good mouser you are!" Caroline exclaimed. She picked up the cat, mouse and all, and held him out as if displaying a trophy. The audience—many of them farm people who understand the value of a good mouser—broke into applause.

"And he's available for adoption, if anyone's interested," Caroline said. She gestured to Clarence, who relieved her of the cat and took him off to enjoy his prey in one of the cat carriers in the adoption area.

"As I was saying," Caroline said. "The lender plans to seize our county government buildings. And now Meg Langslow has discovered that the mayor apparently intends to solve the debt crisis he created by asking the county to seize the property of several local landowners and turn it over to an outside developer!"

All hell broke loose at that hated word, "developer"—and "outside developer" at that. Not that there was anyone living in the county who would publicly own up to being a developer, given the local mind-set on the issue. The county might be divided in many ways over many topics, but nothing would bring the residents together better than the threat of unwanted development.

Caroline let the shouting go on for a few minutes before tapping the microphone for silence.

"Before we discuss what to do about this threat, I'd like to hear a few very brief words from the people most affected by the developer's plans—the people whose land is in danger of being stolen!"

Deacon Washington stepped to the podium and led off with a short but emotional statement about how much it meant to his family that they now owned the very farm on which their ancestors had labored as slaves before the Civil War—and how shocked he was to hear that the county where he'd spent all his life was plotting to deprive him of this important legacy. The New Life Baptist contingent punctuated his statement liberally with shouts of "You tell 'em!" and "Amen, brother!"

Randall Shiffley stood up and, after apologizing for not being much of a public speaker, proceeded to prove himself a liar by making a plainspoken yet eloquent plea for his cousins and their old friend Seth Early to continue farming the land their families had occupied since colonial times. Orville, Renfrew, and Seth stood in a semicircle behind him, looking the very picture of noble, careworn tillers of the earth. The addition of Seth's newly adopted border collie was a nice touch. Someone— probably Cousin Festus—had clearly had a hand in the staging.

Except for one scowling reference to "outsiders with no love for the land," Randall completely refrained from Pruitt bashing. Orville didn't spit tobacco once during the entire performance, and the crowd, having been warmed up by Deacon Washington, peppered Randall's words with enthusiastic amens and encouragement.

"And finally," Caroline said, after the border collie had herded the three farmers off the stage, "Meg Langslow, who discovered this dangerous plot this afternoon when she confronted the surveyors trespassing on the land she and her husband own. Meg!"

She might have warned me that she was planning to ask me to speak. Fortunately the thunderous cheers and applause that greeted my name gave me time to pull my thoughts together. I grabbed the closest twin, balanced him on my shoulder, and strode to the microphone. Not that Josh couldn't have remained in the carriage under Michael's watchful eye, but I figured Cousin Festus would never forgive me if I passed up the chance to show off, on camera, at least one of the adorable infants whose home the developers were threatening. As I stood in front of the microphone, I could see Festus beaming approval at me.

"Michael and I plan for our kids to grow up on this land," I said.

A few amens rang out, and various people shouted "You tell 'em," and "Go, sister!"

"So we have no intention of letting the stupidity, dishonesty, and greed of a few politicians take it away from us. That's why as soon as I heard about the mayor's plan, I called my cousin, Festus Hollingsworth, who has spent his entire legal career fighting similar injustices. Take it away, Festus."

With that I sat down, followed by another thunderous ovation. Festus and Caroline beamed at me. I tucked Josh back into the carriage. Jamie didn't seem jealous that he hadn't had his own moment on camera.

Festus stepped to the podium.

"I would like to thank all of you for putting your confidence in me," he began. "I can't promise to win this for you—no one can—but I can promise I will do everything within my power to do so."

"And bill us for all the time it takes," someone called out from the back. But the heckler didn't sound angry, and the crowd reacted with amused titters.

"True," Festus said. "And I won't lie to you—this is a complicated matter that will require a lot of my time. Unfortunately for me, since it was my cousin who originally called me in, I guess I'm going to have to do this all at the family discount rate."

More laughter.

"The first thing I'll be looking into is whether the town had the legal authority to borrow that money in the first place, and whether the county board had the power to let them use public property as collateral without the voters' approval. I'll also look into whether any of the public officials involved in this scheme committed any indictable or impeachable offenses in connection with this loan. And as far as seizing people's property—we're a long way from that."

A volley of cheers and amens greeted this statement.

"Some of you may have heard about a case where the U.S. Supreme Court upheld a northern town's right to condemn a bunch of modest homes to build a fancy new development. You'll be relieved to know that Virginia was one of the many states to have passed laws making it harder for rogue governments to get away with this kind of outrageous behavior. I'll be looking into whether what these developers are trying to pull has any chance of standing up in court under these new laws. I can already assure you that they won't find approval in the court of public opinion. It won't be easy, but I'm optimistic that we'll prevail."

More ovations. Josh was awake and beaming as if he thought the ovations were all for him. But Jamie woke up and began the soft fussing noises that meant he was about a minute from drowning out the entire meeting unless fed. I grabbed him and a bottle and slipped behind the stage and into my office. I left the door ajar so I could keep track of what was being said without the danger that I'd nod off. Probably not the thing to do in front of a crowd who thought you were a fearless and tireless crusader for justice.

And being out of sight also let me dodge volunteering for all the committees that Festus and Caroline and the rest of the attendees set up over the next hour. A committee to find and set up office and living spaces for the paralegals and clerks Festus would be bringing to town to help. A committee to look through the minutes of the town council and the county board to determine exactly what they were told about the beautification project. A committee, headed by one of Randall's cousins, to analyze the costs of the beautification project, to see if the construction costs were exorbitant. A committee to gather data on the developer that seemed to be interested in our land, particularly any information on their relationship with the lender and with the Pruitts and their financial allies. A committee, including the editor of the *Caerphilly Clarion* and Ms. Ellie Draper, the town librarian, to pull together as accurate a picture as possible of the Pruitts' tangled financial situation. A committee to approach the college administration and talk them into coming out in support of the county's new position, once the county figured out what that was.

Randall Shiffley suggested forming a committee to study the feasibility of doing away with the mayor and the town council entirely on the grounds that they didn't do a lick of useful work and only caused problems for the county board and confused the hell out of people. Festus intervened, suggesting that however appealing this project might be, the citizens needed to focus first on the immediate crisis.

Randall withdrew his motion, but I had the sneaking feeling that he'd be hearing from a whole bunch of people eager to serve on his committee whenever he formed it.

Most important of all was the blue ribbon committee that was staying on after the main meeting adjourned to make a decision on the most urgent question facing Caerphilly—whether to sit tight in the county offices and prepare for a siege or evacuate and form a government in exile. The Fight or Flight Committee, as everyone had already started calling it.

The one option no one even brought up was the mayor's order that everyone go home and behave themselves.

The meeting broke up at around nine thirty, but by half past ten the barn was still far from empty. The Fight or Flight Committee members were still waiting for things to become quiet enough for them to begin their deliberations. Michael and Rob had taken Timmy and the twins up to bed, and I was about to delegate shutting up the barn for the night to Rose Noire, if I could find her. People were straggling out slowly, some still talking in animated clusters, some exchanging phone numbers and e-mail addresses with their fellow committee members.

And many carrying dogs and cats. I was particularly pleased to see the reverend Wilson's wife, a stately steel-haired matron in a formidable church hat, cooing happily to the white kitten with the black patch over his eye. I made a mental note to thank the chief for helping Pirate the second find his home.

I found him talking to Clarence and Grandfather by Spike's pen.

"So I assume you've decided it's okay to release the four-legged evidence?" I asked.

"We convinced the chief that it would be heartless not to take advantage of people being here, and in a generous, volunteering mood," Clarence said.

"I asked that they put every new pet owner on notice that they were responsible for producing the animals if they were needed as evidence," the chief put in. I couldn't tell if he was serious or not.

"Over half of them out of our hair," Grandfather said, with satisfaction. Although he was committed in theory to the welfare of animals of every kind, he tended to be bored rather quickly with individual animals unless they were either dangerous or endangered—preferably both.

"We had a lot of them spoken for already, yesterday or earlier today," Clarence said. "Some of those people took them home tonight, after the chief gave his okay, and a lot more people just adopted on the spot. All of them people I'm well acquainted with, naturally—anyone I can't vouch for has to go through the usual investigation. And when you add in the people from that file you gave me—the people Parker was going to meet to hand over the animals—we've got about three-quarters of them placed."

"Of course, the ones left over are going to be the hardest," Grandfather said. "But we'll manage somehow. We'd better— looks as if we'll have plenty of other work to do." He gestured toward the stage, where the Fight or Flight Committee was starting to assemble.

"Ironic, isn't it?" I asked.

"What do you mean?" Grandfather was frowning suspiciously. I had the feeling he didn't like irony very much unless he was the one wielding it.

"If the committee does decide in favor of evacuation, there's one county agency that won't have a very big moving job, thanks to CORSICA," I said. "You won't see the animal shelter staff scrounging for a new location."

"That's because the mayor fired all the staff," Grandfather said.

"No, they quit," I said. "So isn't it lucky for the mayor you took all the animals away? Otherwise they'd have to figure out what to do with all those animals cluttering up one of the buildings they're seizing."

"Hmph." Grandfather glowered at me and stormed out.

"I plan to take care of moving the shelter equipment," Clarence said.

"I plan to get some sleep," I said.

I decided to check my office to see if Rose Noire was there so I could ask her to lock up the barn after everyone left.

I opened the door and found Caroline and Rose Noire standing on either side of a sobbing Corsican. I recognized her. The weepier of Parker's two known girlfriends. Louise; that was her name.

"Sorry to interrupt," I said, and backed toward the door.

Chapter 15

"No, come in, please," Caroline said. "You might be able to help."

And I might not want to help, I found myself thinking. But Caroline appeared uncharacteristically agitated, and even Rose Noire looked at me pleadingly—Rose Noire who normally basked at the chance of comforting someone else and was always urging us not to hold in our grief.

"What's wrong?" I asked, closing the door behind me.

As if in answer, Louise held out a damp, crumpled wad of paper. After blinking at it for a few moments I realized it was office paper, not tissue, so I reached out to take it from her.

It was a copy of the first page of the infamous contract. Third- or fourth-generation photocopy, by the looks of it. The thing was really making the rounds.

But however maddening I might find the existence of the contract, I wasn't quite sure why it should produce such buckets of tears. I glanced up at Rose Noire. She shrugged and shook her head slightly. Caroline threw up her hands and grimaced.

"There, there." Rose Noire handed Louise another handful of tissues and patted her shoulder comfortingly.

Caroline began edging sideways, as if planning to make a break for the door.

I wondered if I should suggest bringing Louise a kitten to feed. It seemed to have worked well before. Of course, they'd probably already thought of that, and perhaps all the kittens had been adopted by this time.

I took a deep breath and reminded myself to use my gentlest tone—the one I'd use if Timmy were agitated.

"Why does this upset you so much?" I asked.

"Because this proves it," she moaned.

"There, there," Rose Noire said, patting diligently.

"Proves what?"

"He didn't really care about me at all," she sobbed. "He was just using me to get that."

She pointed at the wad of paper in my hands and collapsed onto Rose Noire's waiting shoulder. Rose Noire patted and there-there'd with renewed vigor.

"So you're the one who gave him this?" I said.

"No! I never would!" She whirled and glowered at me as if I'd accused her of animal abuse.

"Sorry, I must have misunderstood you. So how did he get it? And if you didn't give it to him, why would it have anything to do with you?"

"Because I work in the mayor's office," she said, in a tone of utter exasperation at having to explain the obvious. "If Parker was looking for stuff like that—government secrets—then he would know I knew where to find them. And that means he never really loved me—he was just using me."

"Maybe it's just a coincidence," Rose Noire said.

"Yes," I said. "After all, you didn't give him this, right?"

She shook her head.

"And I assume you never gave him anything else confidential?"

Another head shake.

"Then why would anyone assume this has something to do with his relationship with you?"

"The mayor will," she said. "He'll assume I gave it to Parker and he'll probably fire me. And I really need the job—do you think I'd be working for Mayor Pruitt if I could get any other job?"

She collapsed in sobs.

So were these paroxysms of tears for Parker, or for the impending loss of her job? Maybe both.

"But you didn't give him this or anything else confidential," I went on.

"No," she said. "And he never asked me to. Even if he had, I wouldn't have given it to him. I may not like working for the mayor, but that doesn't mean I'd stab him in the back."

"Did Parker ever even ask you to help him get confidential information?" I asked.

She shook her head.

"Then your conscience is clear, right?"

"Yes," she said, sniffling. "But a clear conscience isn't going to do me much good if I'm fired."

"Then again, is it really that bad being fired by the most hated man in the county?" I asked. "And not all that popular in town, either. If they get that recall campaign going, being fired by him could be a badge of honor. And they'll need honest people who know how the office works."

"Really?"

Clearly she wasn't very politically savvy if that angle hadn't occurred to her.

"Louise, even though you didn't give him the contract, is there any chance he could have used you to get it?" I asked. "Did he ask a lot of questions about your work?"

"Oh, yes," she said, sniffling slightly. "He always seemed interested in what I was doing. I thought it was because I was doing it, not that he wanted inside information. But I didn't know that contract existed, so even if I were in the habit of blabbing, I couldn't have told him about it."

"Did he ever come to your office?"

"Yes, he must have been there a dozen or more times. But I don't see how that would help him get the contract. I never saw it before, so it's not as if he could have found it by searching my desk. And all of the staff are always careful not to leave the mayor's door unlocked when he's not there."

"Still—he was there, frequently," I said. "Who knows what happened? Maybe the other staff members aren't all as careful as you are."

"Yes," she said. "It makes you think, doesn't it?"

And she did appear to be thinking intensely. To my relief—and even more to Caroline's and Rose Noire's—she had stopped crying. She still sniffed occasionally, but she was staring at her hands, lost in thought. Trying to figure out if Parker had taken advantage of his access to her office? Considering whether one or more of her coworkers might be rivals for his affection? Or maybe just contemplating how satisfying it would be to throttle him. I wondered if someone should warn Maudie that some of the mourners at the funeral might still have a posthumous bone to pick with the deceased. Maudie probably knew how to deal with that far better than I did, as long as she was forewarned.

"Thank you," Louise said. She smiled briefly at me—not much of a smile, and it didn't reach her eyes, but it showed she was trying. She glanced briefly at Caroline and Rose Noire to include them in it. And then she got up and walked toward the door.

"Louise," I called after her. "Do yourself a favor: talk to the chief. Tell him what you told us. If this contract is connected with the murder, the more he knows how Parker got it, the better. It always goes over better with him if you volunteer information instead of waiting for him to track you down."

She blinked, then nodded weakly.

"And if you can think of anyone else who works down at the town hall that Parker might have been trying to seduce so he could milk her for information, he'd love to hear that, so you might as well make their lives miserable, too."

She smiled faintly at that, and went out, shutting the door carefully behind her.

As I watched her leave, I found myself thinking that adultery wasn't the only reason the woman who had come to Parker's shop might not have wanted to be seen in his company. If you worked for the mayor and had begun to figure out that Parker might be dangerous to know—

"You're a lifesaver," Caroline said.

"Poor thing," Rose Noire said. "It must be so difficult to realize that he was only using her."

"You never know," I said. "When she's not crying, she's rather pretty. I didn't know Parker that well, but I don't think it's impossible that he could have been interested in her for her own sake."

"He wasn't serious about anyone," Caroline said.

"I didn't say serious, I just said interested," I countered.

"So you think he found out about the contract by accident?" Caroline asked.

"Or from some other source," I said. "She strikes me as honest. And she's not the only person in town who would have access to it. What about that other Corsican who was dating Parker. Vivian. Where does she work?"

"Couldn't be her," Rose Noire said. "She's a nurse. Works down at Caerphilly General."

"Oh, right," I said.

"Louise is the most likely," Caroline said. "And I don't care how careful she thinks she was about the mayor's office—it wouldn't be that hard to get around her."

"She has a very trusting nature," Rose Noire said.

"Yes, she's as sweet and innocent as a baby rabbit, and has about as many brains," Caroline said.

"She's not stupid—just gullible about men," Rose Noire said.

"So you don't think she could have killed Parker?" I asked.

They looked at each other.

"I wouldn't go that far," Caroline said.

"You never know, when there's so much negative energy in a situation," Rose Noire said. She was wringing her hands, clearly uncomfortable with the topic. "I don't like to . . . you know."

"You don't like to speak ill of the dead, but you didn't like Parker," I finished for her.

"I don't like to speak ill of anyone," she said. "And I didn't dislike Parker. I just—"

"You just didn't like him hitting on you," Caroline said.

"He hit on you?" I asked.

"Well, of course," Rose Noire said. "He hit on everyone."

"Hell, he even flirted with me sometimes, just to keep in practice," Caroline said. "You learned to ignore him."

"Sounds like a real charmer," I said.

"We could still find out that a jealous lover did him in," Caroline said. "Or a jealous husband or boyfriend."

"But I think Meg has the right idea," Rose Noire said. "Follow the money."

"What happened to *cherchez la femme*?" Caroline countered.

"I will let the chief do both," I said, with a yawn. "I'm off to bed. Rose Noire, can you lock up?"

"Of course," she said.

I headed for bed.

Though I did stop by on the way to say a word to the chief.

"Did Michael get a chance to tell you what he saw in Parker Blair's furniture store?"

"The elusive woman who didn't want to be seen? Yes, thanks. I'm already keenly interested in any of Mr. Blair's lady friends who might not be unattached."

"I can think of other reasons why the woman might have fled," I said. "Have you talked to Louise tonight?"

"No," he said. "Louise who, and why should I talk to her?"

"Dietz, " I said. "Works in the mayor's office. Was seeing Parker. And now thinks he was using her to get information."

"Was he?"

I shrugged.

"Rob said she was their mole in the mayor's office," I said. "I thought she was doing it out of conviction. Who knows? Anyway, I told her to come and talk to you, but perhaps she was too tired to do it tonight."

"She give him that contract you found?"

"No idea. She says not, but even if she's telling the truth, he could have used her to get it. And if she knew he was gunning for the mayor, she might not have wanted anyone to see her consorting with her boss's enemies."

He nodded, and rubbed his eyes.

"I'll track her down tomorrow," he said. "Thanks. For this, and for not trying to make away with the papers you found at Blair's house. Although maybe I shouldn't thank you for expanding my suspect list."

"I thought I'd narrowed it down," I said. "And don't try to convince me that you hate having the mayor at the head of your suspect list."

He smiled slightly.

"The girlfriends are still suspects, too," he said. "And now I pretty much have to interrogate every susceptible female who works down at the town hall, in case one of them gave him the contract and killed him to cover it up. Well, time enough for that tomorrow. Night."

I went back to the house. I was exhausted from getting even less sleep than usual, but curiously energized by the evening's events. I had the sinking feeling that if I went to bed right now, I'd toss and turn for hours.

I decided to fix myself a cup of tea. Herbal tea, of course, but not one of Rose Noire's odd brews. Maybe some old-fashioned rose hip tea.

I grabbed a mug, filled it with water, and put it in the microwave.

Just as I was taking the cup out, Caroline came in.

"That was amazing!" she exclaimed. "I can't believe how well the county is pulling together!"

Clearly she also needed to unwind.

"Would you like some tea?" I asked.

"Love some. You were pitch perfect."

I handed her a couple of boxes of tea bags, set the heated cup in front of her, and put another in the microwave for myself. I leaned against the counter and nodded as she enthused over the meeting.

The microwave dinged. The back door opened.

"Caroline?"

It was Ms. Ellie, the librarian.

"I'm right here," Caroline said. "You look agitated. Meg, fix her some tea."

I put the second mug down at a place for Ms. Ellie and started a third.

Ms. Ellie did look agitated. And I'd never seen her agitated— not even when one of the juvenile delinquent Pruitts turned his ill-tempered dog loose in the children's room during story hour.

"I have favors to ask," she said. "Of both of you. Caroline, may I borrow your truck? The big one?"

"Well, sure, if you need it," Caroline said. "What's up?"

"The big move."

"It's definite, then?" I asked.

"Committee's leaning that way," she said. "And the county board's standing by in the barn to take a vote as soon as the committee makes its recommendation. And your cousin's advising the committee, by the way."

"If Festus thinks the big evacuation is the best plan, I won't argue," I said.

"So we have to move all the books out of the library," Ms. Ellie said. "Not just the books, of course. We have to move everything. But the books are the main problem. So, Caroline, may we use your truck?"

"Of course you may," she said. "And I'll send word down to the sanctuary to bring any other vehicles we can scrounge up. Damn, but this is crazy. How can the lender do this without giving people some kind of notice?"

"According to what we just found out, they did give Mayor Pruitt notice, months ago," Ms. Ellie said. "Not that the mayor told anyone, of course, except for a few of his cronies. He says he's been working to find a solution, but you know damn well he's only been sitting on his rear, assuming that they'd never go so far as to seize the county's property."

I winced slightly. Maybe the mayor had been counting on his eminent domain scheme to keep the lender at bay. Was this demand from the lender that we turn over the county buildings already in the cards, or had my call to Cousin Festus helped trigger it?

I heard a wail from the baby monitor, followed by a murmured "I've got it" from Michael.

The microwave dinged. I shoved my worries aside and made my cup of tea before anyone else arrived to preempt me.

And just in time, too. Randall Shiffley ambled into the kitchen.

"Want some tea?" Caroline asked.

"I'm fine," he said.

I nodded. I hadn't pegged Randall for a tea drinker.

"Beer and sodas in the fridge," I said.

Randall opened the door and helped himself to a Coke.

"Ms. Ellie," he said. "I just wanted to say that as soon as we finish down at the courthouse, we'll come over to the library."

"That will help," she said.

"And Chauncy is sending over some boxes."

Chauncy, I assumed, was the Shiffley in charge of the small family-run moving company.

"I don't suppose we could get the use of Parker's truck for some of this," Caroline said.

"I already asked," Ms. Ellie said. "The chief says it's still part of his crime scene."

"Understandable," I said.

"I just better not see him clearing out the police station with it," Ms. Ellie grumbled. "Meg, there's just one more thing."

I braced myself. I hated that particular phrase, and I had a sinking feeling I knew what was coming.

"We need a place to put the books," she said. "Right now we're just going to box them up, of course. We have to get through emptying the library first. We won't even have time to think about reopening for days—maybe weeks. Not until we either find a new building or fix things so we can get back into the old one."

Weeks might be conservative. If the whole issue had to go through the law courts, we were talking months or years.

"Can we use your sheds? And maybe the hay loft in your barn?"

"We'll have the animals out in a few days' time," Caroline said. "Then you can use the whole barn."

"I don't suppose you could check with Mother and Dad," I

suggested. "They have a barn, too. And I can't think of anything Dad would rather have in his backyard than a library."

"I can," Ms. Ellie said. "He already offered to let the chief use his barn for the temporary police station."

I sighed. I hoped Dad and Chief Burke would both survive the proximity.

"Apparently barn space is at a premium right now," Ms. Ellie said. "Not many people have barns that they don't use for farming."

"True," I said. "Well, then *mi casa es su casa*. Or should that be *mi casa es su biblioteca*?"

"I'd like to make a suggestion," Randall said. "An offer, I guess. A lot of people are going to be pretty unhappy if the county doesn't have a library open. Kids' grades could suffer, people on fixed incomes would have no access to books. If Meg and Michael will agree to host the county's books in their library till we can get past this situation, I'd be willing to build those shelves we've been talking about at the cost of the materials. How about it?"

They all looked at me.

"I'll have to talk to Michael," I said.

"Good." Caroline and Ms. Ellie looked optimistic. Randall seemed to consider it a done deal—had he already talked to Michael? Or did he just know how much Michael coveted the dream library for which Randall had already drawn up plans?

They all took their leave shortly after that. I went out to the barn—which was locked up tight. As I unlocked the door, I made a mental note to thank Rose Noire. I picked up my laptop and a couple of files from my desk, relocked the barn, and took my papers back to the kitchen. Then I fixed myself another cup of tea. Randall's offer had driven sleep even farther away.

I spent the next hour or so poring over our family budget and the Shiffley Construction Company's proposal for our library. Could we afford the library buildout, even at Randall's generous terms? Could we live with ourselves if we passed up the chance?

And wouldn't building out the library be an excellent way to celebrate Michael's tenure? Which wasn't official yet, of course. It wouldn't be official for another month, but it was as close to a certainty as anything could be in the tangled world of academia. So shouldn't I jump at this chance to celebrate his academic success with a library worthy of a tenured professor? A tenured professor and quite possibly, in a few years, a department chairman, since by this fall he would be one of only three tenured faculty members in the newly formed drama department. And the other two were in their sixties and had already come up with a plan for each of them to serve as department chair for a year or two and then retire, leaving Michael in place as their natural successor. Our prospects were rosy.

But right now the bank account wasn't.

And just how long would Ms. Ellie and her books be occupying our library after Randall Shiffley built it out? At the county meeting, Festus had told us to prepare for the battle to last months if not several years. Several years of not being able to use part of our own house?

Of course, that would also mean several years of having wonderfully convenient access to a much bigger library than Michael and I could ever hope to assemble. We already were having bedtime story hour for the boys in the hope that they'd form the same love of reading we had. Everyone always said that the best way to turn children into readers was to surround them with books and adults who considered reading an important part of their lives. What better way to do that than have a library on the premises?

And better in the house than in the barn. I hoped to resume my blacksmithing soon, and I shuddered at the idea of lighting my forge and starting to hammer sparks out of hot iron in a building filled to the rafters with highly inflammable paper. And I could just imagine the conflicts. "Meg," Ms. Ellie would call out. "Can you stop making such a racket? We're trying to have the children's story hour." No, the house was the optimal place for what we'd already promised to do. If only we could afford the buildout.

I alternated between dreams of glory and financial fretting for far longer than I should. Eventually, I must have fallen asleep, facedown on the family budget.

Chapter 16

Something woke me up. I started and almost knocked my chair over. I was in the kitchen. Apparently I'd fallen asleep over my tea. I touched my teacup. It was room temperature. My budget files were still on the table. A few of the papers from the idea file for our library renovation had fallen on the floor.

I glanced at the clock: 2:00 A.M. Past time for the next feeding. Had I been awakened by one of the babies crying?

I got up and went over to the kitchen counter and made sure the volume on the baby monitor was up. Yes, it was, and I could hear only silence, and the occasional soft not-quite snore from Michael. He'd probably done the last feeding or two and fallen asleep in the recliner. I must have been exhausted to have slept through the wailing, even if Michael had turned the monitor off on the nursery end. So what had awakened me?

I ventured out into the hallway. It was empty and silent. So was the living room when I looked inside. But someone had been there. A vase had been knocked off a bookshelf near the door and lay in shards on the floor. Not a vase I particularly liked. I could easily live without it, except that the aunt who given it to us last Christmas would probably notice that it wasn't there the next time she visited. Should I make a big fuss over how upset I was? No, always the chance she'd send a replacement. Best say nothing.

Let her assume I'd moved it to one of the guest rooms. I gave the jagged fragments a wide berth and explored further.

The macaw's cage had been knocked on its side. I went over and peered down at it. The macaw was standing up and looking alarmed but did not, thank goodness, say anything. I righted the cage and adjusted the cover. I heard a soft squawk and a flutter of feathers. I peered in again to see that the macaw was sitting on its perch, head tucked under its wing. I breathed a sigh of relief.

I could see no other damage in the living room. No other new damage—the rug really would have to go to the cleaners. I'd let Mother figure out what to do about the sofas and the gnawed-on end table.

Nothing missing, and no damage. But someone had been here. What were they trying to do? And had they succeeded? Or had they knocked over the vase and fled first?

I went back into the hall and turned on the light there. Only then did I notice that the front door was ajar.

I backed up as far from the door as I could while still keeping it in sight and pulled out my cell phone to call Michael.

"'Lo?" He sounded still asleep.

"I think we may have had a prowler," I said in a low voice. "Are the babies okay?"

"They're fine." He suddenly sounded a lot more awake. "I'll be right down. Call 911."

"I'm not sure," I said. "There doesn't appear to be anyone still here, but the front door's open and some stuff in the living room's been knocked over. And I'd rather stay on the line with you till you get down here."

"Roger."

I inched over to the umbrella stand to grab a stout walking

stick that we kept there for my grandfather to use if the urge to hike hit him while he was visiting.

Then I returned to the living room, though I kept my eye on the front door until Michael appeared. And by that time I'd already found how the intruder had entered.

"Look." I pointed to one of the front windows. "Someone cut the glass and unlatched this window."

"We need a security system," Michael said. "This far out in the country. I'm calling 911."

"Until I saw the glass, I was hoping it was just something else silly the Corsicans were up to."

He came over to inspect the glass, already dialing.

"Hello, Debbie Anne," Michael said. "Yes—I think we've had a burglar."

I returned to the hallway, opened the door and peered out.

"Careful," Michael said. "What if someone's still out there? What if—"

"It's Grandfather." I threw the door open and raced out. "I think he's hurt."

Grandfather was lying facedown at the foot of the porch steps, his tall, angular form crumpled into an awkward heap.

"Send an ambulance, too," Michael said on the phone.

"I'll check his pulse," I said, dropping to Grandfather's side.

It was weak but steady. Was his breathing a little shallow? Or was I just a little panicked?

I could hear Michael talking to Debbie Anne. I reported my findings to Michael, who relayed them to her. I put my hand on Grandfather's forehead. He didn't seem to be overly warm. I wasn't sure if that mattered.

There was something damp and sticky on his temple. I

pulled away my hand to look at it. Was that blood? Hard to tell in the moonlight.

"Turn on the porch light," I said.

"No, we have no idea when," Michael was saying. He reached back inside for the light switch.

I scrambled around to Grandfather's other side and flopped down on my stomach so I could get my head on his level and look at his face.

"She says not to move him," Michael said.

"I'm not," I said. "I want to see if his eyes are open, and if he seems to have hit his head. Tell Debbie Anne you've got to hang up. I want you to call Dad."

"She already did," Michael said. "He's on his way."

Grandfather's eyes were closed. A small trickle of blood ran down the left side of his face. Even though the porch light wasn't that bright, I could see well enough to know it was blood. I brushed a lock of his hair aside and saw a wound on his temple.

"He's bleeding," I said.

"He must have hit his head," Michael said. "Meg can see blood."

"I don't think he hit his head," I said. "I think someone hit him. Angle of the wound," I added, answering Michael's raised eyebrow. "And no, I'm not sure. That's Dad's specialty. I just think it looks suspicious."

Michael nodded and relayed my suspicions to Debbie Anne.

I took Grandfather's hand.

"You're going to be all right," I said, in my calmest voice. "Dad and the ambulance are on their way."

Did he squeeze my hand? Or did I only imagine it?

Michael put his hand on my shoulder.

We stayed like that for what seemed like hours. When the ambulance finally arrived, I wasn't sure whether to be relieved or hurt at how quickly they ordered us aside.

Dad arrived a minute or so after the ambulance. He and the EMTs were grimfaced. They started an IV. Someone mentioned a blow to the head, so apparently I was right. I began to hear words like concussion and subdural hematoma.

"I can keep an eye on things down here," Michael said. "Why don't you stay with the kids. Josh ate about an hour ago, and Jamie should be ready any minute."

I wondered if he was reading my mind. I realized that what I wanted most was to retreat upstairs, pick up one of the boys, and focus on him, blotting out of my mind the picture of Grandfather lying on the front walk.

I spent what was left of the night in the recliner, holding one or another of the twins, waiting for Dad to call and tell us if Grandfather was going to make it.

Chapter 17

"How is he?" I demanded.

It was shortly after dawn on Sunday morning. I had just deposited the boys in the spare crib we kept in the kitchen and was making some decaf when Dad and the chief strolled in, followed by Michael, who had answered the doorbell.

"He's unconscious," Dad said. "But stable."

"Define stable." I sat down, and Michael took over with the coffee.

"His vital signs are good," Dad said. "In fact, they're excellent for his age. He's only got a mild concussion. I just wish he'd regain consciousness."

Dad slumped into a kitchen chair.

"Don't worry," I said, patting Dad's shoulder. "He's much too hardheaded to be killed that way. I'm sure he'll be fine."

Dad sighed, nodded, and squeezed my hand.

"And while we're waiting for Dr. Blake to regain consciousness," the chief said, "I'd like to interview you and Michael about what happened last night."

"I didn't see much," I said.

"Whatever you can remember."

I nodded. Through the kitchen window, I could see Horace and Sammy searching the yard. Presumably they'd finished with the living room, which would now be coated liberally with at least three different colors of fingerprint powder.

"And Horace isn't going to have much luck with the forensics, is he?" I asked. "How many hundreds of people have been in our living room the last two days, or tromped through our yard last night?"

"Which is why I'm going to be relying a lot more on witness statements," the chief said.

"Subtly hinted," I said. "Let's go find a quiet place so I can give mine. You probably already thought of this, but the guy who was driving the church bus was here till the bitter end, ferrying people to their cars. You might ask him what he saw."

"I didn't know he was doing that," the chief said. "That could be helpful."

I doubted if anything else in my statement was, though. Especially since nothing I had to say helped the chief come up with an idea why the intruder had been on our property, or whether or not he'd been in the house.

"Grandfather might have scared off a prowler and been injured in the process," I said to Michael afterward. "Or maybe he interrupted a burglar in the act and gave chase."

I was sitting at the kitchen table, holding Jamie, and ticking the options off on my fingers, which Jamie found curiously fascinating.

"A burglar who hadn't yet taken any of our stuff," Michael said. He was balancing Josh on one shoulder while fixing some breakfast.

"Or a burglar who didn't think any of our stuff was worth taking and was about to leave in a snit," I suggested. "Or a burglar who did take something that we still haven't noticed yet."

"The house isn't that cluttered," he said.

"Could be someone who had it in for Grandfather and came to harm or even kill him," I suggested.

"Or someone who came to talk to your grandfather and lost his temper during the conversation."

I'd filled the one hand and had to count this last possibility on my other hand. Jamie squealed with delight and tried to grab my finger.

"Jamie votes for that scenario," I said. "And I'd put it high on the probability list myself."

"Though most people don't try to settle their arguments with a blunt instrument," Michael said. He put Josh into the baby carriage and set the little disco ball toy spinning to amuse him.

"Good thing," I said. "Or Grandfather would have already had quite a few concussions in his life."

"He'll be fine." Michael came over and held his hands out for Jamie. "Getting the best possible care with your dad on the case. And it's a good hospital, too."

"And thank goodness the hospital isn't county-owned any longer," I said. "Or they'd be clearing that out tomorrow, too. Not so great for someone in the ICU."

"But they're not, so he can stay put, and you can go down and see him. Talk to him."

He set Jamie in the carriage and began bouncing it vigorously, which had the double effect of making the disco ball spin and soothing the boys.

"Talk to him?" I echoed. "On the theory that even though he's unconscious, he'll hear me and rally from his coma?"

"They've done some studies that show it works," he said. "And even if it doesn't, you'll feel better for trying. You'll go crazy, hanging around here all day."

"I wasn't planning on hanging around here all day," I said. "Assuming you can be persuaded to spend your Sunday bonding with the boys, I was planning to help Ms. Ellie pack up the library."

I didn't add that I was planning to do a little fact-finding while I was in town. The chief would probably call it snooping. But the chief didn't have a grandfather in intensive care and a crooked politician trying to take away his home. I wasn't yet sure who I needed to talk to or what I'd ask them, but I knew for sure the action was in town, not here.

"Or if the library's well taken care of, I'll see where else they need me," I added, so Michael wouldn't worry if he learned I wasn't at the library.

"Good plan," he said. "Pack all you like, then visit your grandfather. And when you get tired of packing, we can trade off and you can watch the boys while I help with the packing."

"*If* I get tired," I said. "In my book, packing's a lot easier than riding herd on the kids."

"Pack all you like, then," Michael said. "If I get overwhelmed, I'll draft some help. Your mother recruited a whole bunch of your relatives to help with the packing. She asked if we could put up a dozen or so of them here. I'm sure I can guilt-trip a few of them into babysitting in return for their room and board."

"That settles it," I said. "If a horde of Hollingsworths is descending on us, I'm definitely packing all day."

"Can I come?"

Timmy was standing in the doorway, still in pajamas.

"I'm going to do work, you know," I said.

"I know," he said. "I want to help save the library. I don't want that mean mayor to steal all the books."

"How fast can you get dressed?" I asked.

He vanished.

"I like his priorities," Michael said. "By the way, your mother's already here, and full of energy."

"Damn," I said. "I know I sicced her on the idea of sprucing up the yard, but after last night, I really don't think I can focus on it."

"Relax," he said. "She says she's thinking about her landscaping plans, but right now, she's hell-bent on undoing all the damage the animals did."

"Not to mention what Horace has done this morning while furthering the cause of justice."

"Yes," he said. "I think it was the fingerprint powder that drove her over the edge. She's got a couple of your cousins helping her with the heavy lifting."

"Awesome," I said. "Let's just hope her idea of undoing the damage doesn't involve redecorating in Louis Quatorze."

I grabbed a cup of coffee and ambled into the living room.

To my relief, Mother did seem focused on repair. She was minutely examining every inch of our sofa, while the two burly cousins waited nearby with anxious looks on their faces.

"Needs work," she said at last. "But I think it can be saved. "

Apparently they'd been doing this for a while. The cousins immediately interpreted her words as a signal to hoist the sofa and whisk it off to a waiting truck.

As Michael and I first fixed and then ate breakfast, we could hear her imperious voice giving orders, and every time I went through the hall and glanced in, the room looked a little emptier.

She had the cousins roll up the soiled rug and load it on Dad's truck. Several pieces of chewed-on furniture had joined them, no doubt to gladden the heart and pockets of the little old German man who did all her furniture repairs. Now they were taking down all the curtains while Mother prowled about making sure she hadn't missed anything.

I suspected that some of the things she was taking in for cleaning or repair had needed help before the animals and Horace had arrived, but I wasn't about to quibble.

"Looking better," I said.

"Looking a bit bare, you mean," she said. "I might bring one or two things over to fill in until your stuff comes back. But not till I have a cleaning service in to scrub away all that nasty powder. They might not be able to come out till tomorrow."

"We'll be fine," I said. "We practically live in the nursery these days anyway."

"Well, that will have to do for now," she said. "Are you going into town, dear?"

"Yes," I said. "Going to help with the library."

"Can you drop me off at the town hall?" she asked. "The garden club is gathering there."

"The garden club is having a meeting today?"

"This morning we're packing up the county extension agent's office," she said. "And then we're going to rescue plants."

"Rescue what plants?" I asked. "And rescue them from what?"

"Rescue them from falling into the hands of that horrible company when it seizes all our county buildings," she said. "The county buys all the plants and pays the service that comes by to water and feed them. We got the county board to authorize the garden club to care for the plants during the interim. So we're going to make a sweep through all the government buildings to make sure all the potted plants are moved to more suitable quarters."

"That's nice," I said. Unthinkable, of course, that any of our treasured houseplants might fall into the clutches of the evil lender. But then, I felt the same way about the books in the town library. To each his own.

She followed me out to the hall where she donned a lavender hat trimmed with purple flowers and a pair of purple gardening gloves. Trust mother to have just the right outfit for anything, including a plant rescue mission.

Timmy bounded down the stairs dressed in clothes that looked as if they'd escaped my last roundup of dirty laundry. Mother raised an eyebrow, but I could see no reason to make him put on clean clothes when he'd probably be covered with dust after half an hour of packing at the library, so I led the way to the car. My old car—I'd leave the Twinmobile for Michael, in case he wanted to take the boys anywhere. As I pulled out of our driveway in my tiny Toyota—well, tiny compared to the minivan—I felt a brief surge of guilty pleasure at how free and unencumbered I was.

"Can we stop at the ice cream store?" Timmy asked.

"And the card shop," Mother said. "I want to get a card for your grandfather."

Okay, so much for unencumbered. And the thought of Grandfather lying unconscious in the hospital washed away the last shreds of pleasure.

"Ice cream and get-well cards coming up," I said.

At least I had plenty to distract me. When we got near town, we ran into something rarely seen in Caerphilly, especially on a

Sunday: a traffic jam. So many cars, trucks, and even buses were heading into town that I thought we'd never get a chance to pull out of our country road onto the main highway.

But after a few moments, a farmer in a truck slowed to a stop and cheerfully waved me onto the highway. In fact, the entire crowd was strangely cheerful about the traffic. Perhaps because we all had something concrete and manageable to do. We couldn't solve the county's budget or legal problems, but packing and moving were things we all knew how to do.

"Wow," Timmy said. "Where did they all come from?"

"All the churches sent out calls for help last night and this morning at their services," Mother said. "Not just to their own congregations, but to nearby counties."

And apparently the volunteers had come by the busload. As I made my way through town I saw buses from as far away as Henrico County and Manassas. When we finally reached the town square, I saw various groups gathering under impromptu banners and signs to form work teams. Along with the church groups I spotted uniformed Scout troops and delegations from the nearby Lions, Elks, and Rotary clubs. And to top it off, Mother had sent her all-points bulletin to the Hollingsworth family, who could be expected to answer her call in the dozens if not hundreds. I saw several knots of faces I usually saw only at funerals and family reunions.

I dropped Mother off near one flock of cousins and drove on toward the library.

From the difficulty we had parking anywhere nearby, I deduced that helping at the library was a popular choice.

Ms. Ellie, looking determined, if slightly harried, met us at the door.

"Welcome," she said. "Timmy, would you like to help pack the children's section?"

He nodded vigorously and trotted toward the familiar sunny alcove.

"They're a bit slow back there, but they're having fun," Ms. Ellie said. "And I think it's doing a lot to ease their anxiety about where all their beloved books are going. How's your grandfather?"

"Stable," I said. "Don't ask me what that means. Dad's worried, but not frantic."

A Shiffley cousin wheeling in a four-foot-high stack of moving boxes appeared in the doorway. We both stepped aside into the corridor that led to Ms. Ellie's office.

"And they have no clue who did it?" she asked.

"No," I said. "And no idea whether or not it has anything to do with Parker's murder or the county meeting."

"I'm sure it has something to do with both," she said. "They must be connected. But what happened at the meeting to suddenly make someone want to attack your grandfather?"

I'd been chewing on the same question for hours.

"I don't think it's something that happened at the meeting," I said. "I think it's something that was going to happen after the meeting. The committees, for example. Several of them were organized to dig out information that someone might not want found."

"Good point."

"So which of the committees did Grandfather volunteer for last night?" I asked. "Maybe that would tell us what's got his attacker running scared."

"I don't remember that he volunteered for any of them," Ms.

Ellie said. "Your grandfather's better at giving orders than volunteering."

"Are you sure? Can you ask whoever's keeping the list?"

"I have the list," she said. "Let me check."

I followed her into her office and fretted as she pulled a file folder out of her desk and flipped through the four- or five-page document it contained.

"As I thought," she said. "Not on any of the committees. But he did promise to bring down some auditors to help with some of the financial investigations."

"That's right," I said. "I remember him shouting that out during the meeting."

"I thought he ran a charitable foundation, not an accounting firm," she said, as she tucked the list back in its folder.

"He does run a foundation," I said. "And he'd be the first to tell you that any foundation worth its salt needs top-notch auditors. He gets a lot of funding requests, and he has to have someone to help him sort out which ones are worthwhile and which are not."

And which ones were actually scams. I wasn't sure whether many of the requests they got were crooked or whether Grandfather just talked a lot about the ones that were, but I knew his audit staff was large, skilled, and enthusiastic about unearthing potential fraud. He'd bragged about that at the meeting, too.

"What if someone heard his offer and got scared?" I asked. "Of course it would have to be someone who was at the meeting, which lets out my favorite suspect, Mayor Pruitt."

"Not necessarily," she said. "Could also be someone who got a full report from his spies."

"You think the mayor sent spies?"

"We know he sent spies," she said. "We expected him to—after all, it's a public meeting. We even knew who they were. Poor things—he made them come down to the town hall to brief him once the meeting was over. Kept them there well past midnight, I heard."

"We have spies down at the town hall?"

"One of his spies is actually our spy. Would have joined Corsica if she wasn't on the town payroll. She told us all about it."

"And the mayor wasn't happy?"

"She says he went berserk. I think she'd have mentioned it if he told any of his spies to sneak back and bludgeon your grandfather, but that doesn't mean he didn't order someone to do it as soon as no inconvenient witnesses were around."

We stood in silence for a few moments.

"Are we seriously considering the possibility that one of our elected officials is a cold-blooded murderer?" I asked.

"Yes," she said. "I think he's capable. And if he thought Parker Blair and your grandfather were trying to expose him for the crook he is, he'd sure as hell have motivation. Watch your back. We don't want him going after you next."

The mayor's round red face popped into my mind. When I'd first come to Caerphilly, I'd considered him a comic figure. The prototypical sleazy small town politician. Then I'd realized there was nothing comic about him at all. His was the latest in a long line of Pruitts who'd lived well at the expense of the citizens of Caerphilly, and the idea that he might be about to lose control of the goose that had been providing them with so many golden eggs for a century and a half—that might well turn him homicidal.

"I'll be careful," I said. "But it's not as if he has it in for me particularly."

"He knows you," she said. "He knows you've helped the chief out a time or two. And he knows you won't take the attack on your grandfather lightly."

I nodded.

"So maybe I'll stay here for a while where there are plenty of witnesses," I said. "What can I do?"

"Fiction's pretty well taken care of," she said. "A bit too well. But we could really use someone to work on the nonfiction. Everything except the cookbook section, which is also pretty well covered."

As I made my way to the stairs, I could see what she meant. The fiction shelves, particularly the genre sections, were filled with happy people, and some aisles sounded less like work crews than book club meetings.

"You've never read *The Man in the High Castle*? Don't pack it; check it out before Ms. Ellie shuts down the computers."

"You know, that's an idea. Maybe we should just all check out as many books as we're allowed to. Just for the time being."

"Is this a new Terry Pratchett, or just a British edition of an old title?"

"What do you mean, she's overrated? When was the last time you actually read anything by Christie?"

"Oh, man! They have half a dozen P. G. Wodehouses that I haven't read yet!"

Upstairs it was a lot quieter. With the exception of a group of avid foodies drooling over the cookbooks they were packing over in the 640s, the aisles were largely empty.

I grabbed a stack of boxes—provided, I noticed, by Shiffley Movers—and begin with the 000s, computer science. I was itching to be out doing something else. Something to help foil the mayor's scheme. Something to help Chief Burke solve the murder. Or something to help Grandfather recover. Trouble was, I had no idea what to do on any of those fronts. But packing didn't exactly occupy my whole brain, so I planned to pack until I thought of something better to do.

After half an hour, a couple of employees from Rob's computer gaming company showed up eager to help with the computer books, so I moved over to the 100s (philosophy), where I labored alone for about an hour.

I was just starting on metaphysics (110) when a familiar face peered down my aisle.

"Can I help?"

Francine Mann.

Chapter 18

I had to give Francine credit for nerve. Though I couldn't help wondering what I should deduce from the fact that she was spending part of her Sunday helping to pack the library. Was it a sign that Terence Mann was in sympathy with feelings in the county? Or evidence of a rift in the Mann household?

"Ms. Ellie can use all the help she can get," I said. "Though I think they're having more fun down in the cooking section."

"I think all the chatter is coming from the paranormal shelves," she said, as she began assembling a box from the stack at the end of the aisle. "By the way, I was sorry to hear about your grandfather. Is there any more news?"

"Still unconscious, but his signs are stable," I said. "Thanks for asking."

"If there's anything we can do for him or you, please let me know," she said. "All of us down at the hospital, I mean."

It was a curious clarification. Did she think I'd spurn good wishes and a rather conventional offer of help if it came from her and her husband? I hoped that wasn't indicative of how people had been treating her.

"Terence won't be staying on as county manager," she said, as if reading my thoughts.

"He's resigning?"

"He probably should," she said. "Before they fire him. They

called him on the carpet before an emergency meeting of the county board this morning. He's been there for hours."

Rather useless, if you asked me, but no doubt the board members who had been so nervous at last night's meeting were thrilled to take it out on someone.

"How are you doing?" I asked. I suppose I should have said "I'm so sorry" or "How terrible" or something of the sort, but it wouldn't have been sincere, and she probably would have realized that.

"I just want the whole thing over with," she said. "If they're going to fire him, I wish they'd just do it. I'm going down to the town hall to pick him up in a couple of hours, and if he hasn't resigned by then . . ."

She shook her head and applied herself to the shelves.

I nodded, and searched for something else I could honestly say.

"This has been tough on you," I said finally.

She nodded.

"I have no idea what's ahead," she said. "I'll probably be staying on at the hospital for the time being. Assuming they're okay with it. We need the income. It takes a while to get a job at Terence's level. Of course, when he does get a new job, it will require moving. And right now it's up in the air whether I'll be moving with him."

"I'm sorry," I said. This time I could say that, no matter what I felt about her husband.

"Or maybe I should just leave now," she said. "It's not as if the medical staff ever really accepted or supported me. In fact, they undercut me every chance they get, all because I tried to make a few minor changes in how things have always been done."

I could understand. I'd had a few run-ins myself with "that's how we've always done it."

"I could just go home," she said. Her voice cracked slightly, and I looked up with alarm at the intensity of emotion she'd packed into those five words. She was holding the shelf in front of her as if afraid she'd fall, and biting her lip to keep it from trembling. My first impulse was to give her a comforting hug, and with anyone else I'd have done it, but I was afraid it would shatter the fragile composure she was visibly struggling to regain, and I sensed she wouldn't appreciate that.

"Home would be Boston?" I asked instead.

"Near there," she said with a fleeting smile. "Worcester."

At least I assumed that was what she meant. Sounded more like "Woosteh" in her accent.

We packed in silence for a few moments. Suddenly Francine dropped the rather large book she was packing.

"It wouldn't be so bad if he'd just admit that maybe he was partly to blame," she said, in an undertone. "Not wholly to blame—the county board were fooled, too. And not even mostly to blame—that would be the mayor. But it did happen on his watch."

"Oh, dear," I said.

"And it's ridiculous to go blaming a dead man," she said.

Now that was interesting.

"He blames Parker Blair?"

"He keeps saying everything would have been all right if Mr. Blair had stayed out of it," she said. "And that's ridiculous."

Not only ridiculous, but highly suspicious. When had Terence Mann started blaming Parker for the problems that had eventually lost him his job? Before or after the murder?

I didn't dare ask Francine, though. No matter how innocently I tried to ask it, she'd guess that I was asking if her husband had a motive for murder. I couldn't think of anything to say that didn't sound as if I suspected her husband, though I kept trying for another ten or fifteen minutes as we packed in silence.

I heard a soft dinging sound coming from somewhere nearby.

"Oh, that's my phone," Francine said. She got up and scrambled to the end of the aisle, where she had left her purse.

She answered it, and after a few murmured words, she shut the phone and put it back into her purse.

"I've got to run," she said. "See you later."

My own phone chimed. I scrambled to pull it out of my pocket. Was something up?

It was Rob.

"Meg? Are you with Dad?"

"No, I'm breaking the no cell phone rule at the library."

"Damn. Do you know where he is? We sort of need him here."

"Need him? Why? Rob, if there's a medical emergency, call 911."

"There's something wrong with one of the cats," Rob said. "I paged Clarence ten minutes ago, and he hasn't answered, so I thought maybe Dad could help, but he isn't answering either, and—"

"What do you mean, 'something wrong'?"

"I can't see any wounds or anything, but he's howling in agony. You can probably hear it from there. Wait, I'll hold the phone closer to him."

Yes, I heard it. A prolonged "rrrrowl!" It did indeed sound like a cat in agony.

"Rob, which cat?"

"The fat yellow striped one. He's just lying there in his crate, looking at me and howling horribly."

"Rob, he's a she, and she's not fat, she's pregnant. She's probably about to give birth."

"Oh, my God!"

Maybe I should have broken the news more gently. I could hear Rob beginning to hyperventilate.

"Calm down," I said.

"What should I do? Where's Dad? Why doesn't Clarence answer?"

"Aren't any of the other Corsicans there?"

I knew even as I was asking that of course there weren't. Any of the other Corsicans would have known in an instant what was going on. And since Rob had been known to faint at the possibility of blood, he wasn't exactly the best choice for a feline midwife.

"Fix her a box with something soft in it," I said. "A blanket or a towel—not any of mine, please. Put it someplace quiet, like my office. She'll probably do just fine until Clarence gets there."

"But she sounds as if she's in agony."

Only Rob.

"She *is* in agony," I said. "It's called labor pains. She has my sympathy, but all she needs from you right now is a clean, safe, quiet place to get on with it."

"Okay," he said. "But can you come back and help? You've been through this—you'll know what to do."

"Roger." I hung up. Then I stretched and looked at my watch. Odds were that by the time I got there, someone else would have taken pity on Rob and sent him to boil water or something. But it was probably time to collect Timmy and head home for some lunch.

Timmy was already provided for. Ms. Ellie had ordered in pizzas for her helpers, and a festive, if impromptu, party was in progress. Timmy didn't look happy when I beckoned for him to go.

"You're welcome to stay and have some pizza," Ms. Ellie said.

"I need to check on the twins," I said. To be perfectly accurate, I also wanted to pump some more milk for them in a place less crowded than the library, but I wasn't fond of announcing that fact in public.

"Let him stay and help," Ms. Ellie said. "I can drop him off this afternoon."

Timmy beamed at the chance.

"Fine with me," I said.

I grabbed a slice of the pizza to eat in the car on the way. I had plenty of time—the trip took longer than usual, because the town streets were still choked. Though there were fewer cars and buses bringing in volunteers and more vans and trucks hauling boxes out of town. If I'd had any doubt where the various town and county offices were located, I had only to glance down the street to see which ones had clusters of boxes and furniture on the sidewalk in front of them. The lavender-hatted garden ladies running in and out with potted plants in their purple-gloved hands were another dead giveaway.

While I was waiting for a volunteer to back a very large truck into a very small space at the town hall loading dock, I pulled out my cell phone and called Chief Burke.

"What can I do for you, Ms. Langslow?" he asked.

"I wanted to share something I heard," I said. "Terence Mann has been blaming Parker Blair for his problems."

"According to whom?"

"Mrs. Mann, who was down at the library packing books with me a little while ago."

"Now that is interesting," he said. "Did you find out anything else?"

"I thought of asking her if he'd started blaming Parker only in the last day or so or if he was already mad at him before the murder," I said. "But I figured if I did, she'd know I suspected her husband of murder, and besides, you'd probably rather ask that yourself."

"Good call," he said.

"But she did volunteer that when her husband gets a new job—when, not if, because she's expecting the county to fire him any day now—she may or may not be leaving with him."

"Did she say why?"

"No, but it makes you wonder, doesn't it? What does she know that is suddenly making her want out of a marriage that seemed, up to now, pretty solid? But I figured that's also something you'd rather find out for yourself."

"Thank you," he said. "For the information and for your commendable self-restraint."

He didn't say "uncharacteristic self-restraint," so I decided to accept that as a compliment.

The truck pulled out, freeing up the road ahead of me.

"Got to go," I said. "Good luck."

Halfway home, it occurred to me to wonder where all the visiting Hollingsworths were lunching. Not, I hoped, with us.

To my relief, Mother had only invited a select few out to the house—a mere two dozen—and someone had had the sense to drop by the Caerphilly Market for provisions.

They all took turns trooping upstairs to inspect the twins, and out to the barn to view the animals, including an ever-increasing number of kittens from the yellow tabby. A fine time was had by all with the possible exception of Rob, who had recovered from his panic over the feline blessed event, but was now wandering around the house looking under chair cushions and in wastebaskets and drawers and behind pieces of furniture.

"Hasn't anyone seen my video camera?" he kept wailing. "The most exciting thing to happen in this town since the Civil War, and I'm missing all of it!"

I wasn't sure whether he meant the Great Migration, as Ms. Ellie had started to call it, or the birth of the kittens, in which he'd begun to take an almost paternal pride.

I thought of suggesting that he could borrow our video camera, but Rob was notorious for losing anything smaller than a basketball.

After I'd pumped milk and spoiled everyone's fun by determining that the boys were getting cranky and needed to be put down for a nap, I decided to head back to the library. I checked to see if Mother needed a ride.

I found her standing in the living room, looking around. I noticed that some of the wicker furniture from our sunporch had migrated into the living room to take the place of the missing items. And she'd brought a cheerful indigo-and-white batik tablecloth to throw over the macaw's cage in place of the rather utilitarian canvas tarp that had been there before.

Still, she had that look. The decorating look.

"Perhaps we should repaint while everything's out of the room," she said.

I was about to point out that everything wasn't out of the room. They'd only removed about a fourth of the furniture. Of course, Mother would counter that the burly cousins could come back for another hour or two. I thought of a more practical deterrent.

"Why repaint now?" I asked. "We could just touch things up a little. As soon as the boys start crawling, it's open season on the walls. Makes more sense to repaint after they've had a chance to mess them up."

"That's why I was thinking of repainting," Mother said, with a delicate shudder. "We could use one of those paints that clean up easily with just soap and water. Like the one we found for the nursery. So much more practical for a room where small children will be playing."

I looked at her in astonishment. When had Mother begun taking practicality into account in her decorating?

"And I've never been entirely happy with the shade," she added. "We can adjust that when we repaint. I'll bring you some paint chips later this week."

Aha. She wasn't turning practical; she was using my focus on the practical to talk me into some minor redecorating.

Still, not a bad idea.

"Sounds like a good plan," I said aloud.

She nodded absently. She was still gazing around. I braced myself. She was probably going to suggest that as long as the living room was all torn up anyway, perhaps she could add a few more decorating touches.

"I have to say," she said finally. "I like this macaw much better."

I pondered this a moment. Did she mean that she liked it better than she had before—that the macaw had grown on her? Or that she preferred the macaw to some of the other animals we were fostering? Or . . .

"Better than what?" I asked finally.

"Better than that other macaw."

"We've only ever had the one macaw," I said. "Multiple dogs, cats, hamsters, guinea pigs, and even rabbits, but only one macaw."

"I think you're mistaken, dear." She wasn't really trying to argue—she was using the tone of exaggerated patience that all of my family had taken to using with me. A tone I'd begun to find very, very irritating, because it seemed to suggest that due to the hormones and possibly the sleep deprivation, my brain was on a leave of absence.

I walked over to the mantel and picked up a stack of papers.

"Here's Clarence's inventory." I began running my fingers down the list and flipping through the pages. "First page is all dogs. So's the second. More dogs, Then cats. Then the rodents."

Mother shuddered delicately, as she usually did when rodents were mentioned.

"Here," I said, flipping to the last page. "The birds. Not a lot of them. Three canaries, which I don't remember seeing, so I suppose I should inspect all the cats' whiskers. A pair of racing pigeons. And one macaw."

"Clarence must be mistaken, then," Mother said. "You must have two macaws. Perhaps they're hiding some of the animals from you."

I sighed. That seemed more than possible. Maybe it wasn't

just my imagination that the number of animals seemed to have grown larger every time I went out to the barn. Last night's adoptions didn't seem to have made as much of a dent as I'd hoped. Maybe they were importing them from other nearby shelters to take advantage of public sympathy.

Well, if it helped get homes for the animals . . . I'd worry about that later.

"What makes you think this isn't the same macaw?" I asked aloud.

"The color, dear. The macaw you had yesterday was mostly a very harsh Prussian blue. It didn't fit your living room decor at all. This new macaw is a very lovely shade of turquoise instead. Very nice. Matches the upholstery."

Mother beamed at the macaw. The macaw ruffled its feathers slightly, and I braced myself, hoping it would only say something rude and brash, like "Hiya, toots!" instead of something from the X-rated end of its vocabulary.

The macaw only emitted a soft squawk and began preening its feathers.

"Now that's odd," I said. Yesterday the bird had missed no opportunity to speak. I didn't recall hearing it say anything this morning. Could Mother possibly be right?

And then I realized that of course she had to be right. Mother might have many strange notions and knowledge gaps, but she was absolutely sound on any subject even remotely related to decorating. And color was one of her passions. She had once spent an excruciating hour trying to explain to me the differences between purple, violet, lilac, mauve, heliotrope, magenta, lavender, orchid, grape, puce, pomegranate, Tyrian, wine, solferino, amaranthine, amethyst, fuschia, eggplant, and aubergine. And while other decorators usually carried swatches, Mother always relied on her color memory, which was the chromatic equivalent of a musician's perfect pitch.

So if Mother said that the turquoise macaw had been Prussian blue yesterday, she undoubtedly knew what she was talking about.

But what had happened to the other macaw?

"The break-in," I said aloud. "That's what they were after. The other macaw."

"Why would anyone want to steal a macaw?" Mother asked. "Particularly that rather unattractive one you had here yesterday?"

"Beats me," I said. "I'm with you—I like this new macaw much better. But so far, the other macaw is the only thing missing. Unless you count Rob's video camera, and I really don't think the intruder took it."

"What about the vase your aunt Penelope gave you as a wedding present?"

"It's not missing," I said. "The intruder broke it."

Mother winced.

"Oh, dear," she said. "She's sure to notice it's missing."

"I'll tell her I lent it to you."

Mother winced again.

"She'll never believe that," she said. "Penelope will know I think that vase is hideous."

"Then help me find a solution to the broken vase that doesn't involve buying a replacement," I said. "Because I thought it was hideous, too, and I'm sure it's also hideously expensive, and I'd like to avoid spending a vast sum of money replacing something I didn't want in the first place."

"Don't even think of replacing it," Mother said. "If Penelope ever notices, I think you should just say that you've started putting the breakables away in the attic so they'll be safe when the boys start walking."

I opened my eyes and stared at her in amazement.

"That's perfect," I said. "I mean, in a couple of months, it will be true. In fact, we've already started putting all the breakables up high so the boys can crawl here."

"And you may as well start childproofing now," she said. "Put a few more breakable things aside to make it look plausible. They'll be crawling any day now. You'd amazed how it creeps up on you."

I could tell from the faint wistfulness in her tone that she was still remembering the memorable day that Rob took his first tottering steps and made a beeline for a wobbly table holding a rare piece of Art Nouveau glass.

"Yes," she said. "We'll start childproofing this room tomorrow. Or perhaps later today. I must run. A lot more plants to rescue! By the way, there are a few plants down at the town hall that are too much for the ladies to manage. Could you possibly drop by and help us with them?"

"Glad to," I said. It would make a break from packing books.

"Thank you, dear." She waved cheerfully and sailed away.

After waving back, I returned to pondering the mystery of the missing macaw. Much more interesting than the missing vase, not to mention potentially more important. Maybe Grandfather hadn't been the intruder's target after all. Maybe he'd only been collateral damage in the intruder's quest to steal Parker's macaw.

Which didn't make the intruder any less dangerous.

I followed Mother out to the foyer.

"Don't tell anyone about the macaw swapping," I said. "It could help us catch whoever did it if they don't know we know."

"Of course not, dear." She was arranging her lavender garden club hat at just the right angle in the mirror on our hall coat stand, completely ignoring two kittens who were playing tag on the stand, knocking things off its shelves and doing who knows how much damage to the coats with their tiny little razor claws.

I fetched a box and retrieved the kittens from their playground. Out to the barn with them. As it happened, I was going that way anyway. I needed information about the macaw. And with any luck, there should be at least one animal expert still hanging around the barn.

Chapter 19

I found Clarence out tending the animals. He seemed to have relocated his veterinary practice to our barn. A card table with a clean sheet over it stood ready for any patients who needed examining, and just inside the door, he'd set up half a dozen of the wooden folding chairs we used for parties. No one was waiting on them, fortunately. Clarence was just saying good-bye to an elderly man with a rather stout bulldog in tow. I waited until the two had waddled out the door before interrupting.

I put the kittens back in what was normally Spike's pen and now appeared to be serving as a cattery.

"Clarence, could you come to the house and look at the macaw?" I asked.

"Why?" He looked anxious. "What's wrong with him?"

"Long story," I said. "And I'd rather you just look at him first."

Clarence bustled toward the house so fast I could barely keep up with him. When he reached our living room, he examined the macaw with infinite care. The claws. The beak. The eyes. The inside of the mouth. Under the tail. The macaw bore it all stoically, without saying anything.

"Seems healthy enough," Clarence said. "Not much of a talker, though, is she? Where did you get her?"

"She came with the rest of the animals from the shelter, re-member?"

"Impossible," he said. "The macaw from the shelter was a male blue hyacinth macaw. This is a female blue-and-yellow. Completely different species, not to mention the wrong sex. Although I suppose a layperson can't easily discern the gender."

"Not without getting a lot more familiar with the macaw than I ever want to be," I said.

"Hyacinths are endangered in the wild and very expensive as pets," Clarence went on. "Blue-and-yellows are common both in the wild and in captivity."

"You're positive it was a hyacinth macaw you got from the shelter?" I asked. "Is there any possibility that you could have been mistaken—given the bad light and all the commotion?"

"I'm positive," Clarence said. "Because it wasn't just any hyacinth macaw. It was Parker's. He loved that bird."

I pondered this for a few moments.

"Okay," I said finally. "I give up. Why did Parker dump his beloved, expensive hyacinth macaw in an animal shelter that had just changed its no-kill policy?"

"He didn't. We had one of the Corsicans take the macaw to the shelter, claiming she'd found it in her backyard. The shelter would have had to keep it for a reasonable period to see if the owner claimed it, so the hyacinth was in no danger."

"And just what was the point of this whole maneuver?"

"To reconnoiter," he said. "Get the lay of the land, and so forth."

"But you're the shelter's vet," I said. "You must have been there a hundred times."

Clarence's face fell.

"Apparently I'm not very good at reconnoitering. When I tried to draw a floor plan of the building, it made no sense at all, and I couldn't remember a thing about the locks and stuff. So we sent in Millie with the macaw. She can walk through someone's house in five minutes and then draw you a floor plan to scale. And as it turns out, we didn't even need her floor plan, because they left her alone in the office long enough for her to borrow a spare key."

"Useful skill," I said. "Just what does Millie do when she's not volunteering for CORSICA? I gather she's not a seasoned burglar, or you would have recruited her for the caper."

"She's a real-estate agent."

Okay, that made sense.

"Getting back to the macaws," I said. "If this isn't Parker's macaw, whose is it?"

Clarence studied the macaw for a few seconds. Then he pulled out his cell phone and dialed a number.

"Hello, Jerry? Clarence Rutledge here. How is Martha Washington doing today? No, but could you check on her now?"

He tapped his fingers on the table as he waited for Jerry to report.

"Martha Washington is a blue-and-yellow macaw?" I asked.

He nodded and held the phone away from his mouth.

"Lives in the breakfast room at the Caerphilly Inn," he said. "They have her trained to say genteel things like 'More tea, madam?' and 'Have a lovely day, ducks.' He used his falsetto and a plummy English accent as he imitated the macaw. "Only blue-and-yellow in my practice," he went on in his normal voice, "and I haven't heard of any others in the county, either. What's that Jerry? That's great. Give her a grape for me."

"Ask him if they could use another one," I said, low enough so Jerry shouldn't be able to hear me.

Clarence frowned in puzzlement.

"We've got to get rid of her—er, find a home for her sooner or later," I said.

He nodded.

"By the way, Jer, remember that conversation we had about Martha's feather plucking? Loneliness, yes. They're accustomed to living in flocks, you know. Well, I may have found a companion for her. Yes, another blue-and-yellow who is probably going to be available for adoption. I'm looking for a good home, and I thought of the inn, and poor lonely Martha. No, a first-quality specimen, quite healthy, but the owner . . . left her behind. That's right. If you're interested, I'll put you first on the waiting list."

He and Jerry exchanged a few more pleasantries and hung up.

"One more animal that's going to be safe," he said.

"And one more unsolved mystery," I said. "Can you keep your ears open for any rumors of lost or stolen macaws?"

He nodded.

"But you realize," he said, "that whoever did this macaw swapping probably bought this macaw somewhere for that purpose."

"Yes," I said. "I also realize that whoever bought that macaw viciously attacked my grandfather. So much as I'm sure we're both tempted to start calling pet stores and tropical bird breeders—"

"Understood," he said. "I'm here if the chief needs me, but I'm not going to get in his way. Incidentally, I'm planning to do most of my clinic hours in your barn this week. Lets me keep a closer eye on the animals, and while I'm at it, I can make sure a whole lot of devoted animal lovers get a chance to fall in love with the refugee animals."

"Good thinking," I said. "By the way, don't tell anyone else about the macaw swapping. No use letting the thief know we're onto him." Clarence nodded. "Well, I'm off to help with the evacuation."

"I'm probably going to close down in a few minutes and go to town to help out," he said. "I didn't want to cut my Sunday clinic hours out entirely, but it's been slow as molasses."

"Everyone's in town packing," I said. "See you there."

Though I decided that before I returned to the library, I should drop by and tell the chief what I'd learned about the macaws. I thought dropping by would be better than calling because the macaw swapping would take a lot of explaining, and it's harder to usher a visitor out the door than hang up on an annoying caller.

The roads into town were better than they had been in the morning. Apparently everyone had arrived, and the steady line of trucks heading out of town showed that they were making progress.

Traffic wasn't as bad downtown, either. As I passed the college athletic stadium, I realized why—the parking lot was filled, and a motley fleet of church buses, city buses, and private vans shuttled people to and from their cars. As long as you detoured around the town square, you could travel normally.

Fortunately, the police station was on a side street. Its parking lot was almost filled, but I found a space at the far end. As I trudged toward the station, I saw Sammy Wendell bouncing a hand truck loaded with three cardboard boxes down the side steps.

"Hey, Meg," he said. "If you're coming to see the chief, I should warn you—now's not a great time."

"I gather you're clearing out the police station?"

He nodded.

"Some of the other deputies are relocating our prisoners," he said. "The Clay County sheriff has agreed to take them for the short term. Horace is helping me move the stuff from the chief's office over to your parents' barn. The chief's pretty cranky about the whole thing."

"I don't blame him," I said. "Instead of being out solving Parker Blair's murder, his officers are having to pretend they're movers. If it helps, I have some possibly useful information. Maybe that would cheer him up a little."

"I sure hope so." Sammy continued bumping his hand truck down the steps.

Inside, two other deputies and the chief's wife, Minerva, were packing stuff into boxes. The chief stood with arms folded, glowering. He looked up, and seeing me didn't improve his mood.

"Can I help you?" he asked.

He didn't look as if he wanted to help me. He looked as if he wanted to chew someone out. But Minerva and the deputies were working as hard as they could on something that clearly wasn't their fault, and the only other candidate hadn't done anything to deserve it either. Yet.

"I have some information," I said. "I don't know if it's related to the assault on my grandfather or the murder or both—"

"Been out snooping, have you?" he snapped. "Blast it all—"

"Henry!" his wife snapped.

I almost turned and left. Not that I was afraid of him—I can hold my own in a verbal brawl. But I could see he was in a foul humor, and his snapping at me made me realize that my own temper was rather frayed. Getting into an argument with him wouldn't do anyone any good. I took a deep breath and reminded myself to count to ten before replying.

And then a vision of the chief with the kittens crawling up his trousers sprang into my mind. At any other time I'd probably have burst into laughter, which would really have set him off. It didn't quite have that effect now, but it did take the edge off my anger.

"No." I had no trouble keeping my voice calm. "I was just having a conversation with Mother, and she said something that seemed significant. I thought I'd come and report it instead of using it to go out snooping. If you want to hear it. Clearly you're busy and—"

"Come into my office." He turned on his heel and began stomping down the box-lined hallway. "What's left of my office," he said over his shoulder. "While I still have an office at all."

"Henry," Minerva called after him, in a warning tone. "Be gracious. She's trying to help."

The chief's desk was still there, but most of the contents of his shelves were gone. As were his chair and the two worn but comfortable chairs in which he normally seated his visitors.

"The book boxes aren't too uncomfortable." Under the circumstances, his tone almost counted as gracious. I sat down on a book box. He leaned against the wall and crossed his arms, visibly schooling himself to be patient.

"I think I may know why someone broke into our house and attacked Grandfather. They were trying to steal the macaw."

"And he prevented them?" the chief said. "At too high a cost, if you ask me."

"No, he failed to prevent the theft," I said. "The thief took the macaw that came from the shelter, and left behind a substitute macaw."

"Now that is—" He broke off, closed his mouth and frowned at me. I wondered if, like me, he counted to ten to avoid saying something he'd regret. It felt more like twenty by the time he finished, unless he'd trained himself to count very slowly. Then he started again.

"And you know this because . . . ?"

"Mother noticed they were slightly different colors." I repeated much of our conversation about the Prussian blue and turquoise macaws.

He pondered for a minute or so. The fact that he hadn't chewed me out was encouraging.

"No offense," he said finally. "But is there any chance your mother could be mistaken?"

"About as much chance as you being mistaken about a question of Baltimore geography." The chief, who had grown up in Baltimore and spent several decades on its police force, nodded in acknowledgment.

"But apart from knowing that Mother's absolutely reliable on color, I asked Clarence," I said. "He'd been so busy with the other animals that he hadn't noticed, but he confirmed that the macaw now in our living room is a common blue-and-yellow macaw. The one they took from the animal shelter was a rare, expensive, hyacinth macaw—"

"Are you trying to tell me that someone broke into your house and swapped macaws because the bird from a shelter was some kind of priceless rare parrot?"

"No—" I began.

"Because that makes even less sense than most of what's been going on around here the last few days. They could simply show up and volunteer to adopt the bird for free."

"Whoever did it wasn't stealing the macaw because it was valuable," I said. "It was, but that's irrelevant. They were stealing it because it belonged to Parker Blair."

Now I had his attention.

"What was it doing in the shelter, then?"

"Someone pretended to have found it in their yard and turned it in at the shelter as a ruse for doing some preburglary reconnoitering."

He closed his eyes and growled slightly.

"I have no idea if the reconnoitering was essential," I said. "Maybe the Corsicans just liked the drama of it all. The plan was that Parker would just take back his bird when they turned the other animals over to him."

"It's starting to make a little sense," he said. "But why would the killer—assuming it was the killer—want to steal the bird? You're not suggesting the killer was after the bird all the time? And struck too soon, before Parker had regained possession of it?"

"No, stealing the bird didn't become essential until after the murder," I said. "The macaw talks, remember?"

"I remember," he said. "All too well. Filthy-mouthed bird."

"It's not the bird's fault," I said. "He has no idea what he's saying. An African gray parrot might—there are people who claim that they've taught African grays not just to repeat sounds but to use language. Some of them have linguistic skills equal to that of a three- or four-year-old child, and—"

"But this is a macaw, not a parrot," he said. He didn't quite come out and say "Stick to the point, dammit!" but I got the message. I was starting to sound like Dad.

"A macaw's a kind of parrot," I said. "I gather from what Clarence has said that they're not the best at talking and mimicking other sounds, but not too shabby, either. The killer must be afraid the macaw would repeat something that would give us a clue to his identity."

"Something the macaw overheard?" He sounded dubious. "Like someone plotting to kill Mr. Blair?"

"Maybe," I said. "Usually parrots only repeat things they hear over and over again. The smarter the parrot, the less repetition, but most of the time it still takes some repetition. Sometimes, though, a parrot can pick up something after hearing it just once if it's said with enough emotion. So even if you don't swear a lot, if you shout out a four-letter word when you hit your thumb with a hammer, the parrot finds that interesting and exciting and tends to remember it."

"I don't think that can explain away that macaw's unfortunate vocabulary," the chief said.

"No, that's obviously the result of long-term eavesdropping, or maybe even a dedicated effort to corrupt the poor bird. But if the macaw overheard something that made Parker particularly mad, sad, glad, or whatever . . ."

An image sprang up in my mind: Mayor Pruitt delivering one of his infamous red-faced rants to Parker Blair with a Prussian blue macaw lurking in the background, absorbing every word and repeating a few particularly vehement threats. The chief was frowning, as if completing a similar image.

"Interesting," he said finally. "Of course, it would seem a lot more relevant if we'd found the bird at the crime scene. Since we know that the bird was either at the shelter or in the possession of your grandfather and his accomplices for the entire period during which the murder occurred, it can't possibly be a witness."

He paused for a moment and frowned as if a sudden disturbing thought had occurred to him.

"What's wrong?" I asked.

"I can't believe I'm seriously discussing the possibility that a macaw could be a witness to a murder," he said. "Do you have any idea what the DA would say if I even suggested it?"

I had a brief but vivid picture of the macaw sitting in the witness box at the Caerphilly courthouse, cocking his head as the DA tried to interrogate him.

"Not as a witness," I said. "And lucky for him, too, because I've seen Judge Jane hand out contempt of court sentences for language nowhere near as foul as his. But even though he wasn't there when the murder happened, he could have overheard—and learned to repeat—something that would give you a clue. An argument between Parker and the killer for example."

"Or an argument between Mr. Blair and a completely innocent party," the chief said. "Even if we had the macaw, we'd have no way of knowing if anything it said was relevant."

"The killer must think the macaw knows something," I said. "Something worth the risk of burgling our house."

"And worth assaulting your grandfather." He scribbled a few lines in his notebook. "I'll keep it in mind if—when we apprehend your grandfather's assailant. You seem rather knowledgeable about parrots."

"Only what I've overheard from Dad," I said. "He took an interest in parrots a few years back. He could tell you a lot more about it."

"Yes," the chief said, sounding tired. "I'm sure he could."

"Or Clarence," I suggested. He nodded. Clarence was slightly less likely to give him a two-hour dissertation on the curious habits of the hyacinth macaw—but only slightly.

The chief nodded and scribbled some more. He didn't look particularly happy with the information I'd brought him.

"So to solve the murder," he said finally. "All I have to do is find a miserable talking bird and listen to it until it tells me who did it?"

"That might work," I said. "If the killer is right that the macaw says something significant. But—"

"And if I can even figure out what that significant thing is. Could be difficult. I've interrogated a lot of jailbirds and stool pigeons in my time, but never an actual bird." He was peering over his glasses at me. I wasn't sure if he was joking or not. I suspected not.

"Sorry," I said. "I guess I haven't really explained what I meant. Maybe you don't need to listen to the macaw at all, or even find it. Maybe all you need to do is figure out who bought the blue-and-yellow macaw that they left behind in place of Parker's bird."

He looked surprised.

"Lot of birds in the world," he said.

"But not a lot of macaws in this part of the world," I countered. "There's only one blue-and-yellow macaw in Clarence's practice, and he's already confirmed that it's safe and sound in its usual cage at the Caerphilly Inn."

The chief smiled slightly at this news.

"So the killer had to acquire a blue-and-yellow macaw in the last forty-eight hours," the chief said. "Are they hard to find?"

"Not as hard as hyacinth macaws," I said. "Or maybe the killer would have replaced Parker's macaw with the right kind, and we'd never have known the difference. But I can't imagine even blue-and-yellows are that common. I've never seen one here in town at Giving Paws, and for a small-town pet store they have a reasonably diverse stock."

"It would be pretty stupid of the killer to buy it locally anyway," he said.

"True," I said. "And also pretty impossible to drive more than a few hours and still get back in time to commit the burglary, to say nothing of being seen carrying on with his normal life, whatever that is. There can't be that many places within reasonable driving distance that sell macaws."

"You haven't started checking it out?" he said. "Interrogated a few pet shop owners?"

"No," I said. "And I told Clarence not to, either. And I told both him and Mother not to tell anyone about the macaw swapping."

He nodded.

"I think I'll give him a call." He stood up, signaling that we were through. "See if he knows some of the places that might have macaws."

"And make sure he knows that it's your job to go snooping, not his." I stood up, too.

He paused with his hand halfway to the phone and looked up at me.

"Thanks," he said.

"For bringing you this information or for not going out and trying to find the source of the macaw myself?"

"Yes." He picked up the phone and began dialing.

On my way out, I pitched in by carrying a box of files out to the truck that Sammy was loading. I decided to leave my car in the parking lot and walk the few blocks to the town hall to help Mother and the garden club ladies. After all, helping them would give me an excuse for prowling around the town hall. I had no idea what I hoped to find—the Pruitts hadn't stayed in power for decades by leaving incriminating evidence lying around where the casual passer-by could spot it. But the town hall was where my prime suspect hung out. I felt drawn there.

Chapter 20

I found a cluster of elderly lavender-hatted ladies in a huddle in front of the town hall. They had several rows of potted plants lined up on the sidewalk and were looking up and down the street as if awaiting transportation. Or maybe as if they feared plantnappers might strike before the transportation arrived.

"Oh, look!" one of them exclaimed as I drew near. "It's Meg! I'm sure *she* can manage."

They all turned and beamed at me. I sighed, and wished, just for a moment, that I'd gone back to the library. Or maybe home.

"What's up?" I asked, as I drew up beside their temporary sidewalk jungle.

"Some of the plants that need to be rescued are a bit too much for us to manage," one said.

"Mother told me." I spotted a folding luggage carrier and nodded at it. "Mind if I use that?"

"Of course!" several of them exclaimed, and almost knocked each other down in their haste to deliver it to me.

"So what do you want me to fetch?" I turned to one garden lady who was holding a clipboard with some papers on it. What was it about a clipboard that made its holder look as if she were in charge, or at least knew what she was doing?

"There's a large peace lily in room 201," she said.

"A peace lily?" I repeated.

"Spathiphyllum floribundum," one garden lady said, as if that explained everything.

"Like this," several of them exclaimed, shoving forward a pot containing a peace lily.

I knew what a peace lily looked like, but I was surprised to hear that one had gotten so large that a pair of the abler garden ladies couldn't carry it, especially since they had the sturdy luggage carrier to help them.

I inspected the nearby peace lily. It looked healthy enough, but around the size I'd expect a peace lily to be. Not at all unmanageable. I could see them looking at it and, no doubt, realizing what I was thinking.

"Only bigger," one of them said after a few moments.

"Oh, yes!" another said. "Much bigger."

"Much!" Several others chimed in.

"Enormous!"

"Yes, it should be quite a well-grown specimen," the lady with the clipboard said. "And there's also a large *Ficus benjamina* in room 301. And if you see any other potted plants that we've forgotten, just snag them while you're there."

I was pretty sure now that the problem wasn't the size of the plants but their location.

"Okay," I said. "Rooms 201, 301. Peace lily, ficus, anything else that's green."

"Excellent!" the clipboard lady said. She handed me a pair of purple gardening gloves. Not a bad idea if I was going to be doing manual labor, so I put them on, to the delight of the garden club ladies.

I folded up the luggage carrier and tucked it under my arm.

Coming back with the plants, I could use the handicapped access ramp, but for now it was shorter to climb the marble steps, and easier to carry the folded luggage cart than drag it.

When I reached the top of the steps, I glanced down and saw them all clustered together, staring anxiously up at me as if I were going into battle. I stopped in the lobby at the building directory to see what perils awaited me in 201 and 301.

Aha. Room 201 was the county manager's office.

Room 301 was the office of the mayor.

"Wonderful," I muttered.

"What's that?" chirped a cheerful voice behind me.

I glanced around and saw what looked, at first, like a giant ambulatory spider plant, creeping slowly along the marble floor of the lobby. Closer inspection revealed that the top of the plant was suspended from a purple gardening glove. Presumably one of the shorter garden club ladies was hidden beneath the impressively thick curtain of trailing fronds with baby spider plants at their ends.

"Can I help you with that?" I asked.

"Oh, no," the voice said, and the plant rustled and quivered as if the hidden garden lady was shaking her head vigorously. "I'm doing fine. Carry on! Good luck!"

Good luck? Did she think I'd need it?

I pressed the elevator button and watched as she crept away. As I stepped into the elevator, I found myself thinking it was a pity Rob wasn't here with his little video camera.

When I stepped out of the elevator, I saw, directly ahead of me, a set of stout mahogany double doors with "201" stenciled on them in gold leaf and an old-fashioned Gothic typeface. A brass plaque on the wall beside the doors read "Office of the County Manager." The right door was ajar. Odd that it would be open on a Sunday. Of course, this was no normal Sunday.

I peered in.

I'd expected an antechamber with a secretary, but apparently the county manager didn't quite rate that. Still, it was a largish office, decorated in the same neutral colors and conservative style you found throughout the town hall. And like many other public spaces in the county, the room's walls were blighted by hideous, oversized oil paintings illustrating scenes from Caerphilly's history and geography, painted in the thirties and forties by a Pruitt with artistic ambitions and no discernible talent.

The painting I could see from the doorway showed a group of townspeople with pudgy Pruitt faces and stiff-ruffed early seventeenth-century costumes, being fawned over by several dozen obsequious, scantily clad Indians. Clearly a figment of the artist's imagination rather than a genuine historical scene. Neck ruffs had been passé for decades by the time the town was founded, and the Pruitts hadn't showed up until the late 1800s. Of course, the ruffs did hide the fact that the artist hadn't the slightest idea of how to paint the human neck. Thanks to the ruffs, the townspeople looked fairly normal—normal for Pruitts, anyway—but the Indians all looked as if someone had pounded their heads a little way into their bodies.

I'd have replaced that horror with something more to my taste on day one. Was it significant that none of our recent county managers had?

I took a step into the room and saw Terence Mann standing beside a bookcase, gazing at its contents. His back was to me.

The enemy. Okay, not the major enemy, and probably not one we'd be stuck with in the long term if the opinions expressed at last night's meeting were anything to go by. Still, however satisfying it might be to bash him in absentia, apparently none of the garden club members could bring themselves to confront him in person.

I found I was rather looking forward to it. I took a deep, calming breath and knocked on the half-open door.

"Come in." The look on his face when he turned around was anything but welcoming. Not quite fear, perhaps, but definitely a lot of anxiety.

And then, after he'd studied me for a few seconds, his long, bland face relaxed. Now he just looked melancholy.

"May I help you?" His voice was brittle, but polite.

"I'm here for the plants." I braced myself for what I assumed would be a hostile reaction, but he only shrugged.

"Help yourself." He turned back to the bookcase.

It was only then that I noticed a cardboard moving box at his feet. I thought it unlikely that he was helping with the evacuation.

He glanced back and saw where I was looking.

"Yes, they fired me this morning," he said. "So it's fine with me if you haul away everything in the damned building. I don't even give a tinker's damn whether you're working for the county board or just scrounging for valuables for yourself. Not my problem anymore. Just wait till I pack a few personal items and you can have anything that's left."

"No, not your problem anymore," I said. "Of course, the rest of us will be dealing for years with what you've left behind." And so might he if the talk about taking legal action against him was more than hot air, but I didn't want to tip him off if he hadn't heard about it already.

"I didn't cause Caerphilly's problems," he said over his shoulder. He was running his finger along the spines of the books and occasionally plucking out one and dropping it into the box. "Cause them—I didn't even know about them when I took the job. I thought I was coming to a nice, quiet, affluent county where the biggest problem would be talking the farmers into installing a few more traffic lights. And by the time I found out—hah!"

I wasn't sure if that was a laugh or a snort. He finished with the bookcase and stepped over to the desk.

"No one blames you for causing the original financial problems," I said. "But you didn't do much to help solve them, either, did you? When you figured out how bad things were, why did you try to cover up instead of leveling with everyone?"

"Hah!" he said again. Definitely not what I'd call a laugh. "I thought the board was in on it. I assumed they wanted me to keep it hush-hush. It never occurred to me that every single one of them either couldn't read a spreadsheet or couldn't be bothered."

"So instead you went along with the mayor's plan," I said. "The mayor, and his developer friends, who've been trying to get around the county's antigrowth policies for decades."

He was putting a paperweight in the box. He stood up and looked at me for a few moments.

"Oh, that's right," he said softly. "Your property's one of the ones they'll be seizing."

"One of the ones they want," I said. "We'll see about the seizing."

"It's not personal, Mrs. Waterston," he said. "I know it feels that way to you, but I didn't steer the developers to your land."

"No, I'm sure the mayor did that," I said. "But you could have said, 'No, we can't do that.'"

"According to the legal advice Mayor Pruitt has received, we can," he said. "I didn't think it was reasonable to turn down a plan that would save the county just because a few people are inconvenienced by it. I had to put the welfare of the whole county first. You can see that, can't you?"

He was clever. He struck just the right tone—practical common sense tinged with a hint of regret for the inconvenience he was causing, and a strong suggestion that he was disappointed at my selfishness and obtuseness. For a few moments, I almost found myself buying into his point of view. Who were we to stand in the way of saving the county?

And then I shook free of the spell.

"What you're trying to do isn't saving the county," I said. "You're just trying to get the county out of a temporary financial bind. And to do it, you're willing to sell out to a bunch of developers who want to change the county in ways no one here wants."

He shook his head, smiled his bland smile, and was opening his mouth to speak again. I hastened to drown him out.

"I read up on that Supreme Court case," I said. "The one where they upheld the city's right to seize a woman's house so they could give her land to a developer. You know what's on the land where her house used to be? Nothing. It's a vacant lot now. Circumstances changed, the developer backed out, and now that city has a bunch of vacant lots that used to be people's homes."

"This is a completely different problem," he began.

"And we need a different solution," I said. "Not the one you and the mayor are trying to shove down our throats."

"You don't understand what we're going to do—" he began. And then he stopped and shriveled slightly, his already stooped shoulders hunching even more.

"What *he's* going to do," he said. "Not me and the mayor anymore. Just the mayor. He's the one who got all of you into this in the first place. Go yell at him."

I hadn't been yelling, but maybe he was expecting me to. The county board probably hadn't whispered when they'd fired him this morning.

"I'll be going up to the mayor's office as soon as I take that peace lily downstairs." I trundled the luggage cart over to the plant and hefted it. Not the giant mutant peace lily I'd been led to expect. It wasn't any bigger than the one they'd showed me on the sidewalk.

"That's all I need," I said.

He didn't answer. He had picked up a silver frame from his desk. It held a picture of him with Francine and a slightly younger version of the son who was on Timmy's T-Ball team. He was staring at it with a gloomy expression on his face.

I felt a momentary twinge of sympathy. Not for Mann, but for Francine, and maybe a little for the kid, who was one of the least bratty of Timmy's teammates. What happened to the boy if Francine decided not to move on with her husband when he found a new job? Or maybe when Mann decided that even without a new job he didn't want to stay in Caerphilly another minute?

Not my problem. I glanced around, saw no other plants, and began turning the luggage carrier around.

Mann slipped the silver frame into the box and strode toward the door.

"You can tell them to come up now," he said.

"Tell who?" I asked.

"Whoever the county's sending to inspect my boxes," he said. "I told them this morning I didn't want to take them until someone did that. I want proof that I didn't take anything but my own personal property."

He was standing in the doorway, glaring at me.

"Or is that your job?" he asked.

"No, I'm just here for the peace lily," I said. "But if you like, I'll see if I can find someone to take care of it for you."

He turned and strode off. I had a little trouble getting the luggage carrier over the doorsill, and by the time I got it out into the hall, the elevator had already gone.

"Jerk," I said to the closed doors. "You know how slow these elevators are. You could have held it."

Then again, did I really want to endure a long, slow, awkward elevator ride with the man who had helped the mayor in his plot to seize our home?

A man who just might be a prime suspect in Parker Blair's murder. The mayor wasn't the only one with a motive to stop Parker's investigation. After all, when his discoveries were made public, they had cost Terence Mann his job. What if he'd thought that killing Parker would keep them from coming to light? What if he was the one afraid the macaw's prattle would implicate him? In my eagerness to see our dishonest and obnoxious mayor brought down, was I overlooking the real culprit?

I pulled out my cell phone and called the chief.

"What now?" he said. "A dognapping? Or perhaps a hamster heist?"

"Terence Mann just finished packing his personal effects and wants someone to come and verify that he's only taking what belongs to him."

"And this is your business because . . . ?"

"It isn't, but I was moving a county-owned plant out of his office and he decided to use me as the audience for his dramatic exit. He's left his box of personal effects, and for that matter, his whole office, wide open. I have no idea if the county board really did demand some kind of inspection of what he took—"

"More likely he just wants to cause someone extra work," the chief said.

"But just in case, I figure no one would complain if you did the inspection and made sure anything valuable or confidential was secure."

"And snoop around while I'm there?"

"If you don't want to, tell me who else I should call," I said. "I suppose your lack of interest means he isn't on your suspect list."

There was a silence. I could hear something. Footsteps on a hard surface. Someone saying, "Hello, chief." A truck engine roaring by. The chief was outdoors, apparently, and walking somewhere. It was probably a full thirty seconds before he spoke.

"Unfortunately for Mr. Mann, he doesn't have an alibi for the night of the murder. His wife was working at the hospital and he claims, not surprisingly, that he was home asleep in his bed."

"So he is a suspect."

"He hasn't been ruled out," the chief said. "As it happens,

I'm already on my way to the town hall, so I'll drop in while I'm there. Are you still in the county manager's office?"

"No, I'm right outside the door."

"Stay put."

With that he hung up.

What did he mean by "stay put"? Was he merely ordering me to keep guard over the unlocked door? Or warning me not to go back into the office to snoop around?

Probably both.

I rolled the plant to the side, so someone getting off the elevator wouldn't run smack dab into it. I strolled over to the double doors and took a good long look. The first impression was that the office was suddenly empty. It wasn't, of course—it was still filled with furniture, lamps, drapes, hideous Pruitt oil paintings, and stacks and boxes of paper. The peace lily had only left a small vacancy on the credenza, and there were only a few empty spaces on the bookshelves. There were even files on the desk and papers in the in- and out-boxes. But it contained no personal touches at all, and it was very clear, even to the casual observer, that Terence Mann wasn't coming back.

Which probably meant that if he had any secrets, they weren't here. Or they looked, to the casual observer, like things it would be perfectly normal to pack.

My fingers itched to rummage through the two moving boxes, sitting so casually on the floor, one beside the desk and one by the bookcase.

But I didn't want the chief to catch me doing it. I felt as if I'd earned a measure of trust from him by not doing precisely that sort of thing.

I deliberately turned my back on the double doors and

marched over to a nearby bench that gave me a good view of both the elevator door and the door to Terence Mann's office. Former office.

While I was waiting, I could check on Grandfather's condition. I pulled out my cell phone and hesitated. Should I call the hospital or Dad?

Probably less red tape if I called Dad. And his cell phone number was already on my speed dial list.

He answered in the middle of the second ring.

"Meg! You should see this!" he said.

"Hello to you, too," I said. "See what?"

"Caerphilly's new police station! Isn't it wonderful that we weren't doing anything else with our barn?"

Mother might not think it was so wonderful, since she had plans to convert the barn to a studio for her fledgling decorating business.

"Remember, it's only temporary, Dad," I said.

"We've got the chief's office set up in the tack room, and Debbie Anne's communications console in the first stall, and the fingerprint machine—"

"I'm looking forward to seeing it," I said. "Later. I just called to ask how Grandfather was."

He sighed.

"Stable," he said.

"Stable isn't good?"

"Stable isn't bad," he said. "All his signs are very good, actually. I'd just be a lot more comfortable if he regained consciousness. The longer he's unconscious the more concerned I become."

"Should I go over and visit him?" I asked. "On the theory

that on some level unconscious patients can still hear what we say to them?"

"Yes, please do," Dad said. "I've been running in every time I go to town to fetch another load from the police station, but it might help if more of us did that. Reassure him that everything's going just fine."

Just then the elevator dinged.

"Actually," I said, "I thought I'd tell him to hurry up and get well so he can keep the mayor from seizing all the animals and exterminating them. If you ask me that's a lot more likely to jump-start him than telling him everything's fine."

"But Meg——" he began.

"Gotta run," I said, as the chief stepped off the elevator. "I'll let you know later how my plan works."

Horace followed the chief off the elevator. The two of them glanced at me. Horace waved. The chief nodded, as if to dismiss me. Horace stuck his hand into the doorway to hold the elevator.

I can take a hint. I shoved the cell phone back in my pocket, reclaimed the peace lily, and trundled it onto the elevator.

"Thanks," I said as the elevator door slowly closed. "Have fun."

Back on the sidewalk, the ladies treated me like a conquering hero, and fussed over the plant as if they suspected Terence Mann of dousing it with Roundup and boiling water.

"What took you so long?" the lady with the clipboard asked. "We were frantic with worry!"

"I was just having a little talk with our former county manager," I said.

"Former!" several garden ladies exclaimed. Apparently this

morning's board action wasn't yet widely known. The ladies began coagulating into small groups on the sidewalk, voicing their vehement approval, discussing the significance of Mann's departure, and hotly debating what the county's next move should be. A posse of overalls-clad Shiffleys lugging file cabinets put down their loads to join in the discussion. Participatory democracy at work. Good. The county needed more of that.

I folded up the luggage carrier and marched back into the town hall to confront the mayor.

Chapter 21

I stepped out of the elevator on the third floor. Same layout as on the second floor: mahogany double doors directly ahead, and the hallway stretching out on either side. The doors to room 301 were closed, but clearly the room wasn't empty. I could hear the mayor's voice ranting, slightly muffled by the intervening walls. I couldn't understand everything he said, but I could catch enough to tell that he was probably voicing his opinion of the evacuation.

I could also tell that if we found the missing foulmouthed macaw, the mayor could teach it a thing or two.

I knocked on the double doors. And after about fifteen seconds, when no one came to greet me or sang out "Come in!" I cautiously opened one door and peered in.

The mayor did have an anteroom. The shouting was coming from a closed door to my right—apparently his private office.

I stepped inside and felt a muffled crunch beneath my feet. I looked down and saw that the carpet near the door was littered with bits of broken glass and china. From the larger pieces, I could tell that at least three breakables had met untimely ends here—a white china vase, a green glass vase, and a glass tumbler. Though from the amount of broken glass underfoot I suspected that another item or two had contributed to the debris without leaving any shards large enough to reveal their shape.

There were a couple of new-looking dents on the walls on either side of the mahogany double doors and on the doors themselves.

Apart from the broken crockery, the room looked a lot like the county manager's office. Not as many bookcases and file cabinets, and taking their place were several clusters of guest chairs flanked with end tables bearing neatly fanned selections of magazines. But the furniture, drapes, and carpets were in the same tasteful yet bland style. The desk was as impersonally empty as Terence Mann's. The phone, the in- and out-baskets, and the computer monitor and keyboard suggested that someone could work there if needed, but clearly no one currently did—there were no personal touches, and no other supplies— no pens, pencils, stapler, paper clips, notebooks, while-you-were-out pads, or any of the things you'd usually find on the top of an occupied desk. Even Parker's desk had had a few of the usual items, neatly arranged and squared with the edges of the desk. Clearly the mayor preferred to keep his support staff at a distance.

The hostage ficus was in front of one of the two windows that flanked the vacant secretary's desk. The other window was filled with a large spider plant, almost the twin of the one I'd seen walking through the lobby downstairs.

Between them, spoiling an otherwise perfectly good wall, was another ghastly oil painting. This one showed a pudgy-faced Pruitt in a Continental Army uniform, standing in the prow of a boat being rowed across a vast expanse of turbulent, wintry water by a crew of some dozen burly underlings. General Pruitt crossing the Delaware?

Other, smaller paintings showed turtle-shaped Pruitts in

various settings. Waddling through the wilderness in coonskin caps and buckskins. Peering through their goggles in front of battered World War I biplanes. In one particularly implausible scene, a pudgy Pruitt engineer presented the cotton gin to a grateful South.

A lot of the paintings were obvious imitations of better, more famous works. I had a sudden vision of myself writing an article on the Pruitt painter for the *Caerphilly Clarion*, ostensibly a serious study of the influences that had shaped the artist's career—but of course anyone with half a brain would recognize it as a laundry list of which famous paintings he'd ripped off.

Why was I so focused on the paintings, anyway? I had more important things to think about.

Except that this was all part of the same problem. The Pruitts spending the taxpayers' money on things that were useless, or benefited only them.

Randall had pegged it. Pruitt greed and Pruitt stupidity. Maybe I didn't need to worry about making that article look like serious art criticism. Maybe I should just make it an outright attack and reveal exactly how much county money had been spent on these dubious works. I could call it "Pruitt Pride and Plagiarism."

Then again, if Parker's planned exposé had given one of the Pruitts a motive for murder, did I really want to write an article that would paint the next target on my back?

I tucked the problem away for later consideration. For now, I dragged over a side chair to stand on so I could lift down the enormous spider plant. Then I took the plant out to the hallway, dragging the chair with me so I'd have something to put it on. All the little shoots and baby plants spilled over the sides of the chair and onto the floor, but I smoothed them out and made sure they were as far as possible out of way of foot traffic in the hall. I couldn't remember ever wrangling such a large spider plant before, and yet I had an odd sense of déjà vu—perhaps because it was almost the same challenge as arranging the kind of over-the-top veils several of my friends and relations had chosen for weddings in which I'd been drafted to serve as a bridesmaid.

Then I went back into the antechamber, unfolded the luggage carrier, and wheeled it into position beside the ficus.

As I did, I caught a glimpse of something. There were papers in the in-basket. And the top one had a sticky note on it saying, "Louise—can you get him to sign this? R."

Was this Louise's desk?

I flipped through the top few papers in the in-basket. All of them addressed to Louise or Ms. Dietz. There were even a couple of interoffice envelopes addressed to Louise Dietz, room 301.

The out-box contained only one thing—an envelope addressed to Mayor Pruitt. I picked it up. It was sealed but I could easily see that it contained four loose keys.

Yes, this was Louise's desk. And it looked as abandoned as Terence Mann's desk. She'd cleared out her desk and was turning in her keys. What did—

Just then the door to the inner office slammed open.

"Louise! Where the hell— You're not Louise!"

"Haven't seen her. It's Sunday, remember?"

"I called to say I needed her to come in today. Where the hell is she?"

I shrugged.

"Maybe she's not coming in today," I said. "In fact, maybe she's not coming in at all. Looks as if she's cleared off her desk."

He frowned, then shook his head vigorously.

"No, can't be," he said. "They didn't start all that nonsense about moving out until this morning. Her desk was like that when I dropped by around eleven last night to pick up some papers."

Pick up some papers, my eye. Eleven o'clock would have been when he was debriefing his spies. I looked past him into his private office. I couldn't see much, though I got an impression of ornate mahogany furniture in a space so large it echoed in spite of burgundy velvet upholstery. Was that the room where the macaw snatching and the assault on Grandfather were planned?

And what about Louise? When I'd heard about the mayor's spies, I'd assumed Louise might be one of them. Against her will, of course, but she was desperate to keep her job. But apparently she'd made it back here and cleaned out her desk before the spies arrived.

What if she hadn't cleaned out her desk at all? What if the mayor had done away with her and cleaned out her desk to make it look as if she'd fled?

Okay, probably too melodramatic. But maybe I should ask the chief to find Louise and make sure she was safe.

"She's probably asked the cleaning crew to give it an extra polish or something," the mayor was saying.

I pulled open the top drawer. It contained a stapler and a few pencils.

"I don't think so." I tried the next drawer. A few papers. "If she wanted the cleaners to polish it, she could just have put all her personal things in the drawers. She's cleared out."

"Damnation," he said. "She *is* in on it!"

He turned as if to go back to his office.

I squatted down and gave the ficus an experimental tug. Yes, it was going to be a bear to lift. A gentleman would have seen me fumbling at the plant and asked if I needed help. I wasn't expecting such an offer from the mayor.

"What are you doing with that tree?" he asked.

"County board's recalling all the county-owned plants." I wiggled the ficus a little closer to the luggage carrier. No sense carrying it any farther than I had to.

The mayor responded with a burst of foul language.

I fixed him with my frostiest stare and, in what Rob called my Mother voice, said, "I beg your pardon. If you're trying to talk to me, please do so in a civil manner."

He responded with another torrent of obscenity. I turned my back on him and prepared to hoist the plant.

But wait. Was it really wise to turn your back on someone so angry—someone whose office floor was littered with broken crockery? Someone I suspected of being involved in Parker's death and the attack on Grandfather?

I turned back just in time to dodge a flying vase. It smashed against the wall beside the ficus.

"Assault," I said, in the most annoyingly cheerful tone I could manage. "It will count as battery if you hit me, so I'd put that bookend down if I were you."

Instead, he lobbed it at me. I caught it, easily.

My temper flared.

"And your aim's pretty bad, too." I tossed the bookend in my hand a couple of times, getting a sense of its weight and balance. "Mine, on the other hand, is pretty good. Doorknob," I added, and threw the bookend at it, using my best fastball. Wonder of wonders, I hit the doorknob squarely.

He paled, backed a few steps away, and reached into his pocket for something.

Should I run? What if he pulled out a gun? Was this the time to mention that the garden club ladies knew I was up here and would call the police if I didn't return soon?

His hands were shaking—whether from fear or anger I couldn't tell. And it didn't matter. Either way, I could almost certainly tackle him before he could get a shot off.

I relaxed a little when I saw that he was fumbling with his cell phone. Of course he could be calling whatever thug he'd used to attack Grandfather. Time for me to make tracks.

I returned to the ficus, though without turning my back on him.

"Get someone up here right now, dammit!" he shouted into the phone. "There's another one of them here trying to steal things from my office!"

I hoisted the ficus and plopped it down on the luggage carrier.

"Unhand my plant!" He raced over and grabbed the pot.

"It's not your plant!" I shouted back, grabbing the other side of the pot.

Just then, the chief strolled in, trailed by Sammy Wendell. They both blinked when they saw me and the mayor struggling over the ficus plant. Sammy stood frozen. The chief recovered a lot more quickly.

"You called 911," he said. "What's the nature of the emergency?"

The mayor let go of the ficus so suddenly that I staggered back and ricocheted off the empty desk. I landed in a heap on top of the luggage carrier, with the plant on top of me.

"Arrest her!" The mayor pointed at me and glared triumphantly.

"On what charges?" the chief said.

"She's stealing town property!" the mayor shouted.

"The plants are county property." I shoved the ficus aside and stood up. "Bought with county funds, and maintained under a contract signed by the county. And I'm assisting the Caerphilly Garden Club, which has been authorized by the county to remove the plants for safekeeping."

"Trespassing on town property!" the mayor shrieked.

"These premises are actually county property," the chief said. "At least until that confounded mortgage company shows up on Monday."

"Littering," the mayor said, pointing to some dirt that had spilled out of the fallen ficus's pot. "And assault on a public official."

"Put him down for assault and battery," I said. "You saw him knock me down, right? He's also been throwing vases and bookends at me and the other people who've tried to collect the plants." I pointed to the shards of crockery at their feet.

"She's lying!" the mayor shouted. "Arrest her! Arrest her!"

"I'm not arresting anyone," the chief said. "Not on *your* orders."

He reached into his pocket and took out something. A badge. He held it in his hand for a few seconds, looking at it. No, not looking at it. More like looking inward while his eyes were on it. Then he took a step forward.

The mayor stepped back hastily.

The chief opened his hand to give the mayor his badge.

"I hereby offer you my resignation," he said.

"I'm not accepting it," the mayor said. He backed a few more steps away.

"Let me rephrase that," the chief said. "I quit. Effective immediately."

He put the badge down on Louise's desk and took a step back. The mayor stared at the polished gold shield as if he expected it to turn into a rattlesnake.

"Sammy?" The chief's eyes were still on the mayor.

Sammy, who had been staring in openmouthed astonishment, blinked once or twice and then snapped to attention.

"Yes, sir!" he said.

"Go call Debbie Anne and give her the news," the chief said.

"Yes, sir!" Sammy saluted and dashed out.

The mayor recovered his voice and uttered a few obscenities.

"I'll thank you to mind your language," the chief snapped.

"I don't need you to teach me manners!" the mayor shouted.

"You darn well need someone to," the chief said. "A public official should have more respect for himself and the citizens."

I had the feeling the chief had wanted to say something like that for years.

The chief turned to me.

"That's a mighty big plant," he said. "Let me help you with it."

"I've got a luggage carrier," I said.

We both glanced down at the crumpled metal frame.

"But I don't think it's going to work very well," I went on. "I'd appreciate the help."

"You can't do this!" the mayor shrieked.

"I just did," the chief said. "Let's lift with our knees, not our backs," he added to me. I suppressed a chuckle at the thought of how many times his wife had probably told him the same thing.

"Don't abandon me!" the mayor wailed.

"One. Two. Three. Lift!" the chief said.

The mayor continued to shriek threats and pleas as we lugged the plant out of his office and down the hallway. Halfway to the elevator, the shouts were replaced by thuds, the occasional sound of breaking glass, and more bursts of language nearly as blue as the macaw's. The chief frowned and his jaw muscle twitched a little.

I kept thinking that I should say something, but I couldn't think what, so I saved my wind for hauling. By the time we got the ficus down to the part of the sidewalk where the garden club ladies were staging the plants, I was profoundly glad the chief had offered to help. I could have done it myself, but I'd have regretted it for days—in fact I probably still would.

A small knot of lavender-hatted ladies greeted our arrival with cheers.

"Excellent!" one said. "You braved the lion's den."

"Not without cost," I muttered. "I'm afraid your luggage cart is a goner. And there's a big spider plant in the third-floor elevator lobby that needs to be brought down."

"I'll go!" Several ladies began dashing up the courthouse steps.

"Let's just label this so we know where it came from," another lady said.

She slapped an adhesive label on the pot and, with a triumphant flourish, wrote "Mayor's Office" on it in elegant printing that could almost pass for calligraphy.

"Now all we have to do is get them in the truck," one of the ladies said. The others began rolling up their sleeves and looking determined.

Who had chosen this crew to tackle the town hall's plants, anyway? Not a one of them was over five foot two or under seventy.

The chief and I exchanged looks.

"Let us help you with that," he said. "Meg, you get in the truck. I'll lift them in and you can shove them into place."

The garden club ladies didn't argue much. In fact, as soon as they saw we were hard at work, they went into a brief huddle and then told us they were going to move on to the next building.

The chief and I lifted and shoved for a few minutes in silence. Then a thought occurred to me. I straightened up and looked around to make sure no one else was hovering nearby before sharing it with the chief.

"I'm not trying to interfere with your investigation," I said. "But I was wondering—"

And then I stopped. Technically, the chief wasn't the chief anymore. What happened to the investigation?

"Don't worry," he said, as if reading my mind. "It's still my investigation."

"In spite of your resignation?"

"I'm still deputy sheriff, remember?" he said.

"But this crime's in town," I said. "What if the mayor appoints a new police chief? Not that I'm paranoid, but the mayor's a suspect. Do we really trust anyone he appoints to investigate properly?"

"No," he said. "And since I knew things might come to a head between me and the mayor before too long, I went out to the sheriff's farm last night, and we had a good long talk. He tells me that in the event the town doesn't have a police chief, he has the authority to assume jurisdiction over the case."

And since the sheriff, who was in his mid-nineties, was more or less an elected figurehead these days, delegating everything to his deputy, that meant the chief would still be in charge.

"If he's correct——" I said.

"It occurred to me to wonder about that," he said. "Sounds more like the sort of thing they used to do back in his heyday, twenty years ago."

"I think his heyday was more like forty years ago," I said. "And that's probably how they did things. Of course, maybe it was legal back then."

"I like to know where things stand," he said. "So this morning I ran the whole problem by the county DA. And she assures me that the sheriff is right. As long as there's no police chief, the sheriff's department has jurisdiction. No police chief, and for that matter, no police."

"Your officers are all resigning, too?"

"Most of them don't have to," he said. "Most are already on the county payroll, and the rest will be by Monday morning."

"You were planning to resign, then?"

He sighed.

"Not so much planning to resign as resigned to the fact that sooner or later, the mayor would force me to. So we came up with a plan, just in case. And the DA's plotting out all the legal strategies she can use if the mayor tries to appoint a puppet."

I nodded. I had every confidence that the DA could find a lot of ways to delay things. Still—the sooner the chief could solve the case, the better.

"Getting back to the case," I said. "Did you ever manage to track down Louise? The mayor's secretary?"

"The one you suspect of helping Mr. Blair get his hands on that copy of the contract?" He pulled out his handkerchief and wiped the sweat from his forehead. I wasn't sure if he found my question interesting, or if he just welcomed the excuse to take a break.

"I'm not sure I really suspect her," I said. "She sounded sincere when she said that no matter how much she hated her boss, she wouldn't do that to him. But maybe she fooled me, and even if it wasn't her, she might have a good idea who else would have had access."

He nodded.

"That thought had occurred to me as well," he said. "And I have been trying to reach Ms. Dietz all day. Without success."

My stomach did a somersault at hearing that.

"Maybe she's making a run for it," I suggested. "Or—what if she knows too much and someone decided they needed to get rid of her, too."

"Annoying as it is not to be able to reach her, I think it's a little early to jump to that conclusion," the chief said. He put his handkerchief away and squatted to pick up another plant. "Maybe she just likes to spend her Sundays doing something other than sitting indoors by her telephone."

"Yes, but don't you think it's a little odd that she apparently cleared off her desk and turned in her keys?"

He put the plant down again and turned to me with a frown.

"You're sure of that?"

"That's her desk in the mayor's anteroom," I said. "He was complaining before you arrived that he'd left her a message to come in and she hadn't shown up. I think he assumes she's in on the evacuation, and maybe she is. But according to him, her desk was cleared off by eleven last night. And I don't even think the Fight or Flight Committee had made its decision by that time, much less sent out the word. She must have come down here straight from the meeting."

"Maybe she thought she saw which way the wind was blowing and decided to waste no time," he said.

"Maybe," I said. "But last night when she left the barn, she didn't look like someone who was making a bold decision to risk her job on a principle. She just looked miserable and scared. Maybe she made a run for it. Or maybe whoever killed Parker didn't give her the chance."

The chief studied me for a few moments with a faint frown on his face. Then he pulled out his cell phone and hit a few keys.

"It's me," he said. "Can you get the word out to all our officers that I want to talk to Ms. Louise Dietz? . . . That's right. . . . No, just wanted for questioning. For now . . . Thanks. No, I'm down at the town—I'm down at the county courthouse. I should be back soon."

He hung up, stuffed the phone into his pocket, and went back to loading the neatly labeled plants. But I thought I could see a little more haste in his manner.

"County courthouse," I said. "I like that better than town hall."

"It's what we should have been calling it all along," he said. "Blasted Pruitts!"

About ten seconds after we finished loading the last plant, the smallest and most elderly of the garden ladies trotted back down the sidewalk, beaming with delight.

"Finished so soon?" she trilled. "Wonderful!"

The chief and I watched as she dug into a straw purse, fished out an enormous cluster of keys, and hopped nimbly into the high cab of the truck.

"Thanks again!" she called as she drove off, shifting the truck's gears as effortlessly as if she drove it every day. For all I knew she did.

"I'd better get back to the station," the chief said. "Thanks for the information on Ms. Dietz."

"Don't worry," I said. "The way voter sentiment is running right now, the mayor will probably be recalled long before he has a chance to appoint a puppet."

"Yes. I understand they already have a couple hundred signatures on the recall petitions," he said. "And frankly, even if the mayor does hire a puppet in spite of the DA's efforts, I'll still be investigating the assault on your grandfather, which definitely happened in the county, not the town. We'll manage."

"You bet we will, Chief," I said.

"Deputy Sheriff, you mean."

I tried it on for size.

"No," I said. "You'll always be the chief to me."

He smiled, nodded, and left.

Chapter 22

I decided to make my own escape before the garden club ladies returned with more backbreaking work. I headed for the police station parking lot to collect my car.

As I walked, I fretted over what I'd learned—and how very much we still didn't know. If things were normal, I might have been able to shove the whole thing out of my mind. I'd have reminded myself that the chief, a very smart man and a seasoned homicide investigator, was on the case. And that I had two four-month-old sons at home who needed me a lot more than any investigation did.

But things weren't normal. How much of his time could the chief spend on the murder case, and how much was he being pulled away to referee squabbles like the one between the mayor and me? For that matter, how much time had he and his officers spent packing up the police station when they needed to be working on their investigation? And next there'd be the unpacking, and then the inefficiencies and delays that always happen when you're working out of a different space—even a perfect space, which Mother and Dad's barn most certainly was not. And who knew what would be happening in town tomorrow when the workweek began and the lender found out that instead of paying the interest on its loan, Caerphilly was sticking them with a collection of well-used buildings full of ghastly oil paintings?

If I could think of anything that might help, I'd have done it, even if it got me in trouble with the chief for interfering. But try as I might, I came up empty.

The sun was setting. Part of me wanted to go home and co-coon with the twins. And part of me wanted to stay in town, help with the evacuation, and keep my ears open for stray bits of information that might prove useful.

I decided to compromise. I'd return to the library, do a little bit of packing or maybe only offer to haul a few boxes in my car. Then I'd drop by to pay a brief visit to Grandfather on my way home.

So after phoning home to make sure Timmy and the twins were doing okay with Michael, I headed back to the library.

Around nine in the evening, I was still doggedly packing books when I got a call from Dad.

"Meg? Are you still in town?"

"Unfortunately." I stood up and winced. "I got caught up in the library packing, but we're nearly finished."

"Could you give me a ride home?" he asked. "I'm still help-ing out at the police station. Your brother could take me, but he has to head out now, and I was rather hoping to stop by the hospital one more time."

"Of course," I said. "Want me to pick you up now?"

"No, the chief can drop me off when we finish up here. Your grandfather's in room 242—I'll meet you there."

"Roger."

I felt a pang of guilt. I'd meant to drop by the hospital hours ago. And for all my complaining about how the twins tied me down, I realized I was missing them terribly after a day spent running around without them.

I hunted out Ms. Ellie and apologized for not staying till the bitter end. Then I drove the few blocks over to the hospital.

It might have been faster to walk. I had to pass by the town hall on my way, and the crowds and traffic were worse than ever. In fact, about halfway through the slow crawl around the town square, I turned off on a side street and began picking my way through the less crowded outskirts of town. Taking the long way round would probably save time, and the longest route I could possibly imagine would only take me twenty or thirty blocks out of my way.

My detour led me past the bus station and nearby, the dark building that held Parker Blair's furniture store. I found myself thinking how remarkably close it was to the town hall. It would have been easy for Louise, Mayor Pruitt, Terence Mann, or anyone else working late at the town hall to slip away long enough to kill Parker and then return without anyone being the wiser. Given the elevator's snail-like pace, one of them could easily stretch a supposed trip to the basement vending machine area to fifteen or twenty minutes. And that was assuming there was anyone around keeping close enough tabs that they had to explain their absence.

And the whole bus station area seemed short on both pedestrians and streetlights. Not hard to imagine Parker's killer skulking along these rather run-down sidewalks without being spotted.

A pity Mayor Pruitt hadn't included this part of town in the ruinously expensive beautification campaign. Of course, why would he? None of his family owned property here.

I almost hoped the mayor turned out to be the killer. The tabloids would love it—"Town Elects Psycho Killer as Mayor!"— but it would certainly make the recall campaign much easier.

The hospital and its parking lot were reassuringly bright by comparison. I realized my shoulders were tense and hunched. I didn't normally stress out that much about driving through the bus station area—after all, I'd lived for many years outside Washington, D.C., and driven through neighborhoods that made the worst block in Caerphilly look like a garden spot.

Of course I'd never knowingly driven past a murder site in any of those neighborhoods. Or had to contemplate which of my acquaintances might be the killer.

Then again, maybe my tension wasn't due to my route but my destination. I felt my shoulders tightening even more as I crunched across the gravel of the parking lot toward the hospital entrance.

"I hate hospitals," I muttered.

Caerphilly Hospital was better than most, largely because it was smaller than most, and thus a lot less impersonal. They'd been nice to me when the twins were born. But it was still a hospital. I took a deep breath and strode through the entrance.

The front desk was staffed by a woman reading a copy of *People*. I knew her slightly—one of Randall Shiffley's many cousins. We waved at each other. Since Dad had already told me Grandfather was in room 242, I didn't have to ask directions. I pushed the elevator call button. She went back to her magazine.

No one rode up with me in the elevator. I stepped out onto

the second floor and looked around. No one else in the hall, which was in some kind of night mode—still well lit, but less glaringly bright than it would have been in the daytime. The layout was much the same as it had been on the third floor, where I'd had my brief stay in the maternity ward in December. To my right, the corridor continued a little way. Then, after the nurses' station, it made an abrupt left turn. To my left, it continued on much farther. Room 242, I realized, would be near the end of the corridor.

Why so far from the nurses' station? Then I realized that his room would be directly over the ER, and only a short flight of steps or a quick trip in the service elevator away from whoever was on duty there. Maybe that was their usual place to put patients who were no longer on the ICU but still needed watching.

Or perhaps, even unconscious, my grandfather was enough of a troublemaker that the nurses wanted him as far away from them as possible.

I could see a nurse sitting at the station. Her head was bent, and she seemed to be reading something under the light of a desk lamp.

I decided to ask her about Grandfather's remote location. When I'd taken a few steps toward her, she glanced up and I recognized her. One of the two women Corsicans who'd been so visibly upset by Parker Blair's death. The well-dressed redheaded one. I smiled and searched my memory for her name as I approached the desk.

"Vivian?"

"Yes?"

"I almost didn't recognize you in your uniform." Actually, I had no trouble recognizing her. The red hair was unmistakable, and never had I seen a nurse who made her uniform look more like a Paris original.

Her professional smile froze for a moment, then changed to a more personal one as she obviously recognized me. "Oh, yes. You must be Dr. Langslow's daughter. Maeve?"

"Meg."

"The one who's being so generous about sheltering the animals in your house."

Clearly I hadn't made my desire for the animals to leave clear enough, if the Corsicans were still calling me generous.

"You must be here to visit Dr. Blake," she went on.

"How is he?"

"We were a little concerned for a while, but he regained consciousness about an hour ago and your father says everything's looking good."

"That's wonderful!" Relief washed over me—relief, and just a touch of guilt that I hadn't come down in time to provide moral support while he was still unconscious.

"By the way," I added. "Why is he so far away from your station? Is there some reason you want him right over the ER?"

"We had to move him after he regained consciousness," she said, permitting a slight frown to crease her brow. "He was disturbing the other patients."

"Disturbing them how?" I had a brief vision of Grandfather howling in pain.

"Well, so far he's complained about being left to starve, having to eat inedible food, being awakened for his meds, not being given his meds soon enough, the lack of the Animal Planet channel on his TV, the lukewarm water in his carafe, the bad taste of our ice cubes and—well, I don't know what else."

I winced.

"And I gather he's not complaining quietly," I said.

She shook her head.

"Luckily we're not full up," she said. "We were able to move him to the far end of the hall and the other patients up this way, so we can have a couple of empty rooms on either side of the hall as a buffer zone."

"Sorry about that," I said. "He's a pain in the neck sometimes."

"He's a great man," she said. "A noble crusader for the environment and the welfare of animals."

"Yes," I said. "But that doesn't make him any less of a pain in the neck, does it? Can I go and see him now?"

She nodded and returned to her paperwork.

When I got closer to 242, I heard voices inside. I paused in the open doorway. The room's bathroom door was to my left, off the small entrance hallway, and at the end of the hallway my view into the main part of the room was blocked by a curtain. Not a full-length curtain, though—I could see two pairs of male feet below it, presumably standing at the foot of the bed. One was a pair of glossy black oxfords whose regulation shine had held up well in spite of a long, busy day. The other was a pair of beat-up sneakers that Mother had been trying for years to get Dad to throw away.

"Retrograde amnesia," Dad was saying. "It's not uncommon after a blow to the head."

"What are the chances he'll eventually remember what happened?" the chief asked.

"Impossible to predict," Dad said. "Some people completely recover their memories of the events leading up to the injury, some never get any better, and most fall somewhere in between."

"Can't you get some kind of forensic evidence from the room?" Grandfather said. I was relieved to hear his voice. Vivian had said he was conscious, but hearing him for myself made it more real. His voice didn't sound as bold and resonant as usual, but it wasn't that far from his normal irascible tone.

"Forensic evidence," the chief echoed. "Like what?"

I stepped closer so I could peer through the curtain. Grandfather was sitting up, looking weak but feisty. Dad and the chief glanced my way. Dad waved. The chief nodded to me and turned back to Grandfather. I took this as permission to enter, so I did.

"I don't know," Grandfather said. "Aren't you modern cops always picking up an eyelash hair and using it to prove it was Professor Plum in the library with the candlestick?"

"Only in the movies." The chief sounded remarkably patient, considering. "In real life, forensic science has its limits. For example, in a case like this, just about everyone in town has been in that room, either to help with the animals or to gape at them. So even if we thought we knew who hit you, finding trace evidence that he'd been in Meg and Michael's living room wouldn't prove anything. If we found whatever he hit you over the head with, that might help, but it's a long shot. Horace is working on it, though, on the admittedly unlikely chance that your attacker dropped his weapon in the house or yard."

"And he hasn't found anything?" Grandfather asked.

"Couple pounds of dog hair," the chief said. "Nothing incriminating. So I'm afraid if your memory doesn't come back, we may never catch your attacker."

"What if my memory comes back and all I remember is someone hitting me from behind?"

"Not likely," Dad said. "From the shape of the injury, it looks as if someone hit you from the front. Like this, Chief."

I stepped fully into the room to see better. Dad glanced around, and picked up an object—I couldn't see what. Some kind of medical instrument? He slowly raised it up and brought it down until it gently touched the chief's left temple.

The chief watched this demonstration, then scribbled in his notebook.

"So I was facing my attacker?" Grandfather said. He was frowning as if this didn't sync with what he remembered.

"Facing him and looking up at him," Dad said, nodding.

"Looking up at him?" The chief glanced at Grandfather's long frame—he was well over six feet.

"You mean I was attacked by a giant?" Grandfather asked.

"No, no," Dad looked at me. "Meg, crouch down as if you were tending a dog or something."

I crouched and looked up as Dad brought his demonstration weapon gently down on my left temple. I could see now that he was wielding Rob's missing little video camera.

"Very good," Dad said, beaming at me. I stood up again.

"Crouching and looking up at his attacker," the chief said.

"Crouching or kneeling," Dad said.

"And the attacker was right-handed?"

"Unfortunately," Dad said, with a sigh. "Like ninety percent of the human population."

"I was crouching?" my grandfather muttered, as if he found the thought not only unlikely but vaguely distasteful.

"Tending the animals, I should think," Dad said, in his most soothing tones.

I noticed that he had set Rob's video camera down on the

windowsill. Which was quite possibly where he'd found it, but someone should take it back to Rob. I went over, snagged it, and put it in my purse. I made a mental note to call Rob later to report finding it.

"That does indicate that your attacker was probably someone you knew and trusted," Dad said. "After all, if you didn't trust someone—"

Grandfather yawned suddenly.

"Looks like the sedative is finally working," Dad said. "We should let him sleep."

"If you remember anything, have the nurses call me," the chief said.

Grandfather nodded, his eyes already closed. Dad and the chief began quietly walking out of the room. I was about to follow them when Grandfather mumbled something.

I went to the head of his bed and bent closer.

"What was that?" I kept my voice soft enough that if he'd already fallen asleep it wouldn't wake him.

"I hate hospitals," he said.

I looked around. The management had made an effort to gussy up the room so it didn't look quite so much like most people's idea of a hospital. They'd hung curtains on the windows and art prints on the walls, and painted the walls in soft, dark colors. The room I'd been in with the twins had been forest green with tan woodwork and a framed reproduction of a Rousseau jungle print on the wall beyond the foot of the bed. Grandfather had slate blue, chocolate brown, and Picasso.

Unfortunately, the hospital's efforts didn't do much to disguise the fact that you were in a hospital room—they just made it look like a cross between a hospital room and a budget motel chain. A drop ceiling with acoustic tiles made the room less cold and echoing than the corridors, but it was still clearly something you'd usually only see in an institution. And it was hard to forget you were in a hospital when you were attached to an IV bag and a couple of monitors that beeped or hummed every few seconds.

"I know what you mean," I said. "I'll see you later."

Out in the hallway I found Dad and the chief halfway down the corridor, talking quietly.

"—have to wait and see," Dad was saying.

"What about hypnosis?" the chief asked.

"That can be successful in cases of this kind," Dad said. "But I think trying it right now might be premature. Too stressful for the patient, and not really that likely to produce results. The first thing to do is let the brain heal."

The chief nodded.

"Can you wait a moment, Meg?" Dad asked.

I wanted to say no, I was going home to be with my kids. But he and the chief both looked exhausted and I didn't want to cause either of them any more hassle. So I nodded, and Dad dashed back down the hall toward my grandfather's room.

Chapter 23

"Just a moment. Yeah, right," I murmured, although not loud enough for Dad to hear. I'd known him to say he'd be back in a moment and not turn up for hours. I looked at my watch. Fifteen minutes, I decided, and then I was going looking for him.

I went down to wait by the elevators. There was a bench, but I was afraid if I sat down, I'd keel over fast asleep. So I stayed vertical, pulled out my cell phone, and called Michael.

"Josh and Jamie's residence," Michael answered.

"I'm glad you have your priorities straight," I said. "How are they doing?"

"They woke, they cried, they received new diapers, they ate, they burped, and they've gone back to sleep to work up the energy to do it all over again for you when you get home. How's your grandfather?"

"Conscious, and starting to sound like his old self again. He may or may not ever remember how it happened, but Dad says he'll be fine."

"Good," he said. "I want the boys to get to know their great-grandfather. Even if he is disappointed with how much slower human babies develop compared to the young of other primates. Orangutans, for example."

"He said that?"

"I think he was joking."

"He'd better be," I said. "Or I'll go and whack him a few more times myself. Sorry to leave you to handle so much of today all by yourself."

"No problem," he said. "Rose Noire was here most of the day, and when she had to leave, I recruited help. For the record, Clarence is a fairly promising babysitter prospect, but Caroline's technique clearly shows that she's had a lot more experience feeding creatures with hooves or claws."

"Oh, dear."

"Not to worry," he said. "She was a hoot. That reminds me—in case Rob asks, our little video camera's in the shop."

"In the shop? Why? What's wrong with it?"

"Nothing's wrong with it, and I'll probably let him borrow it once I've had a chance to download all our video. We can replace a lost camera, but I wouldn't want to lose this week's footage of the boys. And Rob already lost his own this weekend."

"Yes, he left it down here at the hospital while he was documenting his grandfather's illness. I've got it."

"I'll tell him. He's been tearing the barn apart and starting to worry that one of the larger dogs might have eaten it or buried it."

"I'll bring it home when I come—which will be as soon as Dad finishes here. I'm supposed to give him a ride. In just a moment, which damn well better be less than half an hour or he can walk home."

"No rush," he said. "I'll be here with the boys."

"And you have a full day of classes to teach tomorrow," I said. "I'll try not to be too late."

"As long as—oops, there's Jamie's early warning sign. Love you!"

With that he hung up. I leaned against the wall, closed my eyes—and realized that one of the light sconces was shining down on my face. I took a few steps to the right until I was midway between the two sconces, at the point of greatest shadow. I leaned back and closed my eyes again. Much more relaxing. I tried to empty my mind. For once it was surprisingly easy.

I was almost asleep standing up when I heard a slight scraping noise. I opened my eyes. Someone was standing at the nurses' station. Not Vivian. And not another nurse. It was the elusive Louise.

She glanced around to see if anyone was watching. I realized that she couldn't see me here in the shadows.

She reached down, pulled out a few drawers, and appeared to find what she was looking for. She pulled it out and set it on the counter.

A purse. Vivian's purse, undoubtedly. It was slim, sleek, and looked hideously expensive. And it was black—just the thing for fashionable mourning.

Louise reached into her pants pocket. She took out a twisted-up bit of white cloth or paper, untwisted it, and shook something out of it into Vivian's purse.

Was it just my imagination, or did the something sparkle as it fell?

She scrunched the paper up again, stuffed it back into her pocket, and tucked the purse in the drawer.

Then she pulled something off her hands. Clear plastic gloves. She shoved those in her pocket, too.

She looked around and scurried over to push the elevator button.

I needed to keep her there till I could tell the chief what she'd done. And I also needed to keep an eye on the drawer containing Vivian's purse.

I waited until Louise wasn't looking my way. Then I began walking toward the elevator and called out to her.

"Hey, Louise!"

She started, then turned and put on a shaky smile.

"Hello, Meg," she said. "I dropped by to see your grandfather but I understand he's asleep."

"Dad's down there right now, checking to see if he's awake," I said. "And if he is I'm sure he'd love to see you. Do stay, please."

"I don't want to be a bother," she said.

"To tell you the truth, he pretends to be grouchy when people stop by, but I think it's really helping his morale, having some of the Corsicans visit. And morale is the key thing at this point. So stay, please; Dad will be back in just a minute."

She smiled uneasily, and perched on the edge of one of the benches by the elevator. I sat down beside her, racking my brains for some way to keep her there.

She gave me the perfect method.

"How are the babies?" she asked.

"Great!" I exclaimed. "Want to see some pictures?"

I'm sure there are people rude enough to say no to that question, but Louise wasn't one of them. Considering that she was probably dying to make her escape, she cooed and exclaimed over the boys with remarkably good nature. I found myself hoping she was only guilty of jealousy and trying to frame her rival, not the murder itself.

After what probably seemed like several decades to her——it

certainly did to me—we heard footsteps in the hallway. We both whirled to see who was coming.

The chief, accompanied by Vivian.

Louise and I both stood. She glanced toward the elevator.

"Thanks for letting me see those photos," she said. "I should be going now."

"Hang on a second," I said. "I've got one more thing to show you."

"Ms. Langslow," the chief said. "Isn't it getting rather late? I thought you were going home."

"I was waiting to give Dad a ride," I said. "And I saw something that I think I should tell you about."

Louise flinched as if I'd struck her.

"Something related to the murder?" the chief asked.

"Possibly," I said. "You know by now that Louise and Vivian were both involved with Parker Blair."

"He got tired of her months ago," Vivian said.

"Tramp!" Louise countered.

"As you see they don't like each other very much," I went on.

"Yes, I'm aware of their . . . involvement with Mr. Blair," the chief said. "They're not the only ones."

The women, who had been glaring at each other, turned to glare at him.

"Although they do seem rather suspicious of each other," he went on. "They each tried to convince me that the other was the most likely suspect in Mr. Blair's murder."

"You lying tramp!" Louise exclaimed.

Vivian contented herself with a superior sniff.

"So maybe it's just jealousy that made Louise put something in Vivian's purse," I went on.

"What?" Louise and Vivian exclaimed in unison.

"Did you see what it was?" the chief asked.

"No," I said. "It was small enough to wrap in a tiny scrap of white paper or cloth that she still has in her pocket. And if you search her, you'll also find the gloves she used to handle the purse."

"What was it?" Vivian demanded. She took a step toward Louise, and reached out as if to shake her, but I stepped between them.

"Sammy," the chief was saying into his phone. "Get up here. And have Debbie Anne send Horace Hollingsworth over."

"We'll see about this," Vivian said. She strode over to the nurses' station.

"Ms. Forrest," the chief said. "Don't touch that."

Vivian ignored him. She yanked open the drawer, pulled out her purse, opened it, and poured the contents onto the counter.

"Leave that alone," the chief snapped.

"I didn't plant anything," Louise said. "She's making it up."

"Oh, my God!" Vivian said. She was pointing to something.

"What is it?" the chief asked.

"Parker's earring," Vivian whispered. "What's it doing in my purse?"

"Don't touch anything," the chief said.

This time it looked as if Vivian would follow his orders. She was backing away from the clutter on the counter, both hands covering her mouth.

Just then the elevator dinged. Louise turned toward the doors. The chief and I both moved toward them. If Louise tried to make a run for it . . .

The doors opened. Sammy stepped out and almost bumped into Louise.

"Detain her, Sammy," the chief said. "Detain both of them."

Sammy looked around in confusion. Counting me there were three possible detainees.

"Ms. Dietz and Ms. Forrest," the chief added. "Ms. Langslow is assisting me."

Sammy looked relieved. He crossed his arms, frowned at his two detainees, and stood in front of the elevator doors.

The chief walked over to look at the clutter Vivian had spilled onto the counter. I followed and peered over his shoulder. The interior of Vivian's purse was probably the one less-than-chic part of her life. She had a slender, elegant wallet and a sleek black cosmetic bag, but around them the counter was littered with bits of cotton and tissue, loose change, pens, individually wrapped mints, empty gum wrappers, and any number of indistinguishable bits of paper and plastic junk. Glittering in the midst of the clutter, like an ill-omened red star, was the ruby earring. I wasn't an expert on gems, but I had a feeling it would turn out to be a ruby, not a red spinel or a garnet. Surely nothing but a real ruby could burn with such a poisonous red fire.

"This does appear to resemble the missing earring," the chief said. He had drawn a pair of gloves out of his pocket and was pulling them on, his eyes fixed on the ruby.

"Complication," I said. I grabbed a pencil from the selection in a plastic cup on the counter and used it to lift up one of the shreds of tissue. The chief glared at me, then glanced down and raised one eyebrow at what I'd uncovered. A second ruby earring gleamed back at us. For a few seconds, the scattered contents of Vivian's purse seemed to form a wizened gnome face, peering up at us from the counter with glowing red eyes.

Then the spell broke, and it just looked like a pile of junk around two glittering red earrings.

Vivian was the first to react.

"Why you . . . you . . . AAAHHH!" She sprang toward Louise, fingernails extended. Louise tried to run, but Vivian caught her, and the two of them began a vicious tussle, complete with hair-pulling, shin-kicking, and fingernail-clawing. Vivian was shouting abuse at Louise in language so blue it would probably have astonished Parker's parrot, while Louise contented herself with shrieking nonstop.

After a brief moment of surprise, both Sammy and I leaped to part the combatants. I didn't have much trouble shoving Louise to the floor and sitting on her, probably because, unlike Sammy, I had no qualms about hitting a woman. And I'd tackled her because she was the smaller of the two. Maybe I should have gone for Vivian. Sammy took quite a lot of damage from her nails before he managed to follow my example.

The chief started around the counter when the fight began, but Sammy and I had things under control by the time he reached the field of combat.

"Good job," he said, glancing from me to Sammy. Then he peered at Sammy's bleeding face and shook his head.

"Can you two . . . people be trusted to keep the peace now?" he asked, frowning down at our prisoners. Normally he'd have called them ladies. Under the circumstances, "people" was as close as I'd ever heard him come to a direct insult.

"Ow!" Sammy shouted. "She bit me!"

"We'll have to cuff her." The chief did the honors himself,

retrieving the handcuffs from Sammy's belt and applying them expertly to Vivian's wrists as she continued to spit insults at them. Once Vivian was safely cuffed, Sammy came over and took charge of Louise.

"Meg, this is a hospital," the chief said. "Do you think you can find some surgical tape, in case Ms. Forrest cannot be persuaded to hold her tongue?"

"Sure," I said. I went into the nurses' station to rummage. A thought hit me.

"Shouldn't we find a replacement for Vivian?" I asked. "Assuming you're probably going to take her away for questioning. Because she seems to be the only nurse on duty on this part of the floor."

"Good point," he said. "Who do we call?"

I pulled out my cell phone and dialed the police station. If Debbie Anne didn't already know who to call, I'd bet she could find out in no time.

I was still filling Debbie Anne in on events here at the hospital when the elevator dinged again. We all whirled to face the elevator, which opened to reveal another deputy peering out, his gun at the ready.

"Put your weapon away, Fred," the chief said. "You can cuff the prisoner Sammy is restraining. Then get some more help up here. Sammy needs medical attention."

"What's wrong with Sammy?" Dad had finally returned and was standing on tiptoes to peer over Fred's shoulder.

"He was assaulted by one of my murder suspects," the chief said. "Are we any closer to getting a nurse for this floor?"

"Debbie Anne's working on it," I said.

"Good job," he said.

Dad hurried out of the elevator. I noticed he was carrying his black bag.

Fred set about handcuffing Louise in a reassuringly businesslike fashion. Of course, he had the easy job. Louise wasn't putting up much of a fight. She was crying softly, and I noticed that the tears she was shedding over her own plight were falling much faster than the ones she'd shed for poor Parker.

Dad exclaimed over Sammy's wounds and patted him on the shoulder.

"She planted those earrings in my purse," Vivian said, appending a few choice words about Louise's character.

"None of that, young woman," the chief said. "Meg, have you found that tape?"

"Here," Dad said, handing me a roll from the medical supplies he was using to patch up Sammy.

Vivian glared at him and fell silent.

"I planted one," Louise said, through sobs. "And only because she planted it in my purse."

"I did not!" Vivian said.

"Did, too!" Louise said. "I was just putting it back. I have no idea where the other one came from."

"You're lying!" Vivian shrieked.

"Quiet!" the chief bellowed. "Hand me that tape."

"I'll be quiet," Vivian muttered.

I handed the chief the tape anyway. He held the roll in his left hand and tapped it slowly against his right palm. Vivian pursed her lips as if to show that she wasn't even thinking of talking.

The elevator dinged again and Horace and yet another deputy stepped out.

"Excellent!" the chief said. "Jasper, you and Fred take these prisoners down to the station . . . er, over to Dr. Langslow's barn and hold them. Separate stalls."

"You can't arrest us!" Vivian yelped.

"We both decline to press charges," Louise said, frowning at Vivian. "You can't arrest us if we both decline to press charges."

"Yes, I can," the chief said. "Disturbing the peace. Assault and battery on poor Sammy here. Interfering with a police investigation. I'm sure I'll think of a few more when I get down to the station. Horace," he said, turning to my cousin, "we have new evidence. Look at this."

The two deputies herded their charges toward the elevator and one pressed the call button.

Horace trotted over to the counter and looked down at the clutter. His face lit up.

"Parker's missing earring!" he exclaimed. Then his face fell. "And another one just like it. Which is the real one?"

"They could both be Parker's," I said. "A lot of places still only sell earrings in pairs. Which is annoying for people who only wear one, I suppose, but at least if you lose one you've still got a spare."

"He wasn't wearing both of them the night he was murdered," the chief said. "He only has a hole in one ear."

"The earring that was ripped from Parker's ear should show traces of blood," Horace said. "And we can probably run DNA and prove that the blood is Parker's. Might even get some DNA from whoever ripped it out."

"And a fat lot of good that's going to do," the chief said. "Since it's been rattling around in these women's purses for heaven knows how long. And we won't even know if the earring that was ripped out was the one Ms. Dietz put into Ms. Forrest's purse or the one that was already there."

"She put both of them in," Vivian said.

"Did not! I only had the one!" Louise countered.

The chief looked at me. I shook my head.

"One earring, two," I said. "All I know is that I saw something sparkly fall into Vivian's purse. And who knows if this is their first round of earring planting or their twenty-first. It's hopeless."

The chief sighed and rubbed his forehead.

"Not hopeless," he said. "Just tedious. I'm betting one of them stole the spare earring from Mr. Blair's house—and locked you in the attic—as part of a plan to frame her rival, not knowing that her rival was already in possession of the real earring. We'll be checking their alibis, examining their clothes for blood spatter, looking for witnesses who might have seen them at your house or Mr. Blair's house, checking for their DNA in the truck cab, trying to prove that one or the other had access to a gun that could have fired the bullet. It'll be legwork and forensics that solves this. Tedious, but effective."

The elevator dinged. The deputies started to herd their charges in, and then had to step back as Francine Mann stepped off and then looked around in surprise.

"What is going on here?" She sounded startled and maybe a little scared. She was wearing a light, loose jacket at least two sizes too large for her slender frame, and with her shoulders hunched and her fists jammed in the oversized pockets, she looked curiously like a frightened young girl.

"Can we help you?" the chief asked.

"I think I'm supposed to be helping you." She straightened her shoulders and some of her usual quiet, competent manner returned. "I'm the night administrative supervisor—that means the duty staff call me if there's a problem."

She looked around and pursed her lips as if suggesting that the duty staff's call was more than a little overdue.

"I didn't call you," Vivian said. There was just a hint of insolence in her tone, as if Francine were the one person in the hallway she could talk back to with impunity. I remembered Francine saying that the medical staff resented her and undercut her at every chance. I'd thought she was being oversensitive, but judging from Vivian's manner, maybe she was right.

"No, you didn't." Francine studied Vivian for a few seconds before turning back to the chief. "I was driving home when Debbie Anne reached me on my cell phone to say that you needed a replacement for Vivian—I thought she'd been hurt. What is she being arrested for—is this about the murder?"

The chief frowned. He hated being interrogated.

"They're in handcuffs because they tried to scratch each other's eyes out," I said. "Long story—I can fill you in later if you like."

"At the moment, we need your help," the chief said. "We don't want to leave the floor unstaffed. I suppose Dr. Langslow can stay here until you can get a replacement for Ms. Forrest."

"There's no need to inconvenience Dr. Langslow," Francine said. "As soon as Debbie Anne reached me I called the first nurse on our roster. She should be here within half an hour if not sooner. And in the meantime, I'll go down and ask the ER to send someone up here to fill in."

"Please do," Dad said.

The elevator had disappeared during the confusion of Francine's arrival. The deputies had punched the button and were watching the floor indicator impatiently. Louise and Vivian were glaring at each other.

The elevator dinged again.

"You might want to take them down one at a time," I said. "Unless you fancy refereeing a cat fight in the elevator."

"Good suggestion," the chief said. "And Fred, call Debbie Anne. We need to get another deputy down here to take over guarding Dr. Blake."

"I thought one of them did it," Sammy said.

"Until we're sure one of them did it, and know which one," the chief said. "Sammy, you can do that after you're patched up."

The deputy guarding Louise ushered her into the elevator. He held the door for Francine. She took a step forward. Then she looked at Louise, paled, and stopped.

"I think I'll take the stairs," she said. "It's just as fast."

She trotted briskly down the hall in the direction of Grandfather's room. The deputies released the elevator door and it left.

"Yankee busybody," Vivian muttered. "As if she gave two pins if anything happened to me. I bet she didn't call the next nurse on the duty roster—just came down to see what was going on. She'll make the call from the stairwell and complain that the duty nurse took too long getting here."

I glanced down the hall to see if Francine had heard, but she was disappearing into the stairwell. Behind us, I heard a buzzing noise.

"Oh, dear," Dad said. "Your grandfather is ringing his call bell."

"I should go and see to him," Vivian said.

"Oh, what a great idea," I said. "Letting one of the people who might have assaulted him look in on him. And just when he's starting to regain consciousness and might be able to identify his assailant."

"I'll go," Dad said.

"I can just go down to the ER," Sammy said.

"Dad, stay here and patch up Sammy," I said, as I set off down the corridor. "Grandpa probably just wants to know what all the ruckus was. I'll call you if he needs anything."

"Right," Dad said. "Come here, Sammy. First we need to clean up that bite wound. You'd be amazed at how filthy the human mouth is."

Chapter 24

When I reached his room, I found Grandfather lying back on his pillows with a thunderous scowl on his face. He was fiercely clutching the little gizmo containing the call button. Since it also housed the TV remote, his death grip was not only sounding the bell at the nurses' station nonstop, it had also turned on the set and was making it flip wildly through all the channels. *The Tonight Show, The Simpsons, Nightline, David Letterman,* a Japanese monster movie, professional wrestling, a music video, *I Love Lucy, SpongeBob,* and the Weather Channel flicked past in the time it took me to reach the bed. He'd also managed to jack the volume up to rock-concert level. Thank goodness for the buffer zone.

"Easy on that thing." I held out a hand for the gizmo. "Do you need a nurse? Or Dad?"

"I'm fine, dammit." He was shouting to be heard over Desi Arnaz and Madonna. "I need to know what the hell all that commotion was out there."

"The chief just arrested some suspects." I eased the call button unit out of his hand, turned off the TV, and hung the thing back on the side of the bed within easy reach. Blessed silence returned, or at least what passes for silence in a hospital—merely the quiet beeping of the three or four machines hooked up to Grandfather.

"Suspects? In my case or the murder?"

"Take your pick." I straightened his pillow. "We're pretty sure it's the same thing."

He nodded and closed his eyes. He seemed fine, but I decided to keep an eye on him for a little while. Dad would know where to find me when he finished with Sammy. And odds were Dad wouldn't dawdle now. He'd be eager to get back to the farm, so he could hang around the barn while the chief interrogated his two suspects.

I felt a small thrill of excitement and relief. It was nearly over.

The chief still had to figure out which of the two women had ripped the earring from Parker's ear. But I had every confidence that between his interrogation skills and Horace's forensic ones, they'd solve that problem before long.

Of course, all the town's thorny financial problems would remain. That would bother me a lot more tomorrow. Tonight, I just breathed a sigh of relief that the murder case was about to be solved. And maybe it was a good thing that neither our mayor nor our county manager had turned out to be killers.

I glanced at my watch. No matter how much of a hurry he was in, Dad would do his best patching up Sammy. That could take fifteen or twenty minutes. Maybe half an hour. I could still get home in time for Michael to get a decent night's sleep. But in the meantime, I'd make myself comfortable.

At least one of the hospital's decorating touches had a practical use. Beside the bed was a chair that looked reasonably comfortable. It even reclined—just the thing for worried family members keeping vigil. My room on the third floor had had one just like it, and in spite of his height, Michael had found it reasonably comfortable for napping, before and after the twins' arrival.

I tiptoed over to the chair, carefully set my purse on the floor beside it, and sank gratefully into the seat, ready to relax.

"Pfffffffft!"

The chair emitted a loud, prolonged noise that sounded for all the world as if an elephant had broken wind.

Startled, I bolted out of the chair.

"What the hell was that?"

I glanced down at my grandfather, who was glaring at me with one open eye.

"It wasn't me," I said. "It was the chair."

"Hmph!" He closed the eye again and settled back into his pillow.

I glared at the chair, and then gave it another try. Instead of slumping into the chair, I sat down slowly and carefully, easing my weight more gradually onto the seat.

"Pfffffffffff!"

This time, the farting noise was softer, but a lot more prolonged. Grandfather made a growling noise but didn't say anything.

I got up again and examined the chair. Had someone hidden a whoopee cushion in it? Rob liked that sort of thing, and I knew from the evidence of the little video camera that he'd been here. But there didn't appear to be any place to hide a whoopee cushion. A small crack in the faux leather was probably the culprit. The chair was making those annoying noises all on its own.

I tried sitting down again. This time I gripped the chair's arms and lowered my body with excruciating slowness. Even with the upper body and arm strength I had from my blacksmithing work it was a grueling process, but I congratulated myself that I'd eliminated nearly all the noise.

I was about ninety percent lowered when my grandfather spoke up.

"Just sit, dammit," he snapped. "Hell and damnation! It's like listening to someone torture a balloon."

I sat. But unless I sat perfectly still, the chair seat continued to make indecorous noises. It squeaked when I crossed my legs. It hissed when I leaned over slightly to see if Grandfather was asleep. Bending down to get something from my purse produced a miniature encore of the original breaking-wind noise. I gave up.

"If you're awake when Dad comes back, tell him I went down to the cafeteria," I said, softly enough that Grandfather wouldn't hear me if he was asleep.

"Hallelujah," he muttered.

I stopped outside his door to scribble a note for Dad and tuck it behind the metal room number plate on the door. Then I headed for the cafeteria, which was on the ground floor at the other end of the hospital. It probably wouldn't be serving hot food at this hour on Sunday night, but the vending machines would be working. And if I picked a booth that emitted unseemly squelching noises when I sat down, no one would care.

I had to turn on the lights when I arrived. The buffet section was empty and scrubbed so well it shone. But there was a large bank of vending machines. I decided on hot tea.

I settled back into a booth to drink it. I closed my eyes and took a few of the deep relaxing breaths I'd learned in yoga class. This was definitely one of those moments Rose Noire kept talking about, when instead of being bored and fretful, the wise person relaxed and turned what could be wasted moments into a relaxing mental haven. For once, there was no one here demanding anything of me—if you didn't count Dad asking me to cool my heels until he was ready to be chauffeured home. The boys were safely asleep, with enough milk stockpiled to feed them if Dad took longer than expected—always a strong possibility. No one was asking me to feed, groom, walk, or clean up after an animal. If she were here, Rose Noire would probably have attempted to lead me in a few restorative yoga poses, but thank God she wasn't, and I could enjoy this rare moment of total peace and quiet in my own way.

After about ten breaths, I opened my eyes and looked around for something to do.

I fished in my purse to find that once again the fat paperback mystery I'd been working on since the boys were two weeks old wasn't there. I'd probably left it on my bedside table. I'd been reading myself to sleep with the opening page of chapter three for the last week.

No book, but I did find Rob's little pocket video camera. I turned it on and began figuring out how to use it.

Not hard. Not that I expected it to be, since my mechanically inept brother seemed to have no difficulty using it.

I sipped my tea and started at the beginning of the camera's memory. Lots of pictures of Rob's feet. One long sequence showing the corner of the refrigerator while Rob and Rose Noire tried to figure out why the camera wasn't on. Their dialogue was muted, but audible in the silent, empty cafeteria.

"Wait a minute!" he said. "It's been on all the time! Great!"

"Do you know how you turned it on?" Rose Noire asked.

Apparently not, because the next sequence showed wildly gyrating scenery and an occasional glimpse of Rob's jeans-clad legs as he strolled along, swinging the camera in one hand, unaware that it was filming.

But after a while his camerawork improved. A sequence of Rose Noire trying to feed both boys at the same time really captured the insanity of life with twins. Though if I were Rose Noire, I'd have made him stop filming and help. I would have to confiscate the sequence of Josh, unwisely left diaperless, happily peeing into the air—and onto his nearby brother. It was cute, but I didn't want Rob sharing it with the immediate world on YouTube.

And then videos of the animals began to appear. Puppies frolicking on our living room rug. A trio of cats grooming themselves in unison like a feline precision drill team. A lot of footage of Tinkerbell, the wolfhound—I wouldn't be surprised at all if she became a permanent resident. And then some footage of the macaw.

The original macaw. I could see now that it was a completely different blue from the one we had now, a darker blue with overtones of gray and maybe a slight tinge of purple. I'd have to take Mother's word for it that this was Prussian blue.

Clearly Rob was amused by the macaw's blue language. I watched several scenes in which the bird swore like the proverbial sailor with Rob giggling in the background. In the first two, the camera jiggled in time with his laughter, but he soon learned the trick of setting it on a piece of furniture. This not only improved the quality of the video, it allowed Rob to get into the action, feeding straight lines to the macaw.

In one shot, I could hear Mother's voice in the background.

"Rob!" she exclaimed. "What in the world are you teaching that poor bird?"

"It's not my fault," Rob said, turning off-camera to look at her. "The bird already knew all that. Parker must have done it."

"Parker, Parker," Mother said. She was still off-camera, but I could almost see her shaking her head in gentle, sorrowful reproof.

The macaw echoed her, repeating Parker's name.

Wait a minute. The bird wasn't just echoing her. Parker's name appeared to have triggered something.

"Oh, Pahkeh," the bird said. "Oh, yes, Pahkeh. Ohhhhh! Pahkeh! YES!"

Rob dropped out of the picture, though his giggles could still be heard. Make that guffaws. Apparently he was so overcome with laughter that he had to roll on the floor. Mother presumably tsk-tsked and left the room, head high, pretending not to hear the macaw.

But the video kept rolling, and the macaw kept repeating Parker's name in what was clearly the heat of passion—and in a strong, nasal New England accent.

Francine's accent. She'd said it herself—she stuck out like a sore thumb because no one else in the whole county sounded like her. And judging from the cries and moans the parrot was uttering, I'd bet anything that Francine knew Parker a lot better than anyone had suspected.

Hadn't Rob recognized her voice? No, Rob probably hadn't met Francine. Even if he had, her accent wouldn't have struck him as strange. His staff at Mutant Wizards were a multicul- tural lot, so he was used to hearing accents from Brooklyn,

Mumbai, Sydney, and yes, no doubt from Boston's Route 128 tech corridor.

I found myself remembering something. Francine's face at the T-Ball game, when the other mothers were laughing over Parker's many girlfriends. I'd assumed her facial expression was disapproval. What if it was jealousy?

And no wonder she'd been fretting so about her accent. She probably knew that the parrot imitated her. Perhaps she and Parker had laughed about it when he was alive. But once he was dead, the parrot might be the only witness to their affair.

What if both Vivian and Louise had been telling the truth? What if someone really had planted both earrings, one in each of their purses? Who better to do it than Francine? She could have had access to Louise's purse while visiting her husband at the town hall, and here at the hospital, she was always flitting about, largely ignored by the medical staff.

She obviously had a very strong motive for stealing Parker's macaw before anyone overheard its imitation of her. And now she knew Grandfather was conscious and might start remembering things any minute.

I scrambled out of my seat and started running.

Chapter 25

Halfway down the long, echoing corridor to the lobby, I realized that I should be calling for help, not racing to the rescue. As I ran, I pulled out my cell phone and dialed 911.

"Hey, Meg," Debbie Anne said. "What's up now?"

"Tell the chief to get back here to the hospital," I said. "My grandfather could be in danger."

"What kind of danger?"

"I think Vivian and Louise were both framed," I said. "Francine Mann is the real killer, and she's somewhere here in the hospital. She's probably going after my grandfather, and—"

Just then I noticed that my phone had gone dead. Not uncommon here in the hospital. Should I run out into the parking lot, where reception was sometimes better? The key word was "sometimes." Did I want to be out in the parking lot, waving around my cell phone and cursing Caerphilly's substandard signal towers while something happened to Grandfather?

Unnecessary. No matter how much of what I'd said had been cut off, Debbie Anne had heard the first sentence. She knew Grandfather was in danger.

I had reached the elevator lobby. No one behind the desk. I punched the elevator call button. Nothing happened. One elevator was gaping open, and the call button didn't light when I pushed it.

Someone had hung an "Out of Order" sign on the open elevator.

Out of order? Or turned off by someone with access to the keys?

I raced for the stairwell.

I emerged on the second floor beside the nurses' station. The vacant nurses' station. What had happened to the replacement for Vivian? If I was right, and Francine was the killer, she could have canceled the request for a replacement once we were all out of the way. Or just waited to make it until after she had done something to Grandfather.

I slowed down to a fast walk on my way to my grandfather's room. I kept glancing left and right as I passed the other rooms on the hall. All were dark. Presumably part of the buffer zone they'd established around Grandfather. Whose idea was the buffer zone, anyway? Was it really something the nurses thought necessary for the other patients' comfort, or had Francine instituted it to make sure my grandfather was as far from help as possible when she made her move? Should I dash into one of the empty rooms and use a land line to call 911 again? No, Debbie Anne knew enough to sound the alarm. I could call again from Grandfather's room.

I paused at the door of 242. No one in sight up or down the hall. I walked in as quietly as I could and paused at the curtain. It suddenly occurred to me that Francine could be armed—after all, they hadn't found the gun that had killed Parker. I bent down and peered beneath the curtain. No feet anywhere in sight. I breathed more easily.

Of course, that didn't mean the danger was over—only that I'd reached Grandfather before Francine had. But I was sure she'd be coming.

And since I'd arrived here before she had, maybe I should see if I could catch her in the act. I could hide along the wall beside the bed and leap out when she came in. Or better yet, in the bathroom—the door was between the inner curtain and the outer door, so I could see her as she crept in.

I was turning to slip into the shadows inside the bathroom door when I heard a familiar noise. A soft "pffffft!" from the whoopee cushion chair.

I parted the curtains slightly and peered in. Francine was standing on the chair and fumbling at the ceiling. I could see her face in profile. She was calm and frowning slightly as if in concentration.

I pulled out my cell phone, turned it on. Wonder of wonders, the wayward signal was back, so I pointed it toward Francine. She moved one of the ceiling tiles aside. There was a space between the drop ceiling and the real one. She was reaching in and pulling something out.

A syringe and a medicine vial.

I snapped a picture of her doing it and hit the button to send it to the baby e-mail list, the one we'd set up so that with one click we could send cute pictures of the twins to dozens of friends and relatives. Good; one bit of evidence safe.

Then I called 911, set the phone down on the floor, and stepped through the curtains. Francine was standing by Grandfather's IV bag, filling the syringe from the little vial.

"You can put that hypodermic needle down now," I said as loudly as I could.

From the floor, I heard faint noises from my phone. Debbie Anne, I hoped, asking what the hell was going on.

"I don't think so," Francine said. She squirted a little bit of the liquid from the syringe, and the drops caught the light and glittered as they landed on the sheet covering Grandfather.

I was racking my brains for something to use as a weapon— and kicking myself for not having stopped to find something on my way. Of course, if I'd stopped to search for a weapon, by the time I'd gotten here, Francine might already have done whatever she was planning to do to Grandfather. Maybe I had something in my purse that I could use.

Or maybe I could just keep her talking until help arrived. As long as I kept her away from Grandfather.

"What were you planning to do to Grandfather?" I asked. "Put potassium chloride in his IV? Or maybe succinylcholine?"

She looked startled for a moment, then her frown deepened.

"Hey, remember, I'm a doctor's daughter," I said, shrugging. "I know a few things. Just as you do, in spite of what the nursing staff think. And speaking of them, were you going to frame Vivian for the theft of whatever's in that vial, or just let the blame fall on the whole nursing staff?"

"I'm sorry you came here." She didn't sound sorry. More like annoyed.

"Just drop the syringe," I said. "You can't get away with poisoning him now."

She sighed, held out her hands, and opened them. The syringe and the little bottle clattered to the floor.

"You're right," she said. She took a fumbling step backward, as if she were about to collapse into the whoopee cushion chair.

Then I realized that when I thought she was reaching back to grab the chair arm for support, she was grabbing something from the oversized pocket of her jacket.

A gun.

"Why bother fiddling with his IV when I can just shoot you both?" she said. "And no, I probably can't get away with that, either, but I'm not sure I care anymore."

"Not since you found out that Parker Blair was only using you to get information about what the mayor was up to," I said.

She winced as if I'd struck her, and her face hardened. Maybe that hadn't been the wisest thing to say. Then again, she seemed to be working up to saying something. Just keep her talking—that was the ticket.

"And I thought you were my friend," she said. "But now—Oof!"

She suddenly lurched forward as if someone had shoved her.

No, someone had kicked her. I could see Grandfather's long, bony leg sticking out from under the sheets. He kicked her again and this time she fell down. As she hit the floor, the gun went off, and I felt a sudden sharp pain in one leg.

"Get her!" Grandfather shouted. "Quick! Before she recovers!"

I was already in motion. I landed on top of Francine and managed to grab her wrist and pin it down. She started shooting, but none of the shots went anywhere near Grandfather or me. One bullet did ricochet off the tasteful chocolate-brown wall and into one of the machines, which died with a small arpeggio of tinkles and beeps.

The gun was now clicking empty. Francine began struggling wildly.

An object sailed past us and struck the wall with a light thud.

"Stop it!" Francine shrieked. "How dare you throw that bedpan at me?"

"Wasn't throwing it at you," Grandfather said. "What'd be the use? Damned flimsy piece of plastic junk!"

I was glad he seemed to be looking for a weapon, but I hoped he'd hurry. I was having trouble holding her down.

"And you're bleeding all over me!" Francine added. This appeared to be aimed at me. "Get away from me!"

Yes, there was rather a lot of blood smeared on the floor where we were struggling. Apparently my leg was bleeding. I felt a momentary twinge of dizziness, and then snapped myself out of it. No time for that now.

I punched her in the stomach, knocking the wind out of her, which had the double effect of halting her struggles and shutting her up. Though both effects probably wouldn't last long.

"Tie her up," Grandfather said.

"With what?" I'd twisted both of Francine's arms behind her back and was sitting on her. I figured I could probably hold her down until help came. Assuming help didn't take too long. She was getting her wind back and starting to struggle again. Desperation gave her more strength than I'd have expected and my leg was starting to hurt like hell. If I lost so much blood that I fainted . . .

"Here." I heard a ripping noise. Some small strips of tape landed near me. I glanced up to see him pulling the IV out of his arm.

"Hey," I said. "Even if you didn't need that IV, there's not enough tape here to hold her. And besides——"

"Then tie her up with this."

He was waving the IV bag with its long trailing cord.

"Great," I said. "Except I've got my hands full here."

It was as much as I could do to hold Francine. And now she had begun kicking everything within reach, trying to knock something down on me. The IV stand barely missed me. Could I manage another stomach punch?

"Damnation," Grandfather said. "Let me do it, then."

To my astonishment, he looped the IV tube around Francine's neck and began pulling it tight. Francine stopped trying to kick the furniture and began struggling wildly.

"Don't strangle her!" I shouted. "The chief will want a live suspect."

"I know what I'm doing," he said. "Used to tackle Burmese dacoits this way."

Francine went limp. Grandfather immediately loosened the tube and began using it to tie her hands. I checked her pulse.

"Okay, at least you haven't killed her," I said.

"Better her than me," he growled.

I retrieved my cell phone.

"Debbie Anne?" I said.

"Meg! What in the world is happening there?"

"Tell the chief to get another stall ready," I said. "We've got the real killer here."

Chapter 26

"You should go back to the hospital, Grandfather," I said. "Dad, don't you think he should be back in the hospital?"

Grandfather ignored me, as he had the last dozen times I'd said the same thing since the chief finished questioning us and let us come here to Mother and Dad's farm for breakfast. I had to admit, from the way my grandfather was packing away pancakes, bacon, eggs, toast, hash browns, and fruit salad, he did look rather like a patient well on the road to recovery.

"He'll be fine," Dad said, from his place by the stove. "He can stay here for a day or two and I'll keep an eye on him. More pancakes, Dad?"

Grandfather nodded, shoved the last bite of his current pancake stack into his mouth, and held out his plate.

I sighed, and looked at my own overladen plate. Maybe escaping a murder attempt had given Grandfather an appetite. Mine was almost nonexistent, thanks to the painkillers Dad had given me for my injury. He assured me that Francine's bullet had only grazed my leg, and it would heal just fine without any scarring, but right now it hurt like hell, and the painkillers weren't helping—just making me woozy.

"Good news!" We all looked up to see Clarence running in, followed by my brother, Rob. "They've found the macaw!"

"The real macaw?" Dad asked.

"Yes, Parker's macaw. An animal shelter outside Charlottesville found his cage on their front step yesterday morning. He's fine. Rob's going to drive up today to collect him."

I peered suspiciously at my brother. Bad enough when he seemed to be on the road to adopting an Irish wolfhound. But better the wolfhound than a foulmouthed macaw.

"Are you still giving the macaw to the Caerphilly Inn?" I asked.

"Parker's macaw? Yes," Clarence said. "He'll still be good company for Martha Washington, even if he's not the same species. But they don't want him till we've done some reeducation. Cleaned up his vocabulary a bit."

"So I'll be taking him down to the Willner Wildlife Sanctuary," Rob said. "Caroline's going to rehabilitate him. She's done it before."

"Excellent idea," I said. "Make sure she teaches him to say 'Monty, you old goat,' just the way she does."

"And while I'm up there, I'm going to spend some time videoing all her animals." Rob had joined us at the breakfast table and was loading his plate with bacon and eggs. "Might even stay over a day or two. Assuming it's okay to borrow your video camera for a while? Just until the chief gives mine back?"

"Fine with me," I said. "Michael's the one who uses it, and he can probably settle for still photography for a few days."

I'd make sure I saved all the videos from it before I gave it to him. And if he lost it, I'd buy a new one and send him the bill.

But it was worth the potential hassle to get rid of the macaw.

And perhaps, if we worked hard, we could get the rest of the animals adopted while Rob was gone—including Tinkerbell, the wolfhound.

"Rob, pancakes?" Dad asked. "And what about you, Clarence?"

Clarence took a seat, and Dad began working on another batch of pancakes, along with reinforcements for the bacon, eggs, and hash browns. Normally I'd be helping, but between my leg injury and the fact that I'd only had about two hours of sleep on a bed in the ER, Dad had put me on injured reserve and was cooking solo.

And as soon as Michael arrived to pick me up, I could go home and start catching up on my sleep. Or at least returning to my normal level of sleep deprivation. Meanwhile, it satisfied the orderly part of my mind to see so many loose ends being tied up.

I thought of another one.

"What about the blue-and-yellow macaw Francine left behind when she stole the hyacinth macaw?"

"Technically, she belongs to Francine," Clarence said with a sigh. "So I suppose she gets to decide the blue-and-yellow's fate."

"Technically, she's evidence." We looked up to see the chief standing in the kitchen doorway. "And as such she will remain in our custody for the time being."

"Great," I said. "If you like, I can drop that particular item of evidence by your new office this afternoon."

The chief winced and nodded.

"Francine will probably need all the money she can get for her legal defense," Clarence said. "I'll talk to the pet store where she got the macaw. They'd probably be willing to buy the bird back once the chief says it's okay. And if not, maybe I can convince the Caerphilly Inn to buy her. We'll work something out."

Knowing that the macaws were not only safe but destined for a cushy life at a five-star hotel raised everyone's spirits even higher.

"Pancakes, Chief?" Dad asked.

The chief hesitated, then sat down.

"Thank you, I believe I will," he said. "It's been an unusual morning."

I interpreted this as a hint that under normal circumstances he did not plan to be having breakfast with Mother and Dad while his police station was in their barn. But Dad beamed with delight, and poured more batter into a skillet. He was in seventh heaven, between having the chance to cosset his father for a few more days and the prospect of hosting the police station indefinitely.

"How's the case coming?" I asked.

"Very well, thank you," the chief said. "A search of Mrs. Mann's home has turned up several bits of useful evidence, including printouts of e-mails between her and the victim and a charge slip that establishes her presence in the vicinity of the pet store where she purchased the substitute macaw."

"She was stupid enough to buy the macaw with her charge card?" Rob exclaimed.

"No, she paid cash for that," the chief said. "But she used her charge card to buy gas six blocks away. I have every confidence that the pet store owner will be able to identify her. And Horace is optimistic that the ballistics on the gun will be useful."

"Good morning, everyone!" Mother sailed into the kitchen. Although it wasn't even seven yet, she was already dressed in what I recognized as working clothes—the dress a little darker and more tailored than her usual wear, and her normal high heels replaced with elegant ballet flats.

"Pancakes?" Dad asked.

"Just a little fruit salad, I think." And then, seeing how his face fell, she added, "Well, perhaps a very tiny stack of pancakes."

Dad returned to pouring and flipping with renewed vigor.

"I gather the garden club has more to do today?" I asked.

"Yes, dear," Mother said, as she took her seat. "We're going to relocate the plants to their temporary homes today. I've put you down for a dozen. They'll fill in the empty spaces in your living room nicely. And don't worry," she added, seeing the look of dismay on my face, "they'll all be neatly labeled so the plant care service will know which ones to tend and water when they come."

"The county's going to keep the plant care service?" I asked. "Instead of asking the plants' hosts to care for them?"

"Some of our garden club ladies have only the vaguest notion of how to tend houseplants adequately," she said, with a tiny shake of her head. "And besides, the county plant care contract is a substantial part of Leah Shiffley's income—we don't want to drive her out of business while this whole thing plays out."

"And just how long do we think it will take the whole thing to play out?" I asked. "Has anyone talked to Festus today?"

"No, but he was singing in the shower when I left," Rob said.

"Of course he's singing," I said. "He's got a potentially lucrative new case. What I want to know is if we should be singing."

"Festus likes money, but he hates losing more," Mother said. "If he's cheerful, that means the prospects are good. On a happier note, Randall Shiffley's coming over today to start on your library shelves."

"So much for catching up on my sleep." The thought triggered a huge yawn.

"I told him he wasn't to make so much as a peep until afternoon," Mother said.

"And I won't." Randall had followed her into the kitchen. "I've got plenty of measuring to do before we start sawing and hammering. And I need to bring over some boxes for the stuff you two have in the room."

"I'm not sure I'm up to packing today," I said.

"'Course you're not," he said. "The Shiffley moving company's doing all that. Free, on account of your valiant service to the county. Which reminds me. Here."

He put a clipboard atop my plate. I peered down at the paper it contained.

"The petition to recall Mayor Pruitt?" I asked. He nodded, and I signed with a flourish. "Long overdue, if you ask me. How many more signatures do you need?"

"Got more than enough," Randall said as he retrieved the clipboard. "But somehow we missed getting your John Hancock yesterday, and I thought maybe you'd like to be in on it."

"Absolutely," I said. "Any idea who'll be running to replace him?"

"I just might," Randall said.

"You live outside the town limits," I said.

"He could move into town," Clarence said.

"Fat chance finding a place," I said. "Do you know how tight the real-estate market is?"

"I do," Clarence said. "And as a responsible executor, I consider it my duty to see that Randall pays full market price when he buys Parker's house from the estate."

Of course, Randall could have a tough, uphill battle. Getting enough signatures on the recall petition today didn't mean Mayor Pruitt was out. And the Pruitts would fight back tooth and nail.

Still, the very notion of a Shiffley replacing a Pruitt as the mayor of Caerphilly made me chuckle.

"Ah!" Mother exclaimed. "There they are!"

I turned to see Michael and Rose Noire strolling in, each carrying a twin.

"Aren't they adorable?" Mother cooed. She held out her arms for Jamie, who actually was looking adorable at the moment. Josh was beet-red and howling like a banshee.

"Sorry," Michael said. He was bouncing Josh just the way he liked to be bounced, to no avail. "He's been cranky all morning."

"I know how he feels," I said.

"You want me to examine him?" Dad asked.

"He probably just misses his mother," Rose Noire said.

"His mother misses him, even if he is being a pill," I said, holding out my arms.

To my astonishment, a couple of seconds after I propped Josh on my shoulder, he stopped crying, hiccupped a few times, and fell asleep.

"See?" Rose Noire said. "He only wanted his mother."

"Coincidence," I said.

Just then Timmy burst into the room.

"Aunt Meg!" he shouted. "Clarence says I can keep her if Mommy says okay! Can you call and ask her?"

Keep her? I peered over to see which of our four-legged residents had captured Timmy's heart.

Tinkerbell the wolfhound. Of course. A dilemma. On the

one hand, it might be a satisfying payback, returning Timmy with a pet wolfhound in tow. On the other hand, who knew how long he and any pet he adopted would be staying with us.

"I have no idea what your mother will say, but I'll ask her," I said finally.

"Yay!" Timmy seemed to think that Tinkerbell's fate had been happily settled. He sat down at the table and looked up expectantly. Tinkerbell settled down at Timmy's feet, no doubt hoping for a few table scraps.

"Pancakes, Michael?" Dad asked, as he slid a plate in front of Timmy without asking.

"Love some," Michael said. "By the way, Festus says we have a long battle ahead of us, but he's optimistic. And he also says we all owe a big debt of thanks to the late Parker Blair. I wasn't quite awake enough to follow his explanation, but I gather if we hadn't found out about the whole debt problem when we did, Festus's job would have been infinitely harder."

Everyone fell silent, and I could hear the bacon sizzling in Dad's skillet. I wondered if the others were fretting about the many problems facing Caerphilly, or feeling sadness over the death of Parker. Or, like me, a little of both.

I lifted my glass of cranberry juice.

"To Parker Blair," I said. "He had his faults, but he loved animals and he did us all an enormous service. I wish we'd all had a chance to get to know him."

"Here, here," Clarence said, and the rest of the breakfasters murmured agreement and toasted Parker with coffee, juice, and in Rob's case, Diet Dr Pepper.

We were all putting our cups and glasses down when Sammy stuck his head in the back door.

"Chief!" he said. "The forensic computer guy's here from Richmond!"

"Great!" Dad and the chief said in unison as they leaped toward the door.

Dad scurried out the back door after Sammy. The chief closed his eyes for a few moments, took a deep breath—I could almost hear him counting to ten—and followed at a more sedate pace.

"Isn't that nice?" Mother said. "Having the police station here is going to be such great fun for your father."

"Welcome to the town that mortgaged its own jail!"

The amplified voice blaring over the nearby tour bus loud-speaker startled me so much I almost smashed my own thumb. I'd been lifting my hammer to turn a nicely heated iron rod into a fireplace poker when the tour guide's spiel boomed across the town square, shattering my concentration.

"Mommy, did the blacksmith lady do that on purpose?" piped up a child's voice.

A few onlookers tittered. I closed my eyes, took a deep breath, then opened them again. I checked to make sure that all fifty or sixty of the spectators were safely behind the fence around my outdoor blacksmith's shop. Then I raised my hammer and began pounding.

Nothing like blacksmithing when you're feeling annoyed. The voice from the tour bus still squawked away, but I couldn't hear what it was saying. And I felt the tension and frustration pouring out of me like water out of a twisted sponge.

Along with the sweat. Even though it was only a little past ten, the temperature was already in the high eighties and the air was thick with humidity. It would hit the mid-nineties this afternoon. A typical early July day in Caerphilly, Virginia.

But in spite of the heat and the interruptions, I managed to complete the current task—shaping one end of the iron rod into the business end of the poker. I flourished the hammer dramatically on the last few blows, and lifted the tongs to display the transformed rod.

"Voilà!" I said. "One fireplace poker."

"But it needs a handle," an onlooker said.

"A handle?" I turned the rod and cocked my head, as if to look at it more closely, and pretended to be surprised. "You're right. So let's heat the other end and make a handle."

I thrust the handle end of the poker into my forge and pulled the bellows lever a couple of times to heat up the fire. As I did, I glanced over at my cousin, Rose Noire. She was standing in the opening at the back of my booth, staring at her cell phone. She looked up and shook her head.

"What the hell is keeping Rob?" I muttered. Not that my brother was ever famous for punctuality.

I wondered, just for a moment, if he was okay.

I'd have heard about it already if he wasn't, I told myself. I pushed my worry aside and kept my face pleasant for the tourists. After all, I'd been making a good living off the tourists all summer. However inconvenient it had been to move my entire blacksmithing shop from our barn to the Caerphilly town square, it had certainly been a financial bonanza. Maybe it wouldn't be a bad idea if the town held Caerphilly Days every summer.

I just hoped we didn't have to continue them into the fall. What if—

I focused on the tourists again and continued my demonstration.

"To work the iron, you need to heat it to approximately—"

"That tent on your right contains the office of the mayor," the tour bus boomed, even closer at hand. "Formerly housed in the now-empty City Hall building."

No use trying to out-shout a loudspeaker. I smiled, shrugged apologetically to the tourists, and steeled myself to listen without expression as the voice droned on, reciting the sad, embarrassing history of Caerphilly's financial woes.

"Alas, when the recession hit," the loudspeaker informed us, "the town was unable to keep up with payments on its loan, so the lender was forced to repossess the courthouse, the jail, and all the other public buildings."

Convenient that they didn't mention the real reason Caerphilly couldn't make its payments—that George Pruitt, our ex-mayor, had stolen most of the borrowed funds for his own use. Actually, a few buses had, until he'd threatened to sue, so now they just mentioned the ongoing lawsuit against him. Not as dramatic, but less apt to backfire.

"And to your left, you can see the Caerphilly Days festival, organized by the citizens to help their troubled town out of its dire plight."

I always winced when I heard that line. It wasn't exactly false—but it did seem to imply that we craftspeople were donating our time and our profits out of the goodness of our hearts, to benefit the town. We weren't—we were making good money for our own pockets. Our real value to the town lay elsewhere.

Not that we could let the tour buses know that—or worse, the Evil Lender, as we all called First Progressive Financial, LLC, the company that had foreclosed on so much of our town. Only our new mayor made an effort to call them FPF, and that was because he spent so much time negotiating with them and had to be polite.

I glanced into the forge and was relieved to see that my iron was hot enough to work. I glanced at Rose Noire and nodded, to indicate that I was about to start hammering again. She bent over her cell phone and began texting rapidly. To Rob, I assumed.

"Come on, Rob," I muttered. "Hurry up."

I pulled the rod out of my forge and began the much more complicated job of hammering the handle end into a sinuous vine-like coiled shape. Mercifully, by the time the iron needed reheating, the amplified tour bus had moved on, and I had only the tourists' questions to deal with.

"What happens if you break it?"

"Don't you ever burn yourself?"

"You shoe horses, don't you?"

"Wouldn't it be faster to do that with a machine?"

I spun out my answers in between bouts at my anvil. Finishing the poker required several return visits to the forge, followed by several vigorous rounds of hammering. I could see Rose Noire, cell phone in hand, keeping a close eye on my progress. I treated the rod—and the tourists—to one last crescendo, a great deal louder than it needed to be, dunked the rod into the water bucket, releasing a small but dramatic cloud of steam, and held up the finished poker for the tourists to admire.

And then I did it all over again. Several times. I answered what seemed like several hundred more questions—or more accurately, at least a hundred iterations of the same half-dozen questions. Finally the clock in the courthouse building chimed eleven, signaling the end of my shift.

I finished up the andiron I'd been making and thanked the

tourists. Then I changed my sign to the one saying that Meg Langslow's next blacksmithing exhibition would begin at 2 P.M. and slipped through the gate in the back of my enclosure. The cousin I'd recruited to mind the booth and sell my ironwork for me dashed in and began quickly shoving the tables of merchandise from the side of the enclosure to a much more prominent place front and center before the crowds dispersed.

Normally I'd have stayed to help her, but Rose Noire was waiting for me. She looked anxious. Not good.

"What's wrong?" I asked.

"Rob's been delayed," she said. "He's fine, and he'll try again later."

"Delayed?" I realized that I'd raised my voice. Several tourists were looking at us, so I choked back what I'd been about to say. "Back to the tent," I said instead.

I strode rapidly across the small space separating my forge from the bandstand at the center of the town square. At the back of the bandstand was a tent. The town square was filled with tents of every size, shape, and description, but whenever anyone barked out "The tent!" as I just had, they nearly always meant this one.

Rose Noire scuttled along anxiously behind me.

As soon as I stepped inside the tent, I felt my fingers itching to tidy and organize. Even at its best, the tent was cramped and cluttered, since it served as the dressing room, green room, and lounge for all the craftspeople and performers participating in Caerphilly Days. Several coatracks held costumes for performers who would be appearing later or street clothes for anyone already in costume. And every corner held plastic bins, locked trunks, totes, knapsacks, boxes, grocery bags, suitcases, and just plain piles of stuff.

"Mom-my!" Josh and Jamie, my twin eighteen-month-old sons, greeted me with enthusiasm. They both toddled to the nearest side of the huge play enclosure we'd set up, holding out their arms and leaning over the child fence toward me, jostling each other, and repeating "Mom-my! Mom-my!"

Eric, my teenaged nephew, was sitting at the back of the enclosure, holding a toy truck and looking slightly hurt.

"They were fine until you came in," he said.

"I know," I said. "They just want to guilt-trip me." Making a mental note to chivvy my fellow tent users into a cleaning spree later in the day, I stepped into the enclosure, sat down, and let the boys climb on top of me. Hugging them calmed me down.

"Thank you for watching them," I said. "And not that I'm complaining, but what are you doing here instead of Natalie?" Eric's sister had been our live-in babysitter for most of the summer.

"Grandpa says Natalie's ankle is broken and she needs to stay off her feet," Eric said. "So Mom drove up this morning to take her home and bring me as a replacement for the next few weeks. Assuming that's okay with you."

"It's fine with me." Having Eric babysit was fine, anyway. Should I feel guilty that my niece had broken her ankle chasing my sons? I'd worry about that later.

"And thank goodness you're here to help out in time for the Fourth of July," I said aloud. "Everything will get a lot easier after the Fourth."

"I thought Caerphilly Days went on all summer," Eric said. "What's so special about the Fourth?"

"I haven't told him," Rose Noire said. "And evidently Natalie is very good at keeping a secret."

"But he's a resident now, at least for the time being," I said.

"Eric, do you swear you won't tell a single soul what I am about to reveal?"

"Yes," he said. "I mean, I swear by . . . um . . ."

"Cross your heart and hope to die?" I asked.

He nodded.

"Okay. Then it's time we told you Caerphilly's sinister secret."